Also by Juliet Blackwell

THE PARIS KEY

THE WITCHCRAFT MYSTERY SERIES
Secondhand Spirits
A Cast-off Coven
Hexes and Hemlines
In a Witch's Wardrobe
Tarnished and Torn
A Vision in Velvet
Spellcasting in Silk

THE HAUNTED HOME RENOVATION SERIES
If Walls Could Talk
Dead Bolt
Murder on the House
Home for the Haunting
Keeper of the Castle
Give Up the Ghost

A TOXIC TROUSSEAU

A Witchcraft Mystery

Juliet Blackwell

AN OBSIDIAN MYSTERY

F
BLA
m

OBSIDIAN
Published by New American Library,
an imprint of Penguin Random House LLC
375 Hudson Street, New York, New York 10014

This book is an original publication of New American Library.

First Printing, July 2016

ISBN 9780451465795

Printed in the United States of America
1   2   3   4   5   6   7   8   9   10

PUBLISHER'S NOTE
This is a work of fiction. Names, characters, places, and incidents either are the product of the author's imagination or are used fictitiously, and any resemblance to actual persons, living or dead, business establishments, events, or locales is entirely coincidental.

Penguin
Random
House

To Chris and Casey, Bill and Brian

*To the marriage of true minds let us not
admit impediments*

Chapter 1

Small business owners have their morning routines. Some people switch on the lights, brew a cup of coffee, and read the paper before engaging with the day. Some count out the money in the register and tidy up the merchandise. Some sweep and hose down the front walk.

Each morning before opening my vintage clothing store, Aunt Cora's Closet, I sprinkle salt water widdershins, smudge sage deosil, and light a white candle while chanting a spell of protection.

Such spells can be powerful, and for a small business owner like me they serve an important purpose: to help customers maintain their composure in the face of fashion frustrations, keep evil intentions at bay, and discourage those with sticky fingers from rummaging through the feather boas, chiffon prom dresses, and silk evening gowns and then trying to shove said items into pockets or backpacks or under shirts.

But protection spells aren't much good against litigation.

"Lily Ivory?" asked the petite, somber young woman who entered Aunt Cora's Closet, a neon yellow motorcycle helmet under one arm. She had dark hair and eyes, and I imagined she would have been pretty had she smiled. But her expression was dour.

"Yes?" I asked, looking up from a list of receipts.

She held out a manila envelope. "You have been served."

"Served?"

"You are hereby notified of a lawsuit against you, Aunt Cora's Closet, and one errant pig, name unknown. By the by, not that it's any of my business, but is it even legal to own livestock in the city?"

I cast a glare in the direction of said pig, my witch's familiar, Oscar. At least, I tried to, but he'd disappeared. Only moments earlier Oscar had been snoozing on his hand-embroidered purple silk pillow, resting up for a busy day of trying to poke his snout under the dressing room curtains while customers tried on vintage cocktail dresses, fringed leather jackets, and Jackie O pillbox hats. Now only the slight rustling of a rack of 1980s spangled prom dresses revealed his location.

"My *pig's* being served with legal papers?"

"Not so much your pig as you. Your property, your worry. At least, that's how it works with dogs, so I assume . . ." The woman trailed off with an officious shrug as she headed for the front door with long strides, already pulling on her helmet. "But that isn't any of my business; I just deliver the bad news. Have a nice day."

"Wait—"

She didn't pause. I followed her outside, where someone was revving the engine of a large black motorcycle. The woman jumped on the back and they zoomed off.

"Duuude," said Conrad, the homeless young man who slept in nearby Golden Gate Park and spent the better part of his days "guarding" the curb outside of my store. In San Francisco's Haight-Ashbury neighborhood, many young homeless people lived this way, panhandling and scrounging and generally referring to themselves as "gutter punks." Over the past year, Conrad—or as he liked to call himself, "The Con"—had become a friend and the unofficial guardian of Aunt Cora's Closet. "You get served?"

"Apparently so," I said, opening the envelope to find some scary-looking legal-sized documents filled with legalese, such as "party of the first part."

My heart sank as I put two and two together. My friend Bronwyn, who rents space in my store for her herbal stand, had filled me in on an incident that took place a couple of weeks ago while I was out scouting garage sales for resalable treasure. It seems a woman came into the shop and started flicking through the merchandise, pronouncing it "unsuitable—too much of that *dreadful* ready-to-wear." Bronwyn had explained to her that Aunt Cora's Closet doesn't deal in high-end vintage; our merchandise consists mostly of wearable clothes, with the occasional designer collectibles. The woman had then turned to my employee Maya and started grilling her about the ins and outs of the store, making none-too-subtle inquiries about where we obtained our specialty stock.

Oscar had started getting in the customer's way, making a pest of himself and keeping her away from the clothes. Bronwyn had tried to call him off, but he'd kept at it, almost as though he'd been trying to herd her toward the exit. Finally the woman had picked a parasol off a nearby shelf and started whacking Oscar, and there had been a scuffle.

The woman had screamed and flailed, lost her balance, and fell back into a rack of colorful swing dresses. Maya and Bronwyn had hastily extricated her, made sure she was all right, and offered profuse apologies. The woman had seemed fine at the time, they both said, and she stomped out of the store in high dudgeon.

But if I was reading the legal papers correctly, the woman—named Autumn Jennings—was now claiming she had been "head-butted" by an "unrestrained pig," had been injured in the "attack," and was demanding compensation.

It was a mystery. Oscar had never herded—much less *head-butted*—anyone in Aunt Cora's Closet before. He wasn't the violent type. In fact, apart from a few occasions when he intervened to save my life, Oscar was more the "let's eat grilled cheese and take a nap" type.

He was also my witch's familiar, albeit an unusual one. Oscar was a shape-shifter who assumed the form of a miniature Vietnamese potbellied pig when around cowans—regular, nonmagical humans. Around me, his natural form was sort of a cross between a goblin and a gargoyle. A gobgoyle, for lack of a better word. His was a lineage about which I didn't want to think too hard.

"Bad vibes, Dude," Conrad said with a sage nod. "Been there. Dude, I hate being served."

"You've been served?" I asked. Conrad was in his early twenties and lived such a vagabond existence it was hard to imagine why anyone would bother to sue him. I could easily imagine his being picked up by police in a sweep of the local homeless population, but how would a process server even know where to find Conrad to serve him papers?

He nodded. "Couple times. But at least yours arrived on a Ducati. That's a nice bike."

"What did you—" My question was cut off by the approach of none other than Aidan Rhodes, witchy godfather to San Francisco's magical community. His golden hair gleamed in the sun, a beautifully tailored sports jacket hugged his tall frame, and a leather satchel was tucked under one strong arm. As he strolled down Haight Street with his signature graceful glide, strangers stopped to stare. Aidan's aura glittered so brilliantly that even nonsensitive people noticed, though they didn't realize what they were reacting to.

This is all I need.

I girded my witchy loins.

Things between Aidan and me were . . . complicated. Not long ago I'd stolen something from Aidan, and I still owed him. And when it comes to debts, we witches are a little like elephants, bookies, and the Internet: We never forget. Even worse, Aidan feared San Francisco was shaping up to be ground zero in some sort of big magical showdown, and he wanted me to stand with him for the forces of good. Or, at the very least, for the good of Aidan Rhodes. It was hard to say exactly what was going on—and exactly what role I was willing to play in it—since the threat was frustratingly nonspecific, and Aidan played his cards infuriatingly close to his chest.

"Good morning," Aidan said as he joined us. "Conrad, it's been too long. How have you been?"

Despite their vastly different circumstances and life-

styles, Aidan treated Conrad with the respect due a peer.
His decency sort of ticked me off. My life would be sim-
pler if I could dismiss Aidan as an arrogant, power-
hungry witch beyond redemption. His kindness toward
my friend was difficult to reconcile with that image.

The two men exchanged pleasantries, chatting about
the beauty of Golden Gate Park when bathed in morning dew and sunshine, and whether the Giants had a
shot at the pennant this year. And then Aidan turned
his astonishing, periwinkle blue gaze on me, sweeping
me from head to foot.

Suddenly self-conscious, I smoothed the full skirt of
my sundress.

"And Lily . . . Stunning as always. I do like that color
on you. It's as joyful as the first rays of dawn."

"Thank you," I said, blushing and avoiding his eyes.
The dress was an orangey-gold cotton with a pink
embroidered neckline and hem, circa 1962, and I had
chosen it this morning precisely because it reminded me
of a sunrise. "Aren't you just the sweet talker."

*"You catch more flies with honey than with vine-
gar,"* my mama used to tell me. Did this mean I was the
fly and Aidan the fly catcher?

"Is everything all right?" Aidan asked. "Am I sensing trouble? Beyond the norm, I mean."

"Dude, Lily just got *served*," Conrad said.

"Served? I fear we aren't speaking of breakfast."

"A lawsuit," I clarified.

"Ah. What a shame. Whatever happened?"

"Oscar head-butted a customer."

"That's . . . unusual." Aidan had given me Oscar
and knew him well. "Was this person badly injured?"

"I wasn't there when it happened, but according to

Bronwyn and Maya the customer seemed fine. But now she's claiming she sustained '*serious and debilitating neck and back injuries that hinder her in the completion of her work and significantly reduce her quality of life*,'" I said, quoting from the document I still clutched tightly in my hand.

"That sounds most distressing. Might I offer my services in finding a resolution?"

"*No.* No, thank you." The only thing worse than being slapped with a slip-and-fall lawsuit—the boogeyman of every small business owner—was being even more beholden to Aidan Rhodes than I already was. Besides . . . I wasn't sure what he meant by "finding a resolution." Aidan was one powerful witch. If he got involved, Autumn Jennings might very well wind up walking around looking like a frog.

"You're sure?" Aidan asked. "These personal injury lawsuits can get nasty—and expensive, even if you win. As much as I hate to say it, you may have some liability here. Is it even legal to have a pig in the city limits?"

"Don't worry about it; I've got it handled," I said, not wishing to discuss the matter any further with him. "Was there some reason in particular you stopped by?"

Aidan grinned, sending sparkling rays of light dancing in the morning breeze. He really was the most astounding man.

"I was hoping we might have a moment to talk," he said. "About business."

My stomach clenched. Time to face the music. I did owe him, after all. "Of course. Come on in."

The door to Aunt Cora's Closet tinkled as we went inside, and Bronwyn fluttered out from the back room, cradling Oscar to her ample chest. She was dressed in billows of purple gauze, and a garland of wildflowers crowned her frizzy brown hair. Bronwyn was a fifty-something Wiccan, and one of the first—and very best—friends I had made upon my arrival in the City by the Bay not so very long ago.

"Hello, Aidan! So wonderful to see you again!" she gushed.

"Bronwyn, you light up this shop like fireworks on the Fourth of July."

"Oh, you do go on." She waved her hand but gave him a flirtatious smile. "But, Lily! Our little Oscaroo is very upset, poor thing! Maybe it has something to do with the woman with the motorcycle helmet who was just here—what was that about?"

"She was serving Lily with legal papers," said Aidan.

"*Legal* papers?" Bronwyn asked as Oscar hid his snout under her arm. "For what?"

"Remember when Oscar"—I cast about for the right word—"*harassed* a woman a couple of weeks ago?"

Oscar snorted.

"Of course, naughty little tiny piggy pig pig," Bronwyn said in a crooning baby voice. "But I have to say she really was bothering all of us. But . . . she's *suing* you? Seriously?"

I nodded. "I'm afraid so."

"Well, now, that's just bad karma," Bronwyn said with a frown.

"You said she wasn't hurt, though, right?"

"She was fine!" Bronwyn insisted. "She fell into the rack of swing dresses. You know how poofy those dresses are—there's enough crinoline in the skirts to cushion an NFL linebacker, and she's, what, a hundred pounds soaking wet? I saw her just the other day, when

I brought her some of my special caramel-cherry-spice maté tea and homemade corn-cherry scones, and she seemed fine. As a matter of fact, when I arrived she was up on a ladder, and she certainly didn't seem to have any back or neck injuries. She was a little under the weather, but it was a cold or the flu."

"When was this?"

"Day before yesterday, I think . . . I thought I should make the effort, since you weren't even here when it happened. I just wanted to tell her I was sorry."

"How did you know where to find her?"

"She left her business card. . . ." Bronwyn trailed off as she peeked behind her herbal counter. "I have it around here somewhere. Turns out, she's a rival vintage clothing store owner, which explains why she was so interested. Her place is called Vintage Visions Glad Rags, over off Buchanan."

"Really. That *is* interesting. What's it like?"

"Very nice inventory, but if you ask me not nearly as warm and inviting as Aunt Cora's Closet. She had some ball gowns that I'm sure were from the nineteenth century. But those are more museum pieces than anything someone would actually *wear*. The whole place was too snooty for my taste, by half. And expensive! Too rich for my blood."

"Did anything happen while you were there? Did she say anything in particular?"

Bronwyn frowned in thought, then shook her head. "Nothing at all. She didn't seem particularly bowled over by my gift basket, but she accepted it. But like I say, she told me she was a little under the weather, so maybe that accounts for her mood. She did have a very sweet dog, and I always say a pet lover is never irredeemable."

"Okay, thanks," I said, blowing out a breath. "If you think of anything else, please let me know. Aidan and I are going to talk in the back for a moment."

"I'll keep an eye on things," Bronwyn said, lugging Oscar over to her herbal stand for a treat. Oscar was a miniature pig, but he was still a porker.

In the back room Aidan and I sat down at my old jade green Formica-topped table. I bided my time and waited for Aidan to speak first. In witch circles, simply asking "What may I help you with?" can open up a dangerous can of worms.

"I have to leave town for a little while," he said.

"Really?" Even though I knew perfectly well that he had lived elsewhere in the past, including when he'd worked with the father who had abandoned me, in my mind Aidan was so associated with San Francisco that it was hard to imagine him in any other locale. "How long do you think you'll be gone?"

"And here I was rather hoping you would beg me to stay," he said in a quiet voice, his gaze holding mine.

"Far be it from me to dictate to the likes of Aidan Rhodes."

He smiled. "In any case, I need a favor."

Uh-oh.

"First," he said, "I'll need you to keep tabs on Selena."

Selena was a talented but troubled teenage witch who had come into my life recently. She reminded me of myself at her age: socially awkward and dangerously magical.

I clenched my teeth. It wasn't Aidan's place to tell me to watch over Selena; she needed all of us with whom she had grown close. But it was true that Aidan and I had both been helping her to train her powers. In her case, as in mine, the biggest challenge was learning to keep control over her emotions and her magic in general. But even as he was asking me to partner with him, Aidan still fancied himself the head of the local magical community—me included. It was very annoying.

"Of course," I said. "I *have* been."

"Of course," Aidan repeated. "And Oscar can come in handy with that as well."

I concentrated on reining in my irritation. It wouldn't do to send something flying, which sometimes happened when I lost my temper. Proving that Selena and I weren't that far apart in some areas of our development.

"You're not Oscar's master anymore," I pointed out.

He nodded slowly. "So true. Alas, I will leave that in your more than capable hands, then. Also while I'm gone I need you to fill in for me and adjudicate a few issues. Nothing too strenuous."

"Beg pardon?"

He handed me a heavy, well-worn leather satchel tied with a black ribbon. "You're always so curious about what I do for the local witchcraft community. Now's your chance to find out."

"I never said I wanted to find out. I'm really perfectly happy being in the dark."

Aidan smiled. "Why do I find that hard to believe? In any event, find out you shall."

I sighed. As curious as I was about Aidan's world, I hesitated to be drawn into it. However, I was in his debt and the bill had come due. "Fine. I'm going to need more information, though. What all is involved in 'adjudicating issues'?"

He shrugged. "Little of this, little of that. Mostly it means keeping an eye on things, making sure nothing gets out of hand. Handling disputes, assisting with certifications . . . Valuable job skills that really beef up the résumé, you'll see."

"Uh-huh," I said, skeptical. At the moment I didn't need a more impressive résumé. I needed a lawyer. "What kind of certifications?"

"Fortune-tellers and necromancers must be licensed in the city and county of San Francisco. Surely your good friend Inspector Romero has mentioned this at some point."

"He has, but since I'm neither a fortune-teller nor a necromancer I didn't pay much attention. So that's what you do? Help people fill out forms down at City Hall? Surely—"

"It's all terribly glamorous, isn't it? Resolving petty squabbles, unraveling paperwork snafus . . . The excitement never ends," he said with another smile. "But it's necessary work, and you're more than qualified to handle it while I'm gone. You'll find everything you need in there."

I opened the satchel and took a peek. Inside were what appeared to be hundreds of signed notes written on ancient parchment, a business card with the mayor's cell phone number written on the back in pencil, and a jangly key ring. I pulled out the keys: One was an old-fashioned skeleton key, but the others were modern and, I assumed, unlocked his office at the recently rebuilt wax museum. "Aidan, what are . . . ?"

I looked up, but Aidan was gone, his departure marked by a slight sway of the curtains. Letting out a loud sigh of exasperation, I grumbled, "I swear, that man moves like a vampire."

"Vampire?" Bronwyn poked her head through the

curtains, Oscar still in her arms. "Are we worried about *vampires* now?"

"No, no, of course not," I assured her as I closed the satchel and stashed it under the workroom table. "Sorry—just talking to myself."

"Oh, thank the goddess!" said Bronwyn, and set Oscar down. Whenever Aidan was around, Oscar became excited to the point of agitation, and his little hooves clicked on the wooden planks of the floor as he hopped around. "Never a dull moment at Aunt Cora's Closet."

Bronwyn and Maya knew I was a natural-born witch, and that, when I focused my intentions, I could do things that most humans couldn't. But they weren't aware of the full extent of my magical life. For instance, they didn't know about Oscar's natural form. I kept them in the dark to shield them, to protect Oscar, and because I was still exploring the scope of my magical abilities. I had still been in training as a teenager when forced to flee my grandmother's home in a small West Texas town and was now playing catch-up. I knew, for instance, that there were woodspeople and other shape-shifting creatures similar to Oscar. But as I continued my studies—working my way through Aidan's extensive library on magics as well as learning at the knee of Calypso Cafaro, a gifted botanist—I was honing my powers and sorting out the real from the fairy tale.

And vampires, I knew, were fictional.

And I fervently hoped they stayed that way. Wayward witches, magic gone haywire, and the occasional demon on the rise were plenty enough to deal with. *And now,* I thought as I considered the purpose of Aidan's visit, *there will be witchy disputes and official certifications to figure out.*

Not to mention whatever supernatural storm was ratcheting up here in the beautiful City by the Bay.

I could hardly wait.

"Vampires scare me," Bronwyn said. "My daughter used to love all those stories; she thought Dracula was sexy. But fanged creatures that drink blood? What's sexy about that?"

"It's a puzzle all right," I said.

"Anyway, Maya's here, so I'm going to take off unless you think you'll need me this afternoon."

"A hot date?"

"Even better—I'm picking up my grandkids after day camp and surprising them with a matinee at the Metreon. Then we're going to go back to my place to make pizza and popcorn and tell scary stories with all the lights out!"

"They're lucky to have you, Bronwyn."

"*I'm* the lucky one."

"By all means, go have fun," I said as we ducked back through the curtains to the shop. "I'll be here for the rest of the day. Hi, Maya, how are you?"

"Doing well. Thanks," Maya said as she shrugged off her backpack, a soy chai latte in one hand. She leaned down to pet Oscar and slipped him a bite of her croissant. "I think I aced my exam."

"That's great!" I said. "Not that we're one bit surprised, mind you."

"Certainly not," Bronwyn said. "Maya, you're a natural-born scholar."

"Nah," she said, though clearly pleased at our compliments. "I just study hard."

"If only that was all it took," I said, remembering

my recent struggles with algebra. I had refrained from using magic to help me pass the GED, but just barely. The temptation to cheat—just a little—had been nearly overpowering.

"Oh! Guess what," said Bronwyn as she filled her large woven basket with her knitting, several jars of herbs, and assorted snacks. "I have the most wonderful news."

"What?" asked Maya.

"You remember my friend Charles?"

"Charles Gosnold?" I asked.

"That's the one!"

Maya and I exchanged glances, and I barely managed to refrain from rolling my eyes. Privately, I referred to him as Charles the Charlatan. Although he claimed to be a clairvoyant, he was about as sensitive to the world beyond the veil as a rhinoceros, and even less graceful when it came to interacting with humans. I couldn't imagine why Bronwyn would consider him a friend, except that she was so bighearted that she saw the good in just about everyone. Except, perhaps, vampires.

Seeing the good in others, especially when it's not apparent, was a lesson I struggled to put into practice.

"Well, you'll never believe this, but for my birthday Charles has arranged for the Welcome coven to spend the night at the Rodchester House of Spirits!"

"The house of what, now?" I asked.

"The Rodchester House of Spirits. It's a haunted house in the South Bay," Maya explained.

"Haunted?"

"*Allegedly* haunted," Maya said.

"*Wonderfully* haunted!" Bronwyn insisted. "You mean you haven't been, Lily?"

I shook my head. I hadn't lived in the Bay Area very long and hadn't managed to visit many tourist attractions. And in any case, haunted houses weren't high on my list of places to see. I had enough of that in my regular life.

"I went years ago," said Maya. "My auntie got a kick out of it, but Mom wasn't thrilled. I remember a staircase that went nowhere, and a door that opened onto a wall. . . ."

Bronwyn nodded enthusiastically. "And six kitchens and *hundreds* of rooms."

"Why on earth did this Rodchester person need six kitchens?" I asked.

"She didn't, really," Maya said. "According to legend, the Widow Rodchester kept building, adding on to her house because she was afraid to stop."

"Exactly." Bronwyn nodded. "Sally Rodchester's husband made his fortune manufacturing the famous Rodchester rifles, the ones that were said to have 'won the West'—which meant, essentially, killing the people who used to live here. After both her husband and her baby died young, Sally consulted a medium who told her the souls of those killed with Rodchester rifles were angry. The only way she could stave off further bad luck was by continually adding onto her house. Which, by the way, was already huge."

"How would adding on to her house appease disgruntled spirits?" I asked.

"I can't remember the rationale, exactly . . . ," said Bronwyn.

"My guess is the medium's brother was a carpenter," said Maya. "But then, I'm a cynic."

"Oh, silly! But can you believe we get to spend the

night there?" Bronwyn may have been in her fifties, but when she got excited about something, she glowed like a little girl. And spending the night in a haunted Victorian mansion was just the sort of thing to excite her sense of wonder. "What a magnificent birthday present!"

"Bronwyn, that sounds . . ." *Dangerous,* I thought. My life hadn't been characterized by the love and kindness my dear friend had known, so I tended to see things in a more complex light. ". . . interesting. How did this even come up?"

"I happened to see a brochure for it the other day and thought to myself, I haven't been there in *ages.* I mentioned it to Charles, and he surprised me with the arrangements! We're going to form the circle and call down the moon. . . . Oh! And mix cocktails!"

Cocktails. Of course.

"What could possibly go wrong?" said Maya, smiling but shaking her head. "The Welcome coven, cocktails, and the spirits of angry gunshot victims?"

"You two will join us, won't you?" Bronwyn asked.

"I say this with the greatest of respect and affection, my friend," said Maya, "but: No. Freaking. Way. How 'bout I take you out to lunch for your birthday? Empanadas?"

"Well, I'm disappointed you won't be there, but I accept your offer of lunch with pleasure. Lily? How about you? This sounds right up your alley."

"Bronwyn," I began. "I really don't think this is a good idea."

"Why not?" Bronwyn looked crestfallen.

"It just . . . seems like a bad idea; that's all," I said, unable to articulate the peril I sensed lurking on the dark horizon of my consciousness, elusive but no less real because of that. But then, as I had just been telling Aidan, I wasn't a fortune-teller. I was probably just put off by the idea of a haunted house. "Won't you rethink it?"

"But everything's all arranged. The whole coven's going! Please say you'll come! I know it's late notice, but they had a cancellation, which is how we got in. It's on Saturday, my actual birthday!"

Traipsing around haunted tourist venues on a lark wasn't my idea of a good time. I dealt with enough supernatural weirdness and danger as it was. But could I let my friend—and her coven—go into a potentially hazardous situation without me?

I rubbed the back of my neck. It was barely noon, and I'd already been slapped with a piggy lawsuit and burdened with Aidan's bureaucratic responsibilities, and now I was faced with the prospect of chaperoning Bronwyn's coven overnight in a haunted mansion.

As Mama used to say: Don't some days just starch your drawers?

Chapter 2

Happily, the afternoon was mellow at Aunt Cora's Closet. We had a steady stream of customers, three or four at a time: a trio of college students browsing the sale rack; a mother and teenage daughter looking for a retro prom dress; a woman seeking an extra-special sundress for a cruise with her fiancé. None of them needed much help, so Maya and I sorted through my latest acquisitions from the 1940s and '50s, a special haul I had had to fight for at an estate auction.

The vintage clothes business used to be easy: I would spend a few hours scouring thrift stores and garage sales for inexpensive items that needed a little love and attention, give them a thorough cleaning and the occasional nip and tuck, and sell them at a generous markup. Nowadays, though, the competition was growing ever fiercer as word spread that Granny's jam-packed attic might just be a potential gold mine. Aunt Cora's Closet wasn't an upscale boutique—nor did I want it to be—but finding inventory that was appealing and affordable was getting tougher every day.

After emptying out the plastic bags on the counter, we divided the clothing into four piles: machine washable, hand washable, in need of dry cleaning, and in need of repair.

"Why is the machine-washable pile always the smallest?" Maya asked with a sigh.

"That's life in the vintage clothes business. It makes a person realize how lucky we are nowadays to have machine-washable clothes, not to mention the machines to toss them into."

"Well, sure," said Maya with a rueful smile, "if you want to look on the *bright* side."

I chuckled. "Ask me how I feel on wash day, when my hands are raw and my arms ache from scrubbing and wringing out wet clothes. I might well be singing a different tune."

"I prefer my mom's dresses. Every label has those three magic words . . ."

"Made by Lucille?"

"Wash and wear."

"So true! I love you in the one you're wearing— that's one of Lucille's creations, right?"

"Yes, isn't it great?" The turquoise halter dress was covered in little sprigs of cherries, and on Maya it looked like she was on her way to some sort of fabulous picnic. Like me, Maya used to be a staunch T-shirt-and-jeans gal, but she couldn't resist her mother's reproduction fashions.

Lucille had joined Aunt Cora's Closet as our expert seamstress, an essential asset for a vintage clothes store since so many older garments needed to be altered to

fit today's stronger, healthier bodies. Charmed by some
dresses that were too far gone to save, she had started
deconstructing them to create patterns she then scaled
up to fit the larger dimensions of many modern women.
Fashioned out of retro-patterned materials, the dresses
were an instant hit with my customers, who loved the
way they combined old-fashioned elegance with machine-
washable comfort. Although she continued to do alter-
ations on our vintage clothes, Lucille had hired and
trained several former residents of the Haight-Ashbury
women's shelter to craft her designs in her spacious
sewing loft. One whole corner of Aunt Cora's Closet
was now dedicated to showcasing Lucille's Loft Designs:
By and for Real Women.

The afternoon passed quickly and by twenty to six
the customers had departed, the new acquisitions had
been sorted, and we'd begun our evening ritual of
straightening up the shop preparatory to closing for
the day. I planned to go speak with Autumn Jennings
face-to-face, but I took a moment to enlist Maya's help
with some background research online. While I was
getting better with computers, I still didn't like—or
trust—them. All those electrons bouncing around . . .
it made a witch like me nervous. Too many ghosts in
those machines.

"Here it is," Maya said. "The Web page for Vintage
Visions Glad Rags. That's her store, right?"

I nodded.

"It's in a nice part of town: not far from the Presidio,
near Pacific Heights," Maya pointed out. "Her rent must
cost a fortune. Either her business is doing well or she's
a trust-fund baby."

"Anything else you can tell me about her?" I asked.

Eyes glued to the computer screen, Maya clicked the mouse rapidly as she moved from one Web site to another. "From what I see here, I'd say she's more of a dealer than a shop owner. She's sold some pretty rare and valuable items to museums. This article mentions a Parmelee Riesling; ever heard of her?"

"She's a clothing conservator at the Asian Art Museum. Carlos Romero introduced me to her."

"Want the phone number of Jennings's shop?"

"Yes, please, though I'm going to drop by her store to speak with her in person. I do better face-to-face." This was another part of my witchy weirdness: I liked to deal with people in person, sense their vibrations and auras. Lately I had started to think I was the last person under the age of eighty who didn't carry a cell phone. The phone robs us of body language and the subtle nuances that are part of interpersonal communication, and I'm sufficiently socially awkward that I need all the clues I could get.

"It says Autumn's store is open for another half an hour," I continued, reading the Web site over Maya's shoulder. "Any chance you'd be up for going with me?"

She gave me a quizzical look. "Do you *want* me to go with you?"

Ever since arriving in San Francisco, I'd been learning how to make friends, as well as how to *be* a friend. I'd always been a bit of a loner, so all this was new to me. Turns out a big part of my being a friend was asking for help when I needed it.

And having a conversation with the woman who was suing me qualified as *needing help*.

"Yes, please. Sailor's working tonight and I'd love to have company. I'll take you to dinner after, my treat."

"I'm all yours," she said with a smile. "I happened to notice that Jennings's shop isn't far from Neecha."

"Ooh, Thai food sounds good." We at Aunt Cora's Closet didn't like to skip meals.

That went double for Oscar, who had picked a truly inspired form when he'd decided to manifest as a pig. The little fellow could eat pretty much full-time.

At the sound of dinner talk, he came trotting over.

"Sorry, Oscar. There is no way you're coming to chat with the woman who's accusing you of bodily injury," I said. He blinked up at me, his pink piggy eyes full of innocence and contrition. I wasn't buying it.

Maya, of course, didn't realize he could understand everything I said.

"*Aw*, look. The poor little guy's hungry," she said.

"Let me take him upstairs, and then we can go."

"I'll lock everything up down here. Good night, Oscar," said Maya, giving him a pat. "Don't let Lily forget to feed you."

"Fat chance of that," I muttered under my breath as I passed through the break room. I grabbed Aidan's satchel from under the table before climbing the back stairs to our living quarters over the shop.

When I paused on the landing to open the apartment door, Oscar transformed into his natural state. Part goblin, part gargoyle, he had green-gray scaly skin, a monkey-like snout, big batlike ears, oversized hands, and taloned feet. He often sat on his haunches, but when standing at full height he reached to my waist.

"OMG," Oscar breathed as I closed the door behind us. Oscar was hundreds of years old but a fan of teen culture. "Is that *the satchel*?"

"You mean this?" I held it up.

He reared back slightly. "It is! It's Master Aidan's *satchel*!"

"Aidan's not your master anymore, remember? But what's so special about this bag?"

His voice dropped and his big bottle-glass green eyes widened. "You *stole* the *satchel*? Mistress, I hate to tell you, but you're gonna be in big trouble. B-I-G, *big*."

"Don't be silly; I'm not a thief."

"You stole my wings," Oscar said, referring to the incident that had freed him from Aidan's control—and placed me in Aidan's debt in the first place.

"That was the exception that proves the rule. Aidan gave the bag to me."

Oscar cast me a disbelieving look from the corner of his eye.

"Oscar, honestly?" I said, exasperated. "You honestly believe I stole this? And then brought it home to paw through it?"

After a beat, he relaxed. "Nah, I guess not. You're crazy but you ain't stupid."

"Thanks for the vote of confidence. Now, let's get you fed so I can get on my way."

"Why would Maaa—iiister Aidan give you the *satchel*?"

"He had to go out of town for a little while, so he asked me to take care of a few things for him. It's no big deal; it's temporary, just while he's gone. Why are you so surprised? You know we're supposed to be working together for the coming . . ." I didn't know what to call it.

"Apocalypse?" Oscar suggested.

"*No*, of course not." In fact, that was the word that came to mind, but I knew it wasn't anything nearly so severe. "Let's just say magical mayhem—it might be tough and require a united front, but it won't be the end of the world."

I looked at Oscar, hoping he'd jump in and agree. But he just gazed up at me, unblinking, with those big green eyes.

"Speaking of which, did you turn up anything?" Oscar was supposed to be my spy. He had connections with other familiars and magical creatures; Golden Gate Park was, apparently, chock-full of woodspeople and the like. I was hoping he'd be able to root out some information as to the looming threat Aidan insisted was on its way to the City by the Bay.

"Nothing yet. Everybody's on edge, but it's all a little . . . vague."

I nodded. "Okay, so what's up with this bag? What's the big deal?"

"Nothing! Um, that's . . . that's great that you would be trusted with that! Really. What's for dinner?"

"Oscar . . . is there something I should know about this satchel?"

"Um . . . er . . . no. Maybe put it in a salt circle, is all. And . . . yeah, maybe a salt circle with some of your crystals around it. And a binding charm; maybe use some tallow. That's all."

Thanks a bunch, Aidan, I thought. Clearly, this was no everyday item. But further interrogation of Oscar would have to wait; Autumn Jennings's shop closed soon and Maya was waiting for me downstairs.

"Okay, I'll put it in a circle of protection, but when I get back we're going to have a little chat, you and I."

"I always enjoy chatting with you, mistress."

"I'll just bet. For the moment, tell me what happened between you and Autumn Jennings."

"Who?"

"Don't play dumb, Oscar. I have to go talk with this woman, and I need to know what happened."

He shrugged and picked at his talons. "I didn't like her."

"That became apparent as soon as you head-butted her."

He snickered. "You said 'butt.'"

"Yes, and I'm trying to save *your* green scaly butt, as well as my own."

He snickered some more. Goblin humor.

"This is serious, Oscar. Autumn Jennings is suing me. I need to know why you didn't like her. Did she do or say something in particular? You've never done anything like this before."

"She was up to no good," he said, opening the refrigerator and poking around for leftovers. "Anyway, I didn't *hit* her, exactly. *She* hit *me* with a parasol! All I did was sorta, like, nose her a little, ya know, to help her leave, and she's got a very challenged sense of balance, from what I could tell. Is there any pizza?"

"In the freezer," I said, turning the old Wedgewood oven on to preheat. "Sorry I don't have time to cook for you. I'll bring you a doggy bag from dinner. Thai food."

"I love Thai food! Don't see why I can't go with you," he added in a sullen tone.

"I think you've done just about enough damage at this point. Now, getting back on topic . . ."

"That Autumn person was looking through the inventory like she was afraid she was gonna catch a *disease* or something," he said, dragging a stool over to the refrigerator and climbing on it. Reaching into the freezer compartment, he brought out two cheese pizzas. "Hey!

You know what we should remember to keep on hand? Taquitos!"

"How about some salad?" I suggested in my unending, though entirely futile, attempt to get Oscar to eat something other than carbs and cheese.

"You shoulda seen her, mistress!" he said, ignoring me. "She said mean things to the Lady." The Lady, in Oscar parlance, was Bronwyn. "And she was rude to Maya. And then she dropped that pretty pink flapper dress on the floor. She pretended she didn't do it on purpose, but she did! I *saw* her!"

Despite my irritation, I was touched by how protective Oscar was toward the store, its employees, and its merchandise. He had become interested in vintage clothes sales and in a misguided attempt to help me make more money had even bought counterfeit couture dress labels from an Internet site. I was still trying to figure out how he had pulled that off. He gave me the labels on his last birthday because, he'd explained as if it were obvious, you're supposed to *give* presents on your birthday, not receive them.

"That's annoying, I'll grant you, but we get rude and careless customers all the time, Oscar. What was it about this one that bothered you so?"

"There was . . . something about her. Something off. Smelled funny."

"Like how?"

He shrugged again. "Just felt wrong, somehow."

"Okay. In the future, if someone seems off or smells funny, I want you to tell me, or go hide in the back room or something. Do *not* head-butt them. Understood?"

His expression was all outraged innocence and he threw up his hands.

"You always tell me I should watch over the place and that 'Oscar's on the job,' especially when you aren't around. How else am I supposed to protect people when I'm a pig, I ask you? Told ya I shoulda chosen the form of a lion, given how much trouble you get into."

"It's not that I don't see your point. Just . . . don't just go around head-butting people anymore, okay?"

He snickered again at the word "butt" and popped the pizzas in the oven.

"Oscar doesn't mind being left alone, does he?" Maya asked as we pulled on our coats and scarves. The sunny summer day had given way to a foggy, overcast evening as the thick marine layer blew in off the Pacific Ocean.

"Nah, he'll eat pizza and watch a movie," I said without thinking.

Maya laughed, assuming I was joking. One of these days I was going to have to come clean to my friends about Oscar's true nature. I kept slipping up recently, which was very unlike me. I had lived so much of my life in hiding that subterfuge had become second nature, but now that I had friends, a home, and a place in the community, I was becoming so comfortable that I forgot to keep my secrets. It was all a bit disconcerting.

"What's Sailor up to tonight?" Maya asked as we headed across town in my cherry red vintage Mustang.

"He has a training session with Patience."

Sailor was the wildly sexy yet frustrating man who held my heart in his big capable hands. He had been a powerful psychic when I first met him, but his abilities had diminished upon breaking free from Aidan Rhodes's influence. Sailor was now training with his "cousin," Patience Blix, who was a female version of Sailor: stubborn and cynical and knowing and absolutely, positively drop-dead gorgeous. The problem was . . . she wasn't *really* his cousin; she was simply Rom, like him. And she was a powerful psychic. And did I mention she was gorgeous? Sailor assured me I had no reason to be jealous of her or the time they spent together, but here's the thing I had discovered about the green-eyed monster: It didn't need a reason. Especially on nights like tonight, when Sailor and Patience spent hours alone together.

But I was working on it. I tried to reframe it as an area of vast potential for personal growth, as Bronwyn would say.

"Too bad," said Maya.

"Yes, but then I wouldn't be enjoying your company."

Maya laughed. "Well, that's true."

"Besides, Sailor and I have Mystery Date night coming up."

"What's 'Mystery Date night'?"

"The last weekend of every month we take turns coming up with a surprise date. Last month was his turn, and date night had a beatnik theme. He took me to the Beat Museum, to Vesuvio's for a drink, then to Tosca for dinner. Afterward we went to City Lights bookstore, and he read me passages from Allen Ginsberg's *Howl*. It was lovely."

"Could you two be any cuter? It's almost enough to bring around an old cynic like me."

"One of these days, Maya, you're going to fall for someone, and then Bronwyn and I are going to tease you mercilessly. I can't wait."

"Of that I have no doubt."

We found a parking space a couple of blocks from

Vintage Visions Glad Rags. The sun was low in the sky
and tendrils of fog wrapped around us as we hurried
along the sidewalk. As we approached the store, I saw
what Bronwyn meant about it being too fancy for her
blood. The shop's name might refer to rags, but the
only clothes on display were pricey, high-end vintage
items. I had never been here before because I didn't
frequent this neighborhood and didn't go out of my way
to hunt down my competition. If I passed by a vintage
store I usually stopped in to scope out what they had to
offer and how they staged their merchandise, but, again
like Bronwyn, I preferred shops that sold wearable
clothes rather than custom vintage garments. At Aunt
Cora's Closet we carried the occasional Chanel or Hat-
tie Carnegie suit, but those were rare. The clothes at
Vintage Visions, in comparison, were the opposite:
more collectible than wash-and-go.

Maya and I exchanged a glance, eyebrows raised,
and entered.

It felt a little like walking into a Christmas tree: Everything was decorated in sumptuous, deep shades of red
and purple, topped with gold and silver gilt. Three vintage crystal chandeliers sparkled overhead, and antique
mirrors gleamed on every wall.

No one was there.

"Hello?" I called.

Behind the cash register was a large hound dog
snoozing on a little red rug.

"Hi there, puppy," I said. She gave me a lazy thump
of the tail but didn't so much as raise her head.

"That's no puppy," said Maya as she peered over my
shoulder. "That pretty girl probably weighs almost as
much as I do."

The dog thumped her tail again.

Maya crouched down and petted the canine, then checked her tags. I heard a tinkling sound. "How cute. Her collar's like a charm bracelet. Let me see . . . according to the tag, it says her name's Loretta."

"Great name."

"Isn't it? Not much of a watchdog, though, are you, Loretta?"

The dog lifted her head a few inches and thumped her tail a few more times.

"Hello? Anybody home?" I called out again. "Surely if her dog's here and the door's open, Autumn Jennings can't be far."

With a final pat for Loretta, Maya looked behind the racks and poked her head into the changing rooms. "No sign of anybody," she said.

"Helloooo?" I called out again, louder this time.

"Maybe she stepped out for coffee or ran an errand or something," Maya said. She flicked through a rack of intricately beaded flapper dresses and held up one in shades of blue and purple. "This is nice."

"That would look great on you." Maya never used to wear vintage clothes, but now that she had gotten into her mother's fashions she'd become more adventurous.

"Ugh," she said. "Check out the price tag. Are there people in this world who think it's reasonable to spend twenty-six hundred dollars on a flapper dress?"

"Let's ask Autumn, if we ever find her. How about this one?" I held up a gorgeous Edwardian-era ball gown, complete with bustle.

"That's amazing," said Maya. "These dresses look like museum pieces, though, don't they? I mean, assuming you were tiny enough to fit into that outfit, where would you wear it? It's a bit much for a cocktail party."

"Opening night at the opera?" I suggested. "Or maybe to the ballet?"

"If you were on*stage*, maybe. I could imagine these dresses being worn as costumes, or in turn-of-the-century London, but they're a little over-the-top for San Francisco's social scene. And wouldn't you need to wear a corset and the whole nine yards?"

I nodded. "Well, as you said, Autumn's a vintage clothing dealer. Maybe she's planning to sell them to a museum or a collector. I've heard collectors will pay good money for just the right piece." I looked around and spied a key ring on the counter beside the cash register. "I know this is a nice neighborhood and all, but doesn't it seem strange that she'd leave the shop wide-open after dark and just . . . take off?"

"Yes, it does. Unless she's through there." Maya pointed to a small door in the wall behind the cash register. "It could be a closet, but maybe it leads to an apartment. Do you think we should open it?"

"I hate to violate her privacy."

"Try knocking."

I knocked on the door, calling out, "Autumn?"

There was no response.

"See if it's locked," Maya said.

I reached for the doorknob and slowly turned it. "It's not locked."

"So open it."

I hesitated, feeling uneasy. Something wasn't right here.

"Do you think we should call the cops?" Maya asked. "Maybe it would be better to be safe than sorry."

"It's hard to believe the dog would be so relaxed if something bad had happened."

"That's true."

"This is ridiculous. I'm opening the door." I pulled the door wide—it wasn't a closet, but the entrance to a narrow staircase.

"Hello? Autumn?" I called up the stairwell. "Anybody home?"

There was a muted thumping from above.

I looked at Maya, who nodded.

"Hello?" I called out again, then started up the stairs, Maya close on my heels. "Anybody up here? Autumn?"

At the second-floor landing, a room to the right was jam-packed with boxes and racks and clothing of all types. One whole movable rack was crammed with clothes, including antique ball gowns; piles of white cotton and lace lingerie were spread out over a small twin bed. Stacks of cardboard boxes lined two walls.

Across the hall a door stood ajar, revealing a plush quilt-covered queen-sized bed, complete with satin canopy; the floor was strewn with papers and clothes.

Autumn Jennings's bedroom? I felt suddenly self-conscious about snooping any further. I could see a kitchen through the open arch at the end of the hall, and that was it. Though the furnishings appeared expensive, the whole place felt sort of . . . *off.* Dingy and messy and more than a little sad, especially compared to the sumptuous luxury of the store downstairs. I lived over my store, too, but my apartment was warm and cozy, with a sunny, old-fashioned kitchen, a charming living room, and a terrace fragrant with herbs and flowering plants. And Oscar, of course. And, increasingly, Sailor.

So even though I was facing a lawsuit, dealing with

whatever Aidan had just dumped in my lap, worried about Bronwyn's coven spending the night in a haunted house, and apprehensive about the magical challenges Aidan felt were imminent, I took a moment to remind myself: All in all, I was one lucky witch. Autumn Jennings didn't seem nearly so fortunate.

"Maya, we should go. These must be her private rooms . . ."

Maya didn't answer.

I looked over my shoulder. Maya stood absolutely still, her hands in the air.

A woman stood in the arch at the end of the hall, pointing a gun at us.

Chapter 3

"Autumn? Autumn Jennings?" I asked, raising my hands as well. "Please put that down. There's no need for a gu—"

"Who are you?" the woman demanded. The pistol waved in the air slightly, as though too heavy for her to keep steady. She was small and birdlike, and her eyes were huge and frightened looking. Her skin was an unnatural shade of gray and she coughed into an old-fashioned handkerchief.

"I'm so sorry. I think we must have stumbled into your private quarters," I said. "It's just that the shop downstairs was open but nobody was around. We thought maybe we'd find you up here."

She looked confused. A sheen of sweat gleamed on her ashen forehead.

"I'm Lily Ivory," I tried again. "I own Aunt Cora's Closet? I was just—"

"You're here *spying* on me?" She looked wildly around the hallway. "What's going on? Are there more of you downstairs?"

"No, no, not at all. Really, it's not like that," I said. "It's just me and Maya. Just the two of us. We mean you no harm. I came here to talk to you in person about the papers I received today. About the lawsuit."

She frowned as though struggling to understand what I was saying, and next thing I knew, she swayed on her feet. I remembered Oscar telling me she seemed "challenged" when it came to balance.

"Autumn, are you all right? You don't look well."

She seemed to be making an effort to stand tall, but she listed to one side so far that she fell against the wall. Then, as if in slow motion, she slid all the way down until she was sitting on the floor. The hand holding the gun went limp, and the heavy weapon clunked on the floor.

Maya approached slowly, crouching in front of Autumn and gently pushing the gun out of her reach. Autumn said nothing. Maya picked up the weapon, holding it gingerly with her thumb and pointer finger. She stashed it atop a high corner cabinet where it was out of sight.

"Autumn, we'll call an ambulance," I said. "You're not well."

"I just . . ." She trailed off. "I can't feel my hands."

Maya already had her phone out and was dialing 911.

Then Autumn slumped over onto her side on the floor.

I knelt next to her and pressed my hand against her forehead. Her skin felt clammy but not feverish. I closed my eyes, trying to convey sensations of comfort and calm, concentrating on sending healing energy through the pads of my fingers, beyond the barrier of skin, clear to the vitality of the blood. I encountered resistance, and my energy dissipated. I swore under my breath. My grandmother Graciela would know what to do in this situation, but I hadn't inherited her talent for curing. Autumn seemed too far gone to accept my special brand of help.

"What do you think is wrong with her?" asked Maya in a low voice, the phone still held to her ear as we waited for the paramedics.

"I have no idea," I said. "It could be anything—a virus, or a chronic health problem. Maybe she's in diabetic shock, something like that?"

"The 911 dispatcher suggests covering her with blankets in case it's shock."

"Good idea." I rushed into Autumn's messy bedroom and pulled the quilt and a pillow from the bed. Several items fell to the floor—jeans and a nightgown and a stack of mail, including a manila envelope. I picked up the mail and placed it on the bedside table but let the clothes join those already covering the floor.

Once we covered Autumn and made her as comfortable as possible, there didn't seem to be much else to do but wait. She mumbled a few unintelligible phrases, and I did what I could to cast a comforting spell, but it wasn't until I heard the faraway whine of an ambulance that I began to relax.

Maya met the paramedics at the shop door to lead them up the stairs.

And then she and I stood back and watched helplessly, hoping the professionals would be able to figure out what was wrong.

"Has she ingested drugs or intoxicants of any kind?" asked one of the EMTs, a young man, as he checked Autumn's vital signs.

"Does she have any chronic health problems?" asked his partner, a young woman.

"I don't know. We found her this way," I responded.

They strapped her onto a stretcher and carefully navigated the steep stairs, Maya and I following behind them.

"I take it you work here?" said the woman, her eyes running over my outfit.

"I, uh . . . vintage clothes are my passion," I answered.

"Lock up after us, will you?" The EMT nodded at Loretta, who still lay on her bed, apparently unconcerned by all the commotion. "And take care of the dog?"

"Yes, of course," I said. "Where are you taking Autumn?"

"UCSF. You can call and check on her later."

After they left, siren wailing, Maya gave me a quizzical look. "Looks like you've been appointed dog sitter and keeper of the keys."

"Looks that way."

"Shouldn't we see if we can find someone closer to her, like a relative or a good friend? I mean, not to put too fine a point on it, but Autumn Jennings is *suing* you. There's a slight chance she might not want you taking care of her shop and her dog."

"Okay, good point. Judging from the apartment upstairs, I'd say she lives alone, but maybe she has family nearby. Let's look for an address book, or a cell phone with a phone number labeled 'Mom.'" Maya and I started searching the store. As I poked around, I took a gander at some of the papers behind the counter. I didn't want to go too far in violating Autumn's privacy, but if something was lying out in plain sight . . .

"Find anything?" asked Maya.

"Not yet."

"You don't think any of this is . . . magic related, do

you? I mean, I thought this was just a sad case of some- one getting sick."

I paused as my hands alighted on some fake haute couture tags, the kind Oscar had given me—he still struggled with the concept that fraud was morally and ethically wrong. Why would Autumn have such things? Could she be involved in some sort of fraud, passing off modern reproductions as genuine vintage couture? Or might there be a benign explanation for her having these tags—after all, at one point I'd had some in my possession, too.

And speaking of familiars . . . I cast a wary glance at Loretta. No, I didn't think Autumn Jennings was a practitioner, but I wouldn't put it past Aidan to have assigned a familiar as protection to a cowan—he'd done it before. Still, if she was under Aidan's protection, why wouldn't he have he told me?

"Lily?" urged Maya.

"What? Oh, sorry. . . . No, I have no reason to believe it's anything out of the ordinary."

"That's a relief."

"Except . . ."

"Except what?"

I shrugged. "Except that *I'm* involved. As the men in my life like to point out, I seem to attract trouble. Magical trouble."

"Maybe it's just a coincidence that Autumn fell sick while we were here. Maybe the trouble is just run-of-the-mill, pain-in-the-neck litigation, and a random ill-ness, not witchcraft."

"It could be. . . ."

"After all, coincidences happen," Maya said.

"Every day, in fact."

Then my eyes fell on a brochure for the Rodchester House of Spirits.

Was this another of the weird coincidences that seemed to follow me around, like a will-o'-the-wisp along the proverbial riverbank? Or might it be a warning, or a clue? Then again, the Rodchester House of Spirits was a popular tourist attraction; maybe one of Autumn's customers had left it here. As simple as that.

"What about Loretta?" Maya asked.

The dog had roused herself to lift her head and still thumped her tail amiably whenever anyone addressed her. But she had remained calm while the paramedics tromped through the store, and she hadn't seemed to notice anything amiss about her mistress.

"Are we even sure she's Autumn's dog?"

"Does it matter? We can't just leave her here."

"True, but maybe Autumn's dog sitting and we can bring Loretta back to her family."

"There was a phone number on her dog tag. Let me give that a try," Maya said, crouching down to pet the pup and check the tags that tinkled on her plaid collar. She stood and used her cell to call the phone number. An electronic version of "Greensleeves" led us to a cell phone on a shelf behind the register.

"Well, that answers two questions: Loretta *is* Autumn's dog, and now we know where Autumn's cell phone is."

"Good, it's not locked," said Maya as she swiped the phone's touch screen and started to search through the contacts list. I watched over her shoulder, impressed by her ease with the mysterious electronic devices called smartphones.

"Anything?"

She shook her head. "No listing for 'Mom' or 'Dad' or 'Great-aunt Betsy.' Looks like mostly business contacts. From her history, though, it looks like she called someone named Jamie a lot in the last couple of days."

"Man or woman?"

"Let's find out," she said, dialing. No one answered, so she left a message that if this was a friend of Autumn Jennings could she or he please try back at this number right away, or at Aunt Cora's Closet tomorrow.

Next we went outside to see if the neighbors could provide any information. On one side was a bank, and on the other a cupcake bakery; both were shuttered for the night. The businesses across the street were similarly dark, so we gave up and returned to Vintage Visions Glad Rags.

"The hospital must have a procedure for finding relatives," I said. "Right?"

Maya nodded and put Autumn's cell phone back where she'd found it. Jamie hadn't called in the time we'd been looking around.

"I suppose we've done all we can. So, I guess we should lock up for now and hope Autumn's feeling better in the morning. I'll leave her a note and also call the hospital to let her know I have her dog and her keys."

The key ring jangled when I picked it up, and at the sound Loretta roused herself from her bed, shook vigorously, wagged her tail, and trotted to the front door.

"Well, I guess we know how to get her moving," said Maya. "Want to go for a ride in the car, sweetie pie?"

"In the past year I've brought home a cat, a baby, and a teenage witch," I mused, letting out a sigh as I gazed down at the dog. "I fear my pig might disown me for good if I bring home Loretta. Any chance you'd be willing . . . ?"

Maya was scratching Loretta behind her big floppy ears. "I would if I could. She reminds me of a dog we had when I was growing up. She could stay at my parents' house, maybe, but now that Mom's busy at the sewing shop every day, and I'm going to school and working at Aunt Cora's Closet . . ."

"What if you brought her to the store during the day?" I said, hoping to talk her into keeping the dog until other arrangements could be made. As Maya had pointed out, we couldn't leave Loretta here by herself, and Oscar might just decide to be another witch's familiar if I brought her home. "She's clearly not aggressive, so she won't frighten the customers. And Autumn will probably be home soon, so it would just be a day or two."

"Didn't you tell the paramedics *you* were the dog sitter?"

"I'm working on learning to ask for help, remember?"

Maya chuckled. "Okay, sure, why not? My folks will get a kick out of her; they've been talking about getting another dog. You want to come home with me, Loretta?"

The dog's adorable, chocolate brown eyes gazed up at Maya and she wagged her tail languidly.

"I'm gonna take that as a yes."

When I entered my apartment, I was greeted by the sound of gobgoyle snores emanating from Oscar's cubby over the refrigerator.

It was a much-needed, homey sound since I was still shaken by the encounter with Autumn. She had seemed so small, so wild-eyed and frightened. The paramedics hadn't given us any clue what she might be suffering from. Based upon her appearance, I would guess her to be in her forties or early fifties, possibly younger. What could be wrong?

Next, I called UCSF hospital, but I couldn't get any information other than that Autumn was in the ICU, which didn't sound promising.

After putting on the kettle for a cup of tea, I reached up to a high shelf and pulled down my huge Book of Shadows, splaying it open on the counter. My grandmother Graciela had gifted it to me, and it was one of the few possessions I had taken when I fled my hometown. The precious tome was so old that the pages felt more like soft fabric than stiff paper under my fingertips; simply flipping through it helped connect me to Graciela and the line of powerful women who had come before us, throughout eternity. Half scrapbook, half witchcraft manual, my Book of Shadows was filled with recipes and spells and quotes and photos and articles cut out of the newspaper, reminding me of many things I would rather forget but that I must remember.

I poured steaming water over a tea ball in my favorite mug and turned the pages. I didn't know what I was looking for, but often the book would help me, flipping open to a particularly significant entry or something entirely new that I'd never seen before.

Not this time, however. I noticed a new recipe for sprite dust, which could come in handy, but I had no idea for what. But nothing that referenced Autumn's symptoms of confusion and paranoia, her paleness and perspiration.

After some more fruitless page turning, I slammed the book closed, placed it back on its shelf, and then showered with handmade lemongrass and rosemary soap. I dressed in a fresh black skirt and blouse. Before I'd fled my hometown at the tender age of seventeen, my grandmother had taught me many things about life and about magics. Chief among the latter was this: "Wear all black or all white when spellcasting. Colors may confuse and alter one's intentions."

It was hard to say how much of what Graciela taught me came from her knowledge and experience as a practitioner and how much was based on old wives' tales, but in the end I had decided it didn't matter. What was crucial was that I be able to focus my intent. Besides, a lot of those old wives' tales were spot-on.

Aidan's leather satchel remained where I'd left it, sitting on top of the old trunk I used as a coffee table in the living room. Before I left earlier I had done as Oscar suggested and encircled it with salt and with stones of ocean jasper, eye agate, and labradorite at the perimeter for protection.

Why was Oscar so worried about the bag being here in my possession? Aidan hadn't indicated there was anything to be concerned about, and I hadn't sensed any warning vibrations.

Still . . . Aidan was a master manipulator, adept at casting magical glamours to mask the truth.

Warily, I sat on the floor in front of the coffee table and studied the bag: It was worn butter soft, a deep, rich brown leather. The black ribbon tied around it appeared to be satin, shiny but fraying slightly at the edges.

I took a moment to intone a grounding spell, stroked my medicine bag, and then finally opened the satchel. The contents appeared just as before. I took out a set of keys, the business card with what appeared to be the mayor's personal number scribbled on the back, and a

folder with multiple copies of the legal statute covering
fortune-telling licensure in the county of San Francisco, along with some application forms.

But what really interested me were the dozens of
pieces of parchment paper. I drew one out: On it, in a
typed font as though from an old-fashioned typewriter,
was *Travis R. Pfost, 2704 Potrero, Apt. 217.* Travis's name
was signed in an illegible scrawl. I took out another:
Kelli Vilaria, 1872 Divisadero (at Golden Gate). Kelli's
signature was loopy and she dotted her *i*'s with little
hearts.

There was something about those scraps . . .

Placing my finger on Kelli's signature, I felt it: a shim-
mer, a quickening. The unmistakable energy of blood
magic.

I took out another piece of parchment, and another.
All had names and addresses; all had been signed in
blood.

Well, now, didn't that just take the rag off the bush?

Were these markers of some kind? People who owed
Aidan favors? If so, they must be very important favors
to have been signed in blood. The magical community
exchanged minor favors all the time; one's word of
honor was usually sufficient. Markers memorialized in
print and signed in blood were reserved for serious
magic. I had always thought of Aidan as the godfather
of the Bay Area's magical community, so perhaps he
was living up to his name in great Hollywood tradition:
Maybe he was making offers folks couldn't refuse and
then forcing them to do as he willed in return.

I sat back, hugged myself, and glared at the satchel.

It was one thing to join forces with Aidan to keep
Selena safe and to go up against whatever magical threat

might be looming over San Francisco. Quite another to be part of a magical shakedown.

So . . . what was I going to do about it?

Exhaustion washed over me. It had been one heck of a day.

I was putting the markers back in the satchel when one escaped from the pile and slowly drifted to the floor. It was signed with a particularly elaborate signature:

Autumn Jennings.

Damn.

Chapter 4

First thing the next morning I called the hospital again but learned only that Autumn Jennings was no longer in the ICU.

Bronwyn wouldn't be in until late, and Maya had a sketch group, so I was alone in the shop. It was quiet, with only one or two customers at a time, so I sorted through business-related paperwork while Oscar snored on his special purple silk pillow. Maya had called to say her mother had taken Loretta to her sewing loft this morning, so I didn't have to worry about her.

I had tried—and failed—to get Oscar to tell me more about the satchel, or to divulge Aidan's location, or at least how to get in touch with him. But Oscar either didn't know, or—more likely—wasn't talking. One of the more disturbing aspects of my relationship to my familiar was that he filled me in only on a need-to-know basis, and his interpretation of my needing to know was often quite different from mine. That was one of the problems of having a familiar who wasn't a real familiar.

A *real* witch's familiar, I grumbled to myself, would do as its mistress said.

Oscar was more like a . . . sidekick. A recalcitrant, garrulous, hungry, stubborn sidekick.

I stashed Aidan's satchel under the counter and promised myself that I'd try to work up the energy to look through it soon, hoping to figure out its significance.

But for now I sipped my coffee, looked around Aunt Cora's Closet, and willed myself to relax.

My shop gave me a deep sense of satisfaction. I felt the welcoming hum of the clothes, breathed in the scents of clean laundry and herbal sachets, and appreciated all the way to the very marrow of my bones just how lucky I was. I had been alone and lonely for so long, but now I had my health, a wonderful job, good friends to confide in and watch my back, Oscar to make me laugh—and occasionally save my life—and Sailor to woo my heart and hold me in his arms. Oscar and Sailor were occasionally infuriating to the point of madness, but still. I honestly had no idea what I'd done to deserve so much.

The memory of Autumn's apartment highlighted my good fortune. Despite the opulence of her store and its wares, her living space had seemed so dreary and depressing and . . . *depressed*.

The bell over the shop door tinkled.

"You Lily Ivory?" demanded a thirtysomething woman, wearing a sort of hippie-chic outfit that included scarves and leather boots. Trailing her into the store was a woman of similar age, dressed like a Goth, in all black.

Not another process server, I thought. *Who did Oscar head-butt this time?*

"Yes," I said. "And you are . . . ?"

"I'm Ebony Trevil," said the one dressed in black. "Aidan said we were supposed to bring our issues to you."

"Ah," I began. "Listen, I—"

"I'm Isadora," said the first. "One name. Like Madonna."

Ebony rolled her eyes and crossed her arms over her chest. "Well, Lily, maybe you could tell the wannabe Madonna here to keep her nose out of my client list?"

"I can't help it if your *former* clients come flocking to me," responded Isadora with a shrug. "Cheaper prices, better service. This is a capitalist system we live in, more's the pity, and that's how capitalism works."

"Pardon me, I really don't—," I began, but they weren't listening.

"Are you even licensed?" Ebony demanded.

Isadora made a face.

"That's what I thought! You're not even licensed! If I wasn't such a team player I would have reported you to the authorities already. You have to be licensed. Tell her, Lily."

Oscar snorted awake, startling both women. As was usually the case for anyone who spotted Oscar in his piggy guise, their surprise turned to laughter.

"It's a pig!"

"So cute! Here, piggy piggy pig . . ."

The brief respite gave me a chance to gather my wits. The women's squabbling was obviously the sort of thing Aidan had asked me to take care of. How hard could it be? I could handle it. I adapted one of the techniques Bronwyn's coven used during group discussions, grabbed a Brazilian rain stick, and held it up high.

"This is the talking stick," I said solemnly, enjoying the sound of the rice inside the stick cascading down, like a torrential rain. "Only she who holds the stick may speak. Am I clear?"

The women nodded.

I handed the stick to the first woman who had walked in. "Ebony, tell me your side of the story, slowly and clearly. You have until the sound of rain stops."

"But—," she said, shaking her head.

"You're wasting your talking time," I warned.

Ebony finally settled down enough to tell me her complaint. "Okay, here's the deal. Isadora used to be my apprentice. She didn't complete her training but opened her own shop nevertheless."

Isadora jumped in: "I don't have to—"

"Do *not* disrespect the talking stick," I ordered, ignoring a snort of laughter from Oscar.

Isadora fell silent.

"Continue," I said.

"I sell love charms and prosperity spells, only for good, never for evil! Isadora's been making up these stupid do-it-yourself kits, which cost half what I charge, and I'm losing business because of it. It's not fair—" The stick fell silent, and so did Ebony.

I took the stick, turned it over, and handed it to Isadora. "Now you."

"My kits aren't stupid!" she said. "They contain herbs and stones, whatever is required for the spell or charm. I have as much right as Ebony to sell whatever I want to whoever I want, thank you very much." She handed the stick back.

Both women looked at me expectantly.

"Hmmmm," I said, wishing I had a long gray beard to stroke to make me look wiser. "Isadora, do you explain to your clients the concept of a witch's ability to

influence reality? That it is the concentration of *intent* that is crucial, not the specific items in a kit?"

"Sure," she said.

I raised one eyebrow.

"Well, I mean, kind of. I mean, I try, but they don't always understand."

"Perhaps that's because you are not being clear," I said. "If spells were as easy as mixing a few items together, then anyone could cast them. But we all know that's not the way things work in the magical world. Now, what's this about you not being licensed?"

"I thought Ebony was just making that up!" Isadora protested.

"Oh, please," Ebony said with scorn. "You want to be a businesswoman, learn about business."

"Fortune-tellers and necromancers must be licensed by the city of San Francisco," I confirmed. "Go down to City Hall and apply for a license, or else you'll be subject to fines and possible imprisonment. Nobody wants to see that happen, now, do we?"

"Fine by me," Ebony said. "Let her spend some time in jail. It'll build character."

"I can't believe this," Isadora said. "You must be mistaken."

"Afraid not." I crouched down behind the counter, opened the satchel, and brought out a copy of the licensure for necromancers. "Article 17.1 of the San Francisco Municipal Code makes fortune-telling permits available in exchange for an application and license fee. Section 1305 states says that the chief of police *'shall grant the permit'* unless the applicant has been convicted of a felony or two or more misdemeanors relating to fraud, etc. in the past seven years."

Isadora was avoiding my eyes and seemed to be thinking.

"Felony fraud conviction?" I asked.

"Oh, wait, *conviction*?" she repeated. "Oh, no, no. I'm good."

By which I assumed she had, perhaps, been brought up on charges at one point. But I wasn't going to open *that* can of worms.

"But I'm no fortune-teller," Isadora continued. "So that stupid statute doesn't apply to me."

"These are civilians we're talking about," Ebony said. "They don't know the difference."

"She's right," I said. "The statute covers that. Listen: *'Fortune-telling shall mean the telling of fortunes, forecasting of futures, or reading the past by means of any occult, psychic power, faculty, force, clairvoyance, cartomancy, psychometry, phrenology, spirits, tea leaves, tarot cards, scrying, coins, sticks, dice, sand, coffee grounds, crystal gazing, or other such reading.'"* I paused to take a breath. *"'Or through mediumship, seership, prophecy, augury, astrology, palmistry, necromancy, mind reading, telepathy, or other craft, art, science, talisman, charm, potion, magnetism, magnetized article, or substance.'"*

Ebony had crossed her arms over her chest and was waggling her head in an "I told you so" gesture.

"Wait," said Isadora. "Coffee grounds? Who *does* that?"

"It's as legit as tea leaves," responded Ebony.

"And that's not all," I continued. *"'It shall also include effecting spells, charms, or incantations, or placing, or removing curses or advising the taking or administering of what are commonly called love powders or potions in*

*order, for example, to get or recover property, stop bad
luck, give good luck, put bad luck on a person or animal,
stop or injure the business or health of a person or
shorten a person's life, obtain success in business, enter-
prise, speculation, and games of chance, win the affection of a person, make one person marry or divorce
another, induce a person to make or alter a will, tell
where money or other property is hidden, make a person
to dispose of property in favor of another, or other such
similar activity.'"*

I put the paper down.

"Dang," said Isadora. "They cover just about everything, don't they?"

"Just about."

"Are *you* licensed?" Isadora asked me, her chin jutting out stubbornly.

"Aidan takes care of all that for me." In fact, I didn't
have a license because I didn't need one. For me witchcraft was a way of life, not a source of income. I had
vintage clothing for that, and lately the store had been
doing really well.

At the mention of Aidan's name the two women
lowered their eyes and seemed less certain.

"Oh, and just in case you're wondering, Municipal
Code 1302 (b) states, *'fortune-telling shall also include
those* pretending *to perform these actions.'"*

They both looked a little stunned.

"Just FYI," I added.

"Okay," Isadora said, picking up the paper and looking it over. "I'll go register for a license. But Ebony has
to get off my back about 'stealing' her customers. It's a
free country, after all."

"But you'll agree to do as Lily says, and inform

them of the difference between hiring a professional—
a licensed, trained professional like me—and doing it
themselves at home with your kit?" Ebony demanded.

"You honestly think they can't figure that out for
themselves?" Isadora asked. "But okay, sure. I'll make
it clearer, and then they can make up their own minds."

"Fair enough," Ebony said.

The women turned to stare at me. What was supposed
to happen next? Acting on instinct, I reached down,
grabbed the satchel, and set it on the counter. Ebony and
Isadora took a step back.

"Whoa," said Ebony.

"Yeah, what she said," said Isadora.

Ebony met my gaze. "So we put our hands on it and
swear? Just like that?"

"Just like that," I said, though in fact I was following
their lead. I was one sorry excuse for an Aidan substi-
tute. To be fair, I hadn't had much in the way of on-the-
job training. And I knew from experience that this was
Aidan's idea of fun, to watch me flailing. Not that he
was actually watching. I hoped.

The women placed their right hands on the satchel
and whispered some kind of oath. Satisfied, they looked
at each other, nodded, and left.

Case closed, I thought with relief. But just as I was
stowing the bag beneath the counter, another woman
stormed into Aunt Cora's Closet. Like Isadora and
Ebony, she didn't have the air of a person looking for the
perfect 1970s outfit for a costume party. She was already
dressed in a distinctive fashion: a colorful dashiki over
bright purple leggings, with lots of chunky tribal jewelry.

"I'm in a time crunch. I need help getting some paperwork through City Hall."

"How am I supposed to do *that*?" I said without thinking.

"If I knew the answer, I'd do it myself, wouldn't I? Aidan always took care of it. Don't you have the mayor's number?"

As a matter of fact, I did. I remembered seeing it in the satchel. But was I supposed to call the mayor now? And what would I say? Offer a bribe? A veiled threat? A campaign pledge?

"Leave me your information. I'll see what I can do," I said, pushing a pad of paper and pen across the counter to her.

What a morning, I thought as the woman scribbled a lengthy note. *I'm ready to call it a day and it isn't even noon. How long is Aidan planning to be gone?*

Just then the scent of roses enveloped me. I looked up to see Sailor opening the shop door, its little bell tinkling merrily.

He paused in the doorway, motorcycle helmet under his arm, hair tousled, dark eyes smoldering, a very slight smile on his face.

"*There* she is," he said in a quiet voice.

Those few words thrilled me to my core. They made me feel as though Sailor had been searching for me his whole life and had finally found me. They made me feel wanted, and . . . loved. And, let's face it; they made me think about things much more delicious than bureaucratic obstructions. . . .

The woman finally finished writing her saga, and I promised to look into the matter. She didn't seem particularly satisfied, but she nodded and thanked me nonetheless. Then she paused and looked from me to Sailor and back to me. She raised her eyebrows, smiled, and left.

Sailor wrapped his arms around me, we kissed, and I lost track of the rest of the world. It took Oscar snorting and bumping our legs to remind us that we were in public and that I had a business to run. My pig didn't approve of public displays of affection, or PDA, as he called it.

"Your visitor seemed agitated," said Sailor when he released me. He took a sip of my now cool coffee and grimaced.

"You should have seen the pair before her. Want me to make you a fresh cup?"

He shook his head. "No, thanks. No time. But tell me, what's going on?"

"Aidan left town."

"For good?" There was a hopeful note in his voice. Despite our recent pledge to work together if and when the need arose, Sailor and Aidan weren't exactly buddies.

"Just temporarily. At least, I hope so."

"Oh, well. How I shall miss his delightful company."

"Meanwhile, he's left me in charge."

"In charge of *what*, exactly? He asks with trepidation . . ."

"I'm still figuring that out. Basically he gave me a satchel and told me to deal with things, then took off before I could ask him questions."

"You've got to be kidding."

"'Fraid not."

"Let me get this straight: You have Aidan's satchel? *The* satchel?"

"Yes. What is it about that stupid bag? Oscar was freaked-out as well."

"What—"

I felt a tingling on the back of my neck.

Sailor felt it, too. We glanced at each other, then turned as one to face the door.

A man and woman entered the store. He was older, probably in his early fifties; she looked to be about my age. Both wore inexpensive dark suits, and neither smiled.

"Lily Ivory?" asked the man.

Sailor planted himself between them and me. "Who's asking?"

"I'm Inspector Stinson," the man said, pulling a leather case from his breast pocket and flashing a shiny SFPD badge. "And this is my partner, Inspector Ng."

Since arriving in San Francisco, setting up shop, and delving into the occasional murder investigation, I had dealt with the police department a fair amount. But usually I was interrogated—sometimes on a good day even asked to help solve crimes—by Homicide Inspector Carlos Romero, who had become a friend. A crazy part of me wanted to ask whether I could request Carlos's presence, as though a person could ask to be questioned by whatever cop she wanted.

"And who are you?" Stinson asked Sailor pointedly.

"A friend," Sailor said, staring him down. After a moment Stinson nodded and looked around him, to me.

"We'd like to speak with you about the circumstances surrounding the death of one Autumn Jennings."

"*Death?* Autumn . . . died?"

He gave a curt nod. Inspector Ng said, "Early this morning."

"What happened?" I asked, shaken. "I mean, it was clear she was ill, but what did she have?"

"That's what we're trying to figure out," said Stinson. "We'd like to get a statement from you."

"Of course."

I told them what Maya and I had seen when we arrived at Vintage Visions Glad Rags yesterday, trying to remember details and reconstruct the timeline. Sailor stood, silent and strong, by my side throughout. I realized I hadn't yet filled him in on what had happened last night, but Sailor was the quiet sort; he would wait to have his questions answered.

Not long ago Aidan had cautioned me that my relationship with Sailor was doomed. He claimed witches like me couldn't be in love without making ourselves vulnerable and therefore sacrificing our power. I had accused Aidan of being jealous, but a small part of me couldn't deny that my life experience supported his theory. Still, I was determined to prove him wrong. Not to toot my own horn, but I was one powerful witch, and becoming more so all the time. Loving Sailor made me stronger, I was sure.

Moments such as this one reinforced that belief. I could feel Sailor's strength humming beside me, warm and welcome, like a psychic hug.

"Nothing else?"

I shook my head. "I can't think of anything."

"Jennings didn't say anything else? Just this sort of paranoid delusion?"

"All she asked was whether we were spying on her, and if we were alone. I really have no way of knowing whether it was a delusion or not, though it did seem that way."

"Okay. We'll need to speak with your assistant, this, uh"—he checked his notes—"Maya Jackson, as well."

"Of course. She'll be in this afternoon, or I can give you her contact information."

"That would be helpful. Thank you. Tell me, why did you go to Jennings's shop yesterday?"

"She . . ." Only then did it dawn on me that the lawsuit pending against me could be seen as a motive for murder. Of course, it wasn't *in fact* a motive because I meant Autumn Jennings no harm, but since these officers didn't know me the way Carlos did, they might not appreciate that. But the truth would come out one way or the other—best to face the music. "She had me served with legal papers yesterday. She was suing me for personal injury in an accident involving a pig."

"A pig?"

"A pet pig. He's a miniature Vietnamese potbellied pig."

"*Huh.* Didn't George Clooney have one of those?" said the woman. "I hear they're real smart."

I nodded and realized that said pig was, once again, making himself scarce. Just as well.

Inspector Stinson didn't seem particularly interested in my pet. "What does a pig have to do with a lawsuit?"

"I'm sorry to say my pig bumped into Autumn, here at the store. She fell into some dresses and seemed fine at the time, but the lawsuit says she suffered neck and back injuries."

His gaze drilled into me. "And you went to talk with her about this? You didn't, maybe, call your lawyer, something like that?"

"I don't have a lawyer," I said. The question hung in the air: *Do I need one?* "I hoped it was a simple misunderstanding, and we could work it out, face-to-face."

"Work it out how?"

"I really don't know. I just . . . I believe in communication, and trying to work things out person to person rather than getting the courts and lawyers involved."

"Hate to break it to you, but if you were served, then the courts and lawyers are already involved. The time to talk is before a lawsuit's filed, not after."

"I— Of course, you're right," I said, wondering where this line of questioning might be leading. "I don't have much experience with this sort of thing."

"Ever speak with the deceased before yesterday?"

I shook my head.

"Nothing at all? No phone calls, text messages, e-mails, Facebook posts?"

"I didn't even know her number until yesterday. And I don't do those other things."

The inspector looked skeptical. "No? Not a twenty-first-century-type gal, eh?"

"You could say as much."

"What about the old-fashioned way? You ever stop by her shop, maybe check out the competition?"

"Yesterday was the first time I was there."

"You didn't send her something, anything at all? An apology of some sort?"

"No," I said, wondering why he was pressing this point; then I remembered something worth mentioning. "Oh, my coworker Bronwyn brought her a gift basket a few days ago, as an apology."

"You weren't involved in this gift basket?"

"No, as I said, I had never been to Vintage Visions, or met Autumn Jennings, until last night."

"We'll need this coworker's information as well."

I nodded.

Inspector Ng inclined her head toward Bronwyn's herbal stand. "You work with herbs and whatnot?"

"No, that's Bronwyn's stand. She specializes in herbal blends, teas, potpourri, that sort of thing."

Meanwhile, Inspector Stinson began perusing the carved amulets and talismans in the glass display counter. Many of the talismans were pentacles, which were signs of protection but which nonmagic folk often mistook for something entirely different—and sinister.

He looked at me, his eyebrows raised. "You're into a satanic-type deal?"

Apparently, Inspector Stinson was one of those people.

"Not in the least." I went over to stand near him but kept an eye on Inspector Ng, who was nosing around Bronwyn's jars and packs of herbs. Sailor was watching as well, arms crossed over his chest like a bodyguard, his gaze shifting back and forth between the inspectors, as though watching a really annoying tennis match.

"None of these items has anything to do with Satan, or evil, or black magic, or anything like that," I said. "They're charms for protection and healing, not for harm. Never for harm. I carve talismans out of medallions cut from fruit trees and expose them to moonlight . . ."

"She's a Wiccan," Ng said, gesturing to the sign hanging over Bronwyn's stand, taken from the Wiccan Rede: *An it harm none, do what ye will.*

I wasn't a Wiccan, but I didn't try to explain further. The difference between witches and Wiccans was generally lost on people not familiar with alternate belief systems, much less the history and moral codes of different forms of witchcraft.

"H'okay . . . ," said Stinson, clearly unimpressed.

"It's a legitimate belief system, Stinson. You gotta change with the times. It's even recognized by the military these days," Inspector Ng said. Then she turned to me: "Lily Ivory, we're going to have to shut this store down for the interim, bring in a forensics crew."

"Shut us *down*? For what possible reason?" I asked, shocked.

"We're gonna need to process these herbs, see if there's a connection."

"A connection to what?"

The inspectors exchanged a look. Then Inspector Ng shrugged, and Stinson said, "To the murder of Autumn Jennings."

Chapter 5

Inspectors Stinson and Ng left their business cards, told me to stay out of the store and not touch anything, and said they would be calling in a forensics team. Happily, I would at least be allowed to come and go from my apartment through the back door that opened onto the alley behind the store. I called Bronwyn and Maya and told them both to expect a visit from the police, and that the store would be closed for a day or two. Then I hung a sign in the shop door that read: *Closed for Inventory. Open soon, please try back!* I had debated what to write and decided a little white lie was probably best. Aunt Cora's Closet was doing a good business these days, but there was no denying we'd had some strangeness associated with us over the past several months, what with pigs going missing and faith-based break-ins and the like. No need to cast even more suspicion over the place.

Afterward, Sailor, Oscar, and I went upstairs. I put my old copper teakettle on to boil while I filled Sailor in on what Maya and I had found at Vintage Visions Glad Rags last night.

"Do you have any reason to believe there's something magical going on?" Sailor asked. "I mean, besides the obvious: that you're a magnet for magical mayhem?"

"No, not really. Except it just seems . . . odd. And Oscar had a problem with Autumn Jennings in the first place. Speaking of which . . ." I turned to my familiar. "What do *you* know about this?"

Oscar, who had remained in his porcine form, ran into the living room, jumped on the couch, and pretended to snooze. He did this sometimes when he didn't want to talk. It really dilled my pickle, but I knew from experience that I wouldn't get anything out of him until he was ready to spill.

"I can't believe I gave up bacon for the likes of you," I grumbled, then turned to Sailor. "But I did find Autumn's name on a marker in Aidan's satchel. What do you think that means?"

Sailor leaned against the kitchen's cobalt blue–tiled counter and spoke deliberately. "I think it means you're right; there might be a reason you're involved in Autumn's death."

"Want to take a look at it?" I asked, reaching for the satchel. "See if you feel anything?"

He held up his hands as though the old leather bag would burn him. "I won't mess with Aidan's things. It wouldn't do any of us any good and might well lead to something . . . bad."

I understood what he meant. Magic was mysterious and unpredictable. Practitioners had different abilities and weaknesses; sometimes these were complementary, sometimes not. Intermingling magical energy from different sources could lead to increased power and strength—or to utter disaster.

Rather like regular human relationships, now that I thought about it.

Not that the outcomes of such interactions couldn't be altered with effort. The first time Aidan and I tried mingling our powers, we wound up melting metal. The second time—after I had gained more control of my powers, I had become more familiar with my guiding spirit, and Aidan was more prepared to deal with my magic—I was able to piggyback on his powers to conjure a vision that helped solve the murder of an innocent woman.

"I would, however, be willing to go to Jennings's store to see if I can pick up any sensations. If Jennings really was murdered, she might well be hanging around."

"You mean . . . her spirit?"

"It's possible."

"But she died in the hospital. Wouldn't her ghost be lingering there? I mean, assuming it's lingering at all?"

"Not necessarily. Sometimes, especially with violent death, such as murder or suicide, the spirit remains near the physical location of death. But many times they manifest in the place of greatest significance to them, typically their home or the locale of a loved one."

"Huh," I said. "Live and learn."

Not being a necromancer, I wasn't up on the rules governing spirits. Ghosts sensed me and often reached out to make contact, but although I could feel them, I couldn't understand them. It was about as frustrating as trying to communicate with Oscar when he went into shutdown mode.

While Sailor poured the hot water over one of Bronwyn's custom loose-leaf teas and into a china teapot, filling the kitchen with the aroma of jasmine and honeysuckle, I phoned Inspector Carlos Romero.

"Sorry; I didn't catch this one, Lily," he said when he answered.

"You heard about Autumn Jennings?"

"Yes, but I was off duty when the call came in."

"What happened, do you know? What did she die of?"

"They're waiting on the final report from the medical examiner, but the doctors suspect it was some sort of poison. Not sure what led them to that conclusion."

"Poison? Was it an accident or on purpose?"

"That would be the question."

"What kind of poison?"

"Still waiting on the toxicology report."

"The inspectors shut down my store, Carlos. They want to process Bronwyn's herbs—I think we're suspects."

"Of course you're suspects. You have a motive, and Bronwyn has knowledge about, and access to, all those suspicious herbs."

"They're not *suspicious*; they're just . . . herbs."

"Sorry—haven't had my coffee yet so I'm not being as clear as I should be. Here's the deal: You would be suspects even if *I* had caught the case, even though I know you. I would be following the same steps, ruling things out. It's standard procedure. I know it's stressful and inconvenient, but try not to get too freaked-out."

"I'll try, but I'm not sure I'm going to have much success. Inspectors Stinson and Ng don't know me like you do, and I'm . . . you know . . . sort of weird. Could you put in a good word for me?"

"I'll do what I can, but I'm sorry to say that my vouching for you with Mark Stinson would probably cause more harm than good. There's some bad blood between us."

"Anyone ever tell you that for a nice man, you sure have a lot of enemies?"

He chuckled. "Maybe I'm not all that nice; you ever think of that?"

"Often. Just not once I got to know you."

"It's an occupational hazard, I'm afraid. We have to ask uncomfortable questions that people would just as soon not answer. But in the case of Mark Stinson it's just nonsense: When he was passed over for promotion a few years ago he made allegations of reverse discrimination, claimed I got the job because I was Latino."

"I'm guessing you got the job because you're a better detective."

"I'd like to think so. You ask me, Stinson was passed over because he's an ass and I'm a better cop. But that's something he'll never accept. Don't get me wrong; he's not a *bad* cop, and he made inspector the following year. But he's had a bug up his butt about me ever since. So you might not want to mention to him that you and I are friends. It won't help your case and might even hurt."

"Understood."

"And in the meantime, I'll nose around, see if I can find out anything on my end."

"Thanks, Carlos. And if you could tell me what Autumn Jennings actually died of, that would be helpful."

"I'll see what I can do."

"Thank you."

"Oh, and Lily? Make sure that pig of yours doesn't go after anybody else. One head-butt can be a mistake; two head-butts constitute a pattern."

"Oscar's not normally that kind of pig. Honest."

"Uh-huh. Make sure he stays that way."

It was only midmorning, overcast as was typical for San Francisco in the summertime. Usually the sun broke through the clouds by noon, warming things up considerably. Still, the City by the Bay was temperate, with temperatures rarely rising above the midseventies even in the summer. Tourists learned this the hard way, and sweatshirt vendors made a killing on the streets of San Francisco.

I decided to take Sailor up on his offer to go by Vintage Visions Glad Rags. Even if the police were processing it as a crime scene, Sailor might be able to read some vibrations from out on the street. It wasn't much of a plan, but at least it was something to do. With Aunt Cora's Closet temporarily closed, I had some unaccustomed free time. Might as well look into Jennings's death a little more. If the authorities happened to see me at Vintage Visions Glad Rags, I supposed I could just say I was nosy. I was already a suspect, after all. How much worse could it get?

Sailor and I headed toward the door, but Oscar got there first. He had transformed into his normal guise, so he could talk.

"Can't *I* go, too?" he asked, his bottle-glass green eyes gleaming in his gray scaly face. "I don't wanna hang around here all day by myself. The store's closed!"

"What do you think?" I asked Sailor.

Sailor shrugged. "Up to you."

"If you come along, you'll have to stay in the car. And make sure no one sees you in your natural form,"

I added. Reports of a gobgoyle in my backseat were all I needed.

He narrowed his eyes. "No one sees the real Oscar," he said, pointing at himself with his thumbs, "unless *Oscar* says so."

I had to hand it to my familiar: He was very good at keeping his true self under wraps. I wondered sometimes if it was because Oscar was that good at being discreet or if it was because most cowans, upon seeing a creature like Oscar, assumed they were hallucinating. People were awfully good at talking themselves out of things that couldn't possibly be, even when those things existed right under their very noses.

Oscar occasionally used his ability to shock people to his advantage, though it was usually while trying to save my life. My heart softened and I felt myself give in.

"Of course you can come, then. We'll take the van so you have more room."

"Be right there!" Oscar said and hurried off to grab a few books and some snacks to keep himself amused while he waited.

"That is one spoiled familiar," Sailor said, shaking his head.

"Well, if a witch can't spoil her familiar, then who can she spoil?" I said sheepishly, grabbing my woven bag and making sure I had the keys to the car and to Autumn Jennings's shop.

"Everybody ready?" I asked. "Then we're off like a dirty shirt!"

Sailor and I stood outside of Vintage Visions Glad Rags, peering in through the plate-glass windows at the shop, which looked as neat and glamorous as it had yesterday. There was no sign of the police or a forensics team tearing the place apart. Autumn Jennings hadn't actually died here, which meant the store wasn't a homicide scene, but it still seemed odd. Then again, I didn't know how official things like chain of evidence and whatnot worked. Still, I hesitated to use the keys and boldly walk in.

"Shall we start with the neighbors?" I asked. "See if anyone there can shed some light on Autumn or her situation?"

"Cupcakes get my vote," Sailor said.

"I do like the way you think," I said with a smile.

A young couple was leaving the bakery as we entered: a woman with pale strawberry blond hair and freckles, and a man with a bushy black beard. The man carried a huge pink box tied with twine but held the door for us with his body.

"Thank you for stopping by, Eleanor, Cody! Isn't it nice to see politeness in young people?" The woman behind the counter aimed that last comment at Sailor and me. She was about Bronwyn's age, plump and red cheeked. As soon as the shop door closed behind the couple, she added in a conspiratorial whisper, "I don't get the facial hair, though. I mean, really? He looks like he's out of one of those historic photos of lumberjacks felling the giant redwoods back in the day. You know the ones I mean? Ha!" She laughed at her own joke. "But he's some sort of high-tech guy, like everyone who can afford to live around here these days."

The small storefront had a traditional black-and-white-checked floor on which sat large glass display cases in a U shape filled with colorful and extravagantly frosted cupcakes. The walls were plastered with posters of Buckingham Palace, Big Ben and the Thames, and British manor houses. The Union Jack featured prominently in a wall hanging and on packages of imported tea. Porcelain teapots decorated with flowers adorned a high, narrow shelf that ringed the room. The whole place smelled like freshly baked cake, vanilla, and spice. I took a deep breath. Heaven.

"So, what can I do you for? I don't believe I've seen you folks here before, have I? I'm Renee Baker," she said. "I'm known around here as the cupcake lady. But as I always say, with a name like Baker, what other line of business could I go into? I absolutely had to *become* a baker!"

I smiled. If that logic held true, I would be working with elephants, or perhaps tuning pianos. And Sailor might well have to take to the sea, though from what I'd seen so far he wasn't much of one for boats.

"It looks like the cupcake business is thriving," I said.

"Hard to believe it myself. Started just two years ago, and already outgrowing my space. Thinking of expanding, but I'd hate to leave the neighborhood."

"Did you know Autumn Jennings, from next door?"

"Yes! *Oh.*" She put a hand over her heart and tsked. "I just couldn't believe it when the police came to talk to me. I mean, she was only about my age, I think, right?" Renee looked to be in her early fifties, though she was so pink and plump and vital it was hard to compare her in my mind to the frail, gray-faced woman I had seen last night. "The poor thing certainly took a turn for the worse recently. She used to *adore* my maple-bourbon-bacon cupcakes, but lately she hasn't had the stomach for anything at all."

"How recently?" I asked.

"Maple-bourbon-bacon cupcake?" asked Sailor at the same time.

Renee winked at Sailor. "Try one?"

"I honestly don't know how I could refuse."

She reached into the display case and selected a perfectly shaped cupcake topped with a generous dollop of maple-colored frosting and crowned with a strip of bacon.

"For here, or to go?"

"To go, please."

"Did you know that in Britain they call cupcakes *fairy* cakes? Isn't that just about the most adorable thing you've ever heard?" Renee asked as she expertly folded a little pink cardboard box. "What else I can get you?"

"Um, let's see," I said. It was nearly lunchtime, and breakfast seemed a long time ago. Besides, it would take a stronger-willed witch than I to refuse the tiny delectable-looking cakes, each with a whimsical name. I pointed out half a dozen different ones: from Granny Bananny Cake to Jack Lemon's Chiffon to Chocolate Suicide. Given the crowd I run with, I wouldn't have a problem finding them good homes.

In fact . . . Oscar was in the van. I ordered a few more.

"Might as well make it a baker's dozen," said Sailor.

Renee placed the assorted cupcakes on a snow-white doily in a pink bakery box, carefully folded in the sides, and tied the box with twine. A tag on the twine was inscribed, *A cupcake a day keeps the doldrums away!*

I paid for the dozen, though she insisted Sailor's maple-bourbon-bacon cupcake was on the house.

"So, is there anything else you can tell us about Autumn?" I asked.

"Well, let's see . . . We were friendly, but not *friends*, if you know what I mean. She was a fine neighbor, but we weren't close. I mean, when you own a cupcake shop you get to know everyone on the block—and I hear some neighborhood gossip, let me tell you!"

"Did you hear any gossip about Autumn?"

"Well, now, like I said, she used to come in occasionally for a cupcake, but although I poked my head into her shop from time to time just to be friendly, she didn't have a single thing I could fit into. I don't think I was her target audience!"

"She seemed to have some lovely things in her shop."

"Oh, that she *did*," Renee said. "And she just got a new lot in, too, just before she passed. She was very excited about it. A great big old trunk that hadn't been opened in decades, apparently, just chock-full of clothes that had never been worn. She said it was an actual *trousseau* from the Victorian era. Can you imagine?"

"A trousseau?" I asked.

"Don't you know what a trousseau is? Ah, modern young people just don't know the old traditions."

Of course I knew what a trousseau was. I was surprised because it was rare to find a trousseau from the past intact, precisely because the contents were usually put to use as soon as the owner was married. But Renee was on a roll, so I didn't interrupt.

"In the olden days," Renee explained, "a girl would work on her trousseau from an early age, embroidering linens and lingerie and whatnot and folding them away in a hope chest or armoire, waiting for that most special day when she would be *married*." Renee clasped her hands under her chin and let out a loud sigh. She was clearly a die-hard romantic. She was like the anti-Maya.

"I see," I said. "So Autumn had acquired an intact Victorian trousseau? Did she mention where she got it from?"

"Goodness, if she did, I don't remember. But it contained some lovely things. Not just clothes but all kinds of items, even adorable hand-embroidered tea towels, can you imagine?" Renee continued. "I suppose that was common for a trousseau, all the linens, too. Autumn showed me the items upstairs; she said she was taking her time to price them properly before putting them out on the floor for sale. She tried on one of the ball gowns, which looked beautiful on her. I wouldn't have minded trying on one myself, but, like I say, those vintage clothes aren't made for a substantial woman like me. I could have used those tea towels, though."

"You should check out Lily's store," Sailor said. "Aunt Cora's Closet, over in the Haight-Ashbury, offers plenty of selections for womanly women."

I gawked at Sailor. Who was this person charming bakers, ordering cupcakes, and promoting Aunt Cora's Closet? Where was the cantankerous, brooding psychic I had met in a dive bar who didn't have a kind word for anyone?

"Oooh, 'womanly women,' eh? I like that," Renee Baker said with another wink. "You'd better watch your man, Lily, or I might cover him in frosting and eat him right up."

"Um, yes, well, thank you for the warning," I said. I had no idea how I was supposed to respond to Renee's last statement, and I could feel the telltale burning that meant my cheeks were ablaze. "And for your help, Renee. And the cupcakes."

"Enjoy! Have a sweet day! Keep the doldrums away!"

Out on the sidewalk, I turned to Sailor. "What's gotten into you?"

"To what, specifically, do you refer?"

"Why are you being so . . . nice?"

He chuckled. "I'm a nice guy."

"Since when?"

Sailor clutched at his heart and pretended to stagger. "You wound me most grievously, madam."

"There are many ways I would describe you, my dear Sailor, but 'a nice guy' is not the first phrase that comes to mind."

"I suppose I should take that as a compliment. Don't they say women don't want a nice guy?"

"No, I don't think it's that we don't want a nice guy. It's just that . . ." I trailed off as I spied a dog walker peeking into the window of Vintage Visions Glad Rags. She had half a dozen dogs on leashes, big and little, all apparently well cared for and pampered. A Dalmatian boasted a sparkling rhinestone collar, a full-sized poodle had a Fifi haircut, and a tiny mop of a dog had blue ribbons in his long, shining hair.

But it was the woman I most noticed. Where did I know her from . . . ?

She turned toward us, and her eyes widened.

It was the woman who had served me with legal papers.

She dropped the leashes and ran.

Chapter 6

One of the smaller dogs tried to run along with her, but his leash was attached to the others, and the bigger dogs weren't moving. On the contrary, they stood like good little soldiers awaiting orders.

"Hey!" I yelled. "I need to talk to you!"

Sailor shoved the box of cupcakes at me and took off after her, but she disappeared around a corner before he caught up. Seconds later the black Ducati zoomed out of the alley and down the street in the opposite direction. She wore no helmet, and her dark hair streamed out behind her. Sailor trotted back to Vintage Visions Glad Rags, where I stood holding the cupcake box in one hand and six leashes in the other.

"That was odd behavior in a dog walker," Sailor muttered, taking the bakery box from me and checking the contents. "Friend of yours?"

"Not hardly. She served me with the legal papers from Autumn Jennings yesterday morning. Why on earth would she run away like that? If anything, *I* should be the one trying to get away from *her*."

"Maybe she thought we were here to beat her up."

I did my best at lifting one eyebrow. "One look at me was enough for her to abandon her dogs and flee?"

"Maybe not you, but your bodyguard." He shrugged. "I'm pretty scary looking. Or so I've been told."

"According to Renee the cupcake lady you're more yummy than scary."

"I feel as though I should be insulted. Okay, maybe it *is* you she's scared of. Maybe she found out you're a witch and is afraid of being hexed."

"I never hex," I scoffed. Then I shrugged. "Well, almost never."

He grinned. "I know that. I just like how annoyed you get when I suggest you might. Anyway, I got the license plate of the bike, for what it's worth."

"You're so smart. I knew there was some reason I allowed you to hang out with me."

"That and the bodyguard thing."

"Oh, yeah. I keep forgetting," I said with a smile and a kiss.

I borrowed Sailor's phone to call my private investigator, Sam Spade, and asked him to use his contacts to run the plates. Spade didn't exactly live up to his literary namesake; in truth, he was a pretty lousy private eye. Nonetheless, he came in handy from time to time. He said he would see what he could find out and get back to me.

"So, what are we going to do with the dogs?" Sailor asked.

The six canines were sitting patiently, watching us.

"I suppose . . . if they have tags with addresses, we

could bring them home. If not, I don't know . . . Land sakes, this wasn't exactly how I had hoped to spend the day."

I checked the Dalmatian's collar, but while he had tags and a phone number, there was no address. Same with the dachshund. Sailor dialed the numbers but received no answer. The poodle had a city-issued dog license but no contact information at all.

Sailor crouched down in front of a cocker spaniel and spoke quietly. "Hey there, little fella."

He caressed the dog's silky head, then cradled it in his hands for a moment, concentrating.

After a moment he gave me a rueful glance and a quick shake of his head. "Figured it was worth a try, but all I ever pick up from dogs is thoughts of food and generalized love and affection."

I smiled. "Doesn't sound like a bad way of being, all things considered."

The Dalmatian started barking, and the spaniel joined in.

Renee emerged from her store, drying her hands on a towel. "I saw what happened. That's the strangest thing! The dog walker usually comes by this time every day and picks up Loretta, Autumn Jennings's dog. There's a dog park around the corner."

"Do you know the dog walker's name or how to get ahold of her?" I asked.

She shook her head. "I always waved and said hi, and she waved back, but that was about all. But then, I'm more a cat person. Such a shame she abandoned these little pups like that. I never would have thought it. She seemed so devoted to them!"

"Do you know where any of them live?" Sailor asked.

"Only the poodle. His house is down the street," she said, pointing to a white Victorian. "He belongs to an elderly lady, Mrs. Morgan. Doesn't get out much. Can't handle the stairs."

"Okay, we'll start there. Thanks."

"Oh, wait just a minute." Renee ducked back into the store and returned moments later holding a small pink bakery box tied with twine. "Orange-rosemary. Mrs. Morgan's favorite. Tell her hi from Renee!"

"We will, and thanks again."

Sailor and I headed down the block, each holding a bakery box and the leashes for three dogs. When we reached the white Victorian, I held on to the poodle's leash and handed the others to Sailor, then climbed the long flight of stairs to the front door.

It took several minutes for the door to open. Mrs. Morgan was an elderly woman who wore her thinning gray hair in a braid twisted into a bun atop her head. She was dressed in a smart white linen pantsuit and expensive-looking gold jewelry. Behind her I could see a high-ceilinged foyer with a gleaming round table, a small love seat, and a tiled fireplace. Like many of the homes of the elderly I visit, this one also held several boxes and stacks of newspapers and catalogs.

She lit up at the sight of her dog, who greeted her so enthusiastically I feared he'd knock her over.

"Oh! Hello, Colonel Mustard! You're back early!"

I smiled. "Your dog's name is Colonel Mustard?"

"Yes, from the board game Clue."

"Oh, of course," I said, though I'd never played it. My childhood hadn't included a lot of the standard-issue kid experiences, such as board games or campfires or bake sales. I had spent my time avoiding my peers and learning the fine art of spellcasting at my grandmother's knee. I couldn't recite any patty-cake rhymes, but by the age of ten I knew exactly how much dragon's blood resin to add, and when, while concocting a prosperity charm and how to call on—and keep in line—a helpful demon during a binding ritual.

"Renee Baker asked me to bring you a cupcake," I continued, holding out the little box and happy to have a nice opening gambit. "She says hello. It's orange-rosemary."

"Well, isn't that thoughtful! My favorite. Thank you." Mrs. Morgan looked past me, her eyes alighting on Sailor, who stood on the sidewalk with the other dogs. "But . . . where's Scarlet?"

"Is Scarlet the dog walker?"

"Yes. We laughed because my dog is named Colonel Mustard, and she's Miss Scarlet!" She chuckled.

I smiled, pretending I understood the reference and making a mental note to look up this Clue game. I would add it to my mental list of Things to Do to Seem More Normal.

"Do you know how I might get in touch with Scarlet?" I asked. "Or even her last name?"

"Did something happen? I don't understand. I pay her ten dollars to take the Colonel to the dog park, and he hasn't been gone very long; I can't believe he even made it to the park. Where is Scarlet, and who are you?"

"I apologize, I should have introduced myself." I brought out a card. "I'm Lily Ivory."

"You're in the vintage clothes business?" she said as she read it. "Like the shop across the street?"

"Yes. Do you know the owner of that store, Autumn Jennings?"

"She bought several things from me last time I cleaned out my closets. I must say she was rather picky. Turned up her nose at some perfectly lovely items, which seemed a bit snooty for someone who sells used clothes, if you ask me. She said she only wanted historic pieces, or those with designer tags."

"A vintage clothes dealer's rationale can be hard to understand," I said with a nod. I was still outside on the landing; Mrs. Morgan remained in the open door. On the one hand, I thought I might be able to learn something further if I imposed upon this woman for a cup of tea, but on the other . . . Sailor and I had five dogs to escort home, not to mention, Loretta was homeless. Aunt Cora's Closet was closed for forensics, and in light of Autumn Jennings's death and Scarlet's bizarre behavior . . . I was beginning to think something fishy was afoot.

"Not that I need the money, particularly," Mrs. Morgan was saying. "I just want them to go to a good home. In fact, I was going to call someone else to come pick them up."

She nodded at a couple of plastic black bags in the corner of the porch landing. "Or . . . I don't suppose you'd like to take a look, since you're in the same business? I had everything freshly laundered."

"I . . . sure," I said, making a snap decision. Based upon Mrs. Morgan's home and the way she was dressed, I made the assumption her clothes would be of high quality. As soon as I opened one bag and peeped inside, I saw I was right. They were neatly folded linens and woolens, and at least one cashmere sweater. As I touched them I picked up subtle vibrations of single-mindedness and ambition, which made me smile. It was too easy to assume "little old ladies" were pliable and dithering; Mrs. Morgan was clearly made of sterner stuff.

"These look great," I said. "If you're just trying to get them out of your house, I could give you a flat price instead of going through and looking at each piece. The things I can't sell I make sure to donate to a good cause."

"Really? That would be lovely! Autumn took the older items, so if you take the rest, I can relax knowing my closet-cleaning project is complete."

I always carried my Aunt Cora's Closet checkbook with me because I never knew when I'd pass by a promising garage sale or flea market. "Strike while the iron's hot" was my unofficial store motto. After Mrs. Morgan and I agreed on a price and I wrote her a check, I steered the conversation back around to the runaway dog walker.

"So, Mrs. Morgan, the strangest thing happened with Scarlet. She actually abandoned the dogs on the sidewalk, just took off on a motorcycle, for no apparent reason. Do you know how I might get ahold of her to make sure the dogs are returned to their owners?"

"Scarlet? I can't believe she would do such a thing," she said, shaking her head. She gazed at me for a moment; then her eyes shifted to Sailor standing with the other pups on the sidewalk. "I guess she must have, mustn't she? It's just so hard to believe. She seems so mature, very capable for one so young. She's done other odd jobs for me and I've never had a problem."

"Do you have a number for her?" I urged. "Or any kind of contact information?"

Mrs. Morgan pressed her lips together for a moment, then asked me to wait and closed the door. I held up one finger to tell Sailor it would be another moment. He was stroking the Dalmatian's fur; the dogs seemed calm with him, panting and waiting patiently.

The door opened again, and Mrs. Morgan handed me a card with a number written in pencil. "Here's her phone number."

"Thank you," I said. "Do you happen to know where any of the other dogs live?"

She shook her head. "No, I'm sorry. I'm no help at all. That was Scarlet's job."

"One last thing—could you tell me what kind of odd jobs Scarlet did for you?"

She shrugged. "Helped me to clean out the attic and my closets, that sort of thing. I'm an absolute sucker for antiques—I love looking through catalogs, and they're so heavy I never manage to get them out to the recycling. Scarlet was good at things like that. I know she did some occasional work for Autumn across the street as well. She's from Missouri, as am I. We Missouri folk are hard workers."

I nodded and smiled. "Does Scarlet live around here, too?"

"She mentioned working part-time at the Legion of Honor. I assume she lives near there because I think she's an artist, doesn't have a car." She shook her head. "I simply can't believe she ran off and left the dogs. There must have been some kind of emergency."

"I'm sure you're right. Well, thank you for your time."

"Good luck to you," she said, closing the door.

As I turned to leave I heard her speaking to Colonel Mustard in a high-pitched voice: *"Does my good boy want a cookie? Who's the good puppy? Colonel Mustard is, that's who."*

Sailor watched as I came down the stairs carrying a big plastic bag in each hand.

"Let's trade," Sailor said. I put down the heavy bags and he handed me the bakery box and the leashes.

"Doing a little scavenging, are we? I admire your commitment."

"She who hesitates is lost," I replied. "In my line of business you never know where you'll find your inventory. Plus, I thought it might help Mrs. Morgan to open up a little."

"What did she say about the dog walker?"

"First name's Scarlet, no last name. I've got a phone number but no address," I said, leaning over to say hello to the dogs. "And call me a cynic, but I sincerely doubt Scarlet is going to hop on her motorcycle and come roaring back in response to a sternly worded phone call."

"Worth a try, at least," Sailor said with a shrug, pulling out his phone and dialing. A mechanical voice said the phone was out of service. "Well, that's a bust."

"Mrs. Morgan seemed quite surprised that she would run off and leave the dogs. Says she's done small jobs for her and that she's responsible and hardworking."

"So this all seems out of character," Sailor said. "And she was the one who served you with papers? I don't think that takes any special training; she probably just did it as a favor to Jennings, or for payment."

I nodded. "But why would she run when she saw us? And not just run away, but abandon the dogs?"

"That's the question, isn't it? First things first, though: Let's stash the clothes in the van. Then we can use our sleuthing skills to find the families of these pooches here."

* * *

We had parked in the shade, made a nest out of blankets, and brought along snacks and a stack of mysteries
for entertainment—Oscar was currently making his
way through Ray Chandler's entire oeuvre—but even
so, as we opened the van doors to toss the heavy bags
of clothing inside, my familiar was literally tapping his
foot, outraged that we were "spending the day with a
bunch of dogs" while he was cooped up in the van.

Then his gaze locked onto the pink bakery box like
a bottle-glass green heat-seeking missile.

"What's *that*?" he asked.

"Cupcakes. They're for later. Seriously, Oscar, you
can have one—*just* one—right now. And then I'm going
to leave the box in here with you, and I declare, if any
of the others are touched, there will be no more cupcakes in your life, ever. *None*. You know I can make
that happen, so don't test me." He still hadn't looked
away from the box, but he nodded. "I'm serious, Oscar.
Also, don't forget, I'm the keeper of the satchel."

At this he met my eyes, gulped audibly, and nodded
again.

I opened the box and held it out for him to choose.
He dithered so long I had to threaten him again.

"Oscar, you are jumpin' on my last nerve. We've got
a pack of dogs waiting on us, not to mention a suspicious death to investigate. I'm fixin' to just take the box
with us."

"All right, all *right*," he said, squeezing his eyes shut.
"It's between the chocolate and the lemon chiffon . . .
eenie meenie minie . . ."

"Hell's bells, Oscar. Just *choose*!"

Sailor took the box from me, grabbed the chocolate one, shoved it at Oscar, and fastened the twine tightly around the box.

"There. Bon appetit. Also," Sailor said, pointing at Oscar before saying in a threatening tone, "you will not touch the maple-bourbon-bacon one, understand? You do *not* want to find out what will happen if I return and the maple-bourbon-bacon cupcake is missing. I am *not* a nice guy. I have that on good authority."

Oscar's response was muffled by a mouth full of cupcake.

"What was that?" I asked.

"I *said* I don't eat bacon. Hello: *pig*. Remember?" He rolled his eyes.

"Good thing there's chocolate, right? How is it?"

"*Really* good. Hurry back so we can eat the rest!" He picked up the book that was splayed facedown, crawled into his nest, and started reading.

It took us the better part of the afternoon, but Sailor and I finally got all the dogs to their respective owners. A few inquiries at stores up and down the street yielded the name of the cocker spaniel's owner, an optometrist who had an office a block away. The receptionist there knew where the Pomeranian lived, and the Pom's housekeeper knew the Dalmatian. From there it was like pulling at a loose thread.

Unfortunately, no one knew anything more about Scarlet than Mrs. Morgan did: no last name or address, just a phone number. Several speculated that Scarlet might be an artist but didn't know what kind, only that she "seemed artistic" and had mentioned working at the Legion of Honor.

"What now?" I said after the final pooch was handed over to the loving arms of her person.

"You still have the keys to Jennings's shop?"

I hesitated. "Yes."

"Let's go inside, see if I feel anything."

I hesitated. "I'm pretty sure the police wouldn't approve."

He let out a bark of a laugh.

"What?" I asked.

"Seriously? If you did only what the police would approve of, Lily, my love, you'd be tucked safely into your apartment above Aunt Cora's Closet. Or perhaps even still cooling your heels in a small-town Texas jail."

"I suppose you're right. Still . . ."

"Besides, I thought you were taking over for Aidan. Rhodes wouldn't worry about the police when he had the keys to a shop that wasn't even marked with crime scene tape."

"I'm not *taking over* for Aidan; I'm just filling in while he's out of town. It's *temporary*." I looked at him askance. "Besides, aren't you the one who usually warns me away from something like this?"

"I'm evolving," he said.

"Since when?" I demanded.

"Since I started accepting the fact that you're a magnet for supernatural mischief," he replied, gently pushing a lock of hair out of my eyes. My long hair was up in its usual ponytail, but wrangling the dogs had freed a few errant strands. "And besides, at the moment you've got me for backup. I feel much better about the whole thing if I can make sure you're safe."

I offered him a smile, and then I used Autumn's ever so slightly purloined keys to let us into the shop.

Chapter 7

The first thing I noticed was the smell. The shop didn't smell bad, exactly. But I was so used to the scent of Aunt Cora's Closet, a combination of fresh laundry mixed with the fresh sachets I made—this week's were rosemary and lavender mixed with pine needles—that Vintage Visions Glad Rags seemed almost . . . sepulchral. I hadn't noticed that when I was here before, with Maya. Could my memories be clouding my perceptions?

Last time I hadn't expected anything worse than a conversation with the woman who was suing me. But now when I entered the store I remembered tiny, shaky Autumn Jennings holding a pistol in the upstairs hallway before collapsing in a heap on the floor. Her sweating, ashen face and wild eyes. She had seemed so frightened, so small.

Could someone have meant her harm? Had she been murdered, or was her death a tragic accident? Or, perhaps, even . . . suicide? The living quarters upstairs were depressing enough; that was for sure.

Sailor was walking slowly around the store, brushing by the expensive flapper dresses and smart Jackie O–era linen sheaths. I stood still, watching him closely. I probably had an edge on sensing vibrations or conjuring visions from textiles, but Sailor was a necromancer, keyed in to the world of the beyond in a way I could never hope to be.

"Anything?" I asked when he completed a loop around the shop floor.

He shook his head. "Where did you encounter her?"

"Upstairs."

"Let's check it out."

I took a moment to stroke the soft red leather medicine bag on a braided cord of multicolored silk strands that I kept tied at my waist. In it was a small collection of items from my past—a stone, a feather, a little of the red dirt connecting me to my childhood in West Texas—as well as a few objects tying me to my present. I "fed" the bag regularly, anointing it with oil from time to time, whispering to it my hopes and fears. No matter the situation, touching it helped to ground me.

"You okay?" Sailor asked after a long moment.

"Yes, I'm fine. Let's go."

I opened the little door behind the register and led the way up the dim stairs. In the upstairs hallway, enough light sifted in through the grimy windows so we could see where we were going.

"It's depressing up here," Sailor said quietly.

"I thought so, too. But really, this from the man who lives just beyond a homicide scene in Chinatown?"

"It's a very old homicide. It isn't going to hurt anyone."

I cocked my head. "You think something here is going to hurt someone?"

He shrugged, as though distracted, and went to stand in the doorway of the first room to the right. I peeked around his shoulder.

The room was still packed with boxes and portable clothes racks, and a heap of lingerie lay on top of the bed. A plastic bin held old-fashioned brown and black leather shoes, the scent of shoe polish combining with that of cardboard and dusty textiles. Several Victorian-era ball gowns hung on cushioned hangers from hooks jutting out from the wall, silks and satins in shades of emerald green, butter yellow, and mauve. The freestanding full-length mirror was tilted slightly back in the corner.

Everything was exactly as I remembered. A few things might have been moved around, but there was no finger-print powder residue, no overt signs that anyone had con-ducted a thorough search. Why hadn't the forensics team been here, collecting evidence?

Sailor crossed the room slowly, turning his body slightly sideways, like a gunslinger, as he approached the mirror.

I remained, silent and unmoving, in the doorway.

Sailor stood in front of the looking glass for a very long time. Finally, he raised one hand and placed his palm flat against the mirror's slick glass, hung his head, and let out a deep breath.

I had witnessed Sailor making contact with the dead before, but he'd always sat cross-legged on the floor when entering a trance. Perhaps this was a new technique he'd been developing with Patience. Mirrors can be powerful and sometimes serve as windows to the backward world and the spheres beyond the veil. This was why they were traditionally covered in a house where someone had died recently, for fear that the deceased's soul might become trapped.

Sailor remained, unmoving, in front of the mirror for so long I began to wonder if he was all right and fought the urge to break the spell, to intervene.

Sailor is a big boy; he knows what he's doing.

So I stroked my medicine bag again and focused my intent on supporting Sailor's psychic explorations. I had no idea whether my energy could help him, but I decided it couldn't hurt to try. Having Oscar anywhere in the vicinity helped me when I was brewing.

We were enveloped in a silence so profound that the buzzing of an insect and the ticking of the old pendulum clock in the hallway filled the air and surrounded us. I looked around, noting a stack of cardboard boxes that had been labeled by hand with a thick black marker: *Shoes*, *Hats*, and three large ones labeled *Silverware*, *Dishes*, and *Napkins*. I peeked into one labeled *Stockings*. Inside was a jumble of old-fashioned stockings, many of them striped. They were very old, and more than a few were moth-eaten beyond repair. If this was representative of the quality of the items in the Victorian trousseau Autumn had been so excited about, she would have been very disappointed.

At long last, Sailor lifted his head, his arm fell away from the mirror, and he turned to look at me.

My blood ran cold: For an instant his eyes were blank, devoid of any signs of Sailor-ness.

"Are you all right?" I ventured. "Sailor?"

And just like that, Sailor was back. He nodded. "I made contact. Autumn wasn't able to tell me what had happened to her. She's . . . confused, I'd say."

"Is she here now?" I looked around, as though expecting to be able to see her. "Or did you connect with her on a spectral plane?"

"No, she's here. I expect she will be for a while; she's not convinced she's dead. I have to hand it to you vintage clothes dealers—you're extraordinarily dedicated. She's intent on taking care of her latest acquisition. I couldn't get her to focus; she kept obsessing about it."

"So, then . . . she's haunting this shop?"

He hesitated. "I'm not sure 'haunting' is the best way to describe it. She's . . . hanging around. I don't think she intends to bother anyone; not sure she's really aware of the living, though as she becomes more focused, she might accidentally spook someone."

"Okay." I blew out a breath. "As it turns out, I know someone who specializes in ridding houses of their ghosts, so if need be we could call her in."

"It occurs to me that between the two of us we have quite an interesting roster of friends and acquaintances. We could throw one hell of a Halloween party."

"You aren't kidding. But for the moment let's get back to Autumn. You're saying she can't tell you what happened, or how she was poisoned?"

He shook his head. "I didn't really expect that she could. It's rare for the departed to know what happened. I think of it as a kind of amnesia, a kindness our brains extend to us so we don't proceed to the next stage of existence accompanied by pain and fear. The only time a victim of a homicide can be helpful in naming the guilty party is when they had been stalked or harassed previously. That didn't happen to Autumn, at least not that she could remember."

"Could she tell you anything at all?"

"It's not like we're sitting down and having a chat. It's much more amorphous. I get a series of impressions or symbols, and then do my best at interpreting them. One thing that did come through loud and clear: Autumn's confused, perhaps because of the poison."

"That's not surprising—she was confused when Maya and I found her."

He nodded. "Probably the same thing. Time moves at a different pace on the other side of the veil as well, so I imagine getting over something like that might be unpredictable."

"She couldn't tell you anything else?"

"She's very focused on some of the lingerie on the bed. Oh, and towels."

"Towels?"

He shrugged. "Like I said, we don't actually *talk* about it. It's more a kind of . . . mind melding, for lack of a better term. I see images, get sensations. And I saw towels, with embroidery on them."

"Wait a minute—didn't Renee mention something about tea towels?"

The buzzing sound grew louder as I approached the bed and started sorting through the pile of assorted items—old-fashioned lingerie such as corsets and bloomers and petticoats, as well as embroidered linen towels, both large and small.

As I picked up and held the items, one after the other, I felt their vibrations. There was a distinct sense of dread and pain and . . . fear.

It was muffled, faded through the ages, but, like most strong sensations, it endured.

"These are very old sensations," I said. "Probably original to the young woman whose trousseau this was."

"And are we to assume she simply never married? Or is there a more sinister interpretation . . . ?"

"Given these sensations, I'm afraid she passed away. I feel pain and fear and a sense of . . . otherworldliness. Madness, maybe? Or someone on the brink of death, with one foot in this world and one beyond."

I reared back as a bee flew by.

"Hey, how'd you get in here?" I held out my hands. "C'mere, sugar."

It flew to me, landing on my palm. The bee walked around, exploring for a moment, her tiny feet tickling my palm.

I could feel Sailor's eyes on me. "You converse with bees now?"

"Um . . . not exactly. I mean, it's not like they talk back."

"You're not afraid it will sting you?"

I shook my head.

"This a witchy thing?"

I smiled. "I don't know about all witches, but I've always been close to honeybees. And they're not doing well; have you heard about the colony collapse? We need all the bees we can get. Would you open the window, please?"

Sailor obliged, forcing up the stiff sash with brute strength. I held my hand out the open window, and after a moment the bee lifted off and buzzed away.

I looked back to find Sailor's intense gaze upon me.

"What?" I asked, suddenly self-conscious.

"Nothing," he said softly, giving me a smile. "Let's look through the rest of the place."

Our search didn't turn up much more, and we didn't want to rearrange anything before the police had a chance to investigate, for fear of disturbing evidence. The kitchen was large enough to double as a family room, with a nicely upholstered couch, thick oriental carpet, and huge flat-screen TV in one corner, but despite shiny black granite countertops and cherry cabinets, it was as gloomy and off-putting as the rest of the apartment. A few nice paintings hung on the wall, slightly askew. A mahogany table and two chairs were set up by the window, the table half-covered by a stack of old newspapers; dirty dishes lined the counter, and the sink was full of pots.

Autumn's bedroom was similar: nicely furnished but messy. The bed had been made before I yanked off her quilt yesterday to warm her up while we waited for the paramedics, but several items of clothing had been tossed on the floor as though without thought, and the top of a sleek vanity was littered with bills and letters and store flyers, in addition to a jumble of lotion and perfume and a hairbrush. The stack of mail I had picked up yesterday was where I had left it: mostly bills, and the thick manila envelope that I now noted was marked *Jamie*.

We went back downstairs, where I riffled through the things behind the counter in earnest, because now that Autumn was dead I wasn't concerned with respecting her privacy. I was hoping to find a receipt for one very odd, very old trousseau. But there was no sign of a ledger, and I wasn't nearly adept enough at computers to try to figure out a bookkeeping system, even if I had been brave enough to try to e-snoop.

In the pile of papers behind the register, along with

the brochure for the Rodchester house, was a receipt from the Legion of Honor. It indicated that Autumn had lent some pieces to the museum. And Mrs. Morgan had mentioned that Scarlet worked there as well.

I jumped when an electronic version of "Greensleeves" filled the shop. As soon as I realized where it was coming from, I grabbed Autumn's phone and checked the screen.

"Jamie?" I answered the call.

"I saw you called last night," said a man's voice. "You've changed your mind? Price is the same."

"I . . ." *Dangitall*, I should have thought this through. Did that manila envelope hold cash for Jamie? If so, was it for something banal like a used bicycle? Or could it be for some nefarious purpose? Should I play along, pretend I was Autumn? "Yes, I believe I have changed my mind. How much was it again?"

"You playing with me?"

"I'm just a little confused lately."

"Not surprised, given the size of what you're dealing with. Tell you what—today's nuts for me. Meet me tomorrow night, nine o'clock, Pier 39. Buy a ticket to the mirror maze. I'll find you inside. What do you look like?"

"Long brown hair. I wear vintage dresses usually."

"Good for business, I'm guessing. All right, I'll find you. Bring the money."

He hung up.

"May I ask why you're describing yourself to a stranger on the phone?" Sailor asked.

"I guess we're meeting a man named Jamie tomorrow night at the mirror maze on Pier 39. Do you know it?"

He nodded.

"I mean, if you're available? I shouldn't assume."

"Suffice it to say that if you're going to meet a strange man at night in a mirror maze, *I'm* going to meet a strange man at night in a mirror maze. Who's Jamie?"

"I don't know, but there's an envelope for him upstairs in Autumn's bedroom. I'm guessing it contains cash."

"How much do you think that is?" I said, gazing at the stack of hundred-dollar bills in the envelope.

"A few thousand dollars? Maybe more? We could, of course, count it."

We could, but I was afraid to touch it.

"I suppose it could be legitimate," I said. "Maybe Autumn was planning to buy some clothes from him."

"Paying for merchandise in cash instead of by check? And holding business meetings at the Pier 39 mirror maze? Pretty sure that's not how it's done in Fortune 500 companies."

"It does seem fishy, doesn't it? Could I use your phone again?"

After Sailor handed it over, I called Sam Spade and asked him to track down whatever he could about someone named Jamie, and gave him his phone number.

"So what now?" Sailor asked.

"Want to go to a museum?" I asked him.

"Is this just for our erudition or . . . ?"

"Mrs. Morgan mentioned Scarlet worked at the Legion of Honor. And there's a receipt here indicating Autumn loaned some garments to an exhibit there. So maybe that's where they met? Or . . . something? I don't know. Maybe we can find Scarlet there?"

He checked his watch. "Your wish is my command. At least until six o'clock."

"What happens at six?"

"I've got a couple of readings lined up. Time for me to make some money."

"That's great, Sailor."

He shrugged. "Some of these folks are a bit worrisome. But it's a living."

Chapter 8

"What's the story, morning glory? What's the word, hummingbird?" Oscar demanded impatiently when we returned to the van.

Sailor raised an eyebrow.

"We had a 1960s musicals film festival last week," I explained. "*Bye Bye Birdie* was Oscar's favorite."

"Of course," Sailor said dryly. "I should have guessed."

I cast a suspicious glance at the pink bakery box, which appeared to have remained the way we left it. Oscar was the very picture of innocence, though I thought I spied a little green frosting on his snout. Still, it was hard to tell against his greenish scales. While we were gone he had made his way through an entire bag of ranch-flavored Doritos, two apples, and a king-sized Snickers bar. I was pretty sure the apples had been the last to go down his gullet, and then only because he'd already eaten all the good stuff.

"What's the tale, nightingale?" Oscar insisted.

"It was a bit of a water haul, when it comes right down to it," I said. "But we found a few leads. We're heading over to the Legion of Honor now. Want to come along, or should we drop you off at home?"

"The Legion of Honor's over near the ocean. Can we go to the beach after? Or maybe hike Lands End trail? Or get brunch at Cliff House?"

"I . . ." I glanced at Sailor.

"Sounds like a plan to me," he said. "No reason to hurry back to the shop, remember? When's the last time you went to the beach?"

"As I'm sure you recall, I was recently shot at and nearly trapped and killed in a tunnel at the Sutro Bath ruins," I said. "Does that count?"

"Not exactly what I had in mind," said Sailor with a chuckle. "I was thinking more along the lines of lolling on the sand with a picnic basket, watching the waves roll in, searching for seashells . . ."

"Who *are* you?" This was a whole new side of a man I thought I had come to know.

"Did someone say picnic?" Oscar, at least, was true to form. There was no distracting this gobgoyle from talk of food. "Picnics have potato chips! And cookies! And the cupcakes for dessert!"

"Okay, boys, I tell you what," I said, laughing. "I'm getting hungry, too. First let's see what we can find out about the mysterious Scarlet the Dog Walker at the Legion of Honor, and then if we have time we can pick up some fixin's for a picnic on the beach, like regular Californians."

"I hate to burst your bubble," said Sailor, "But regular Californians do not picnic at the beach in the fog."

"I'll bet some of them do."

"Tourists, maybe."

"All right, fine. We'll act like tourists, then."

"And then it'll be cupcake time?" Oscar asked.

"And then it'll be cupcake time."

"Nope," said the tired-looking middle-aged man behind the desk in the offices of the Legion of Honor. "Nobody named Scarlet on the payroll."

"Could she be a volunteer, maybe?"

"Maybe."

"Could you check?"

"You'd have to talk to the volunteer coordinator. But she doesn't work today."

"Is there any way you could check for me? It's a matter of some urgency."

The man let out a long, exasperated breath, as if the burden of my request sat heavily upon his well-padded shoulders. Leaning forward, he started typing and squinted at the computer screen.

"Lotta volunteers in a place like this," he grumbled, still clicking on the keyboard and the mouse. "Every art history graduate in the world thinks, 'Super, I want to be a museum curator!' Like that makes any sense at all. They had the smarts God gave a goose they would go into computer programming like everyone else in the world. Whoever heard of art history as a major?"

I bit my tongue to keep from asking why, given his disdainful attitude, *he* was working at a fabulous art museum like the Legion of Honor. As my grandmother used to say, *"Some people can't even enjoy their ice cream cone for the drips."*

He scrolled through a list on the computer screen,

tilting his head back to read through the bottom section of his bifocals.

Finally, he wrote something on a Post-it and handed it to me.

"That's all I got."

I read the note aloud: "Victorian clothing?"

He nodded. "Only one Scarlet listed, and she was a volunteer for the Victorian clothing exhibit, Vintage Victoriana. You need a special ticket for that."

It cost an extra ten dollars apiece to get into the special exhibit, but I figured it was for a good cause. I intended to take a quick spin through the show, just long enough to see if anyone knew Scarlet or if some other clue as to how to find her might appear. But to my surprise Sailor lingered, even after the security guards and ticket takers explained that they didn't know the volunteers who had helped set things up. He seemed content to study the contents of the glassed-in cases. I had assumed he hung around Aunt Cora's Closet mostly because of *me*; it hadn't occurred to me that Sailor might be a vintage clothing buff. Then again, vintage clothes did have a way of winning people over.

"What?" he asked me.

"What, what?" I asked in return.

He smiled, his gaze fixed on a placard reading,

Mantle, Paris, c. 1891; Emile Pingat, France, active 1860–1896. Wool; simple weave with silk velvet studded with embroidery of silver-and-gold thread, pearl beads, ostrich-feather trim

and

Visiting Dress, France, c. 1855. Silk; simple weave adorned with weft-float brocade patterning upon satin background, silk-and-metallic-thread ribbon trim

"Why are you looking at me like that?"

"I didn't realize you were interested in old clothes. You don't seem nearly so enamored with the merchandise at Aunt Cora's Closet."

"That's because I don't want to be invited to join you on wash day. I've seen how you recruit helpers for the laundry."

"Very funny. But seriously, do old clothes appeal to you?"

"Not the textiles themselves. What draws me is the history, what the fashions say about the time and place, the social and cultural mores. That sort of thing. Lots of people find it fascinating, obviously; look how crowded the exhibit is."

It was a weekday, so the throngs were probably at their thinnest, but there were still plenty of visitors milling about.

"Are you picking up on anything?" Sailor whispered.

"Not really. I wish I could touch it."

"I know what you mean," said a woman who had overheard me. "Can you imagine being that tiny and wearing something like that? The last time I was that small I was still in middle school. I know a few women who could fit into it, though."

I smiled.

But the woman's comment made me think: Autumn had been quite petite. I bet she could have worn these garments.

"You know," I said to Sailor in a low voice, "Renee

mentioned Autumn had tried on the Victorian ball gowns from the antique trousseau. Usually ball gowns were worn over corsets and petticoats, and a woman who could afford a gown like that also had servants to help her get dressed."

"Must have been nice," Sailor said.

"Not just nice—necessary. It was impossible for a woman to put on a fancy dress like this given all the accoutrements and scores of tiny buttons or hooks that fasten the dress in the back."

"The invention of the zipper must have changed all that," Sailor mused. "So where are you going with this?"

"It occurred to me that Autumn would have needed help getting into those Victorian ball gowns. So maybe Scarlet tried on the dresses with Autumn and they helped each other."

"And if she did—what would that tell us?"

"I have no idea."

The dresses were works of art, full of fanciful poufs, swags, and drapes. But as pretty as they were, the idea of actually wearing one held no appeal. Wealthy women of the era were clad in many pounds of fabric and ornamentation, such as beads and jewels. And that wasn't even counting the physical restraint of being encased in tight-fighting corsets and clothing, not to mention the absurdly narrow high-heeled shoes they wore, wildly unsuited to cobblestone streets and slippery surfaces. I'd take the comfort and ease of movement of modern clothing and footwear any day.

We moved on to a display of gloves and shoes, which seemed almost comically elongated.

Gloves and Shoes, Austrian, 1850s. Empress Elisabeth of Austria was considered the most beautiful woman in the world. Her elongated figure set the standard for constricted, elegant beauty. This pair of almost fantastically slender Adelaides and gloves were given to her by one of her many admirers. The fashion for straight shoes was a boon to cobblers as it freed them from the need to make two versions of the shoe, the left and the right; they needed only a single last per shoe size.

"Can you believe this? Who could possibly fit into something like that?" I asked, imagining that even a child's hands and feet would be wider than the gloves and shoes on display. When Sailor didn't answer, I glanced up and saw he had drifted off to the next case.

"Sorry," he said. "I was distracted by the sleeve plumpers."

"The what, now?"

He gestured at a mannequin wearing a cotton sateen corset, frilly petticoats, and large down-filled balloons fitted high on the arm. "Sleeve plumpers."

"Well, in the 1980s women wore shoulder pads. I guess it's the same concept." I gave him a sidelong look. "You sure you aren't perusing the corset?"

He gave me a crooked grin. "I'm not going to deny this stuff might lead a person to certain . . . ideas. You get some corsets in the shop occasionally. Ever try one on?"

"Now, just never you mind," I said, but I made a mental note for our next Mystery Date.

We wandered along, marveling at the items in the glass display cases. One held a pair of mannequins dressed for a night out on the town, Victorian-style. The woman held a pair of mother-of-pearl opera glasses and was dressed in a gown of long green organza with a silk-satin border and imitation-pearl glass beads. According to the sign, the male mannequin was wearing a *Gentleman's Suit (Coat, Waistcoat, Breeches), France. Silk cut, uncut, and voided velvet on satin foundation.*

"You'd look pretty spiffy in something like that," I said. If the man wanted to see me in a corset, turnabout was fair play. I loved his motorcycle gear, but it would be fun to see him all dressed up.

"That getup reminds me of your pal Aidan."

"Yes, Aidan does look nice in formal wear. Not *this* formal, of course."

Sailor gave me an odd look.

"What?"

He shook his head. "What have you heard from him?"

"Nothing, and I wish he'd get back. I walk the streets in fear someone will flag me down and ask me to bribe the mayor or some such."

"Just say this: 'I'll get right on that.' Repeat as necessary."

"Think that'll work?"

"Nine out of ten bureaucrats approve."

I laughed. "I'll give it a try."

We moved on to the next showcase, which held a black moiré silk and jet mourning gown with a black lace veil.

"That's so sad," I sighed.

"The Victorians died early and often," Sailor said. "They had a lot of rules and traditions for mourning. Check out the lacrimatory."

"I'm sorry?"

He pointed to an elaborate glass tube decorated with silver and gold filigree. "You don't know about lacrimatories?"

I shook my head.

"They're tiny bottles to collect tears. Examples were found among the ancient Romans, and the Victorians revived the tradition."

"How in the world do you know about something so obscure?"

"My aunt was intrigued by them for a while, even tracked down a couple of used ones. They can be utilized in some magical systems, though she was never able to figure out exactly how to use them. Lacrimatories are equipped with special stoppers that allow the tears to slowly evaporate. When the bottle's empty, the mourning period is over."

"I've never heard of such a thing." I was imagining the power such a bottle could have, holding so much grief and love, as well as the very real physical connection of a person's salt residue in the glass.

"It says here," Sailor continued, reading from the catalog, "'The widow hidden under her black mourning clothes and behind her veil invited not only sympathy, but also predacious behavior. As an unmarried woman with sexual experience, she was intriguing to the men of her social circles, and beyond. But as such, she was also considered by many to be a threat to the status quo.'"

"Well, that stinks," I said. "She loses her husband, has to put up with unwanted sexual advances, *and* is considered a threat to society because of it?"

"Society has had a hard time with independent women. Witness the way witches have been treated through the ages. Things are better these days, but there's still a double standard. An independent man is admired but an independent woman is often pitied or considered suspect."

I squeezed his hand. "You are an extraordinary man."

"Maybe that sort of statement is simply calculated to coax you into my bed—ever think of that?"

"Are you making predacious male advances?"

He grinned. "If you were a grieving widow I'd be all over you. . . ."

I shook my head. "You are capable of many things, Sailor. But that? I think not."

"And as I've said before, you are awfully trusting for one who's seen so much."

"It's not trust so much. It's more that you don't need subterfuge to coax me into your arms."

"'Will you walk into my parlor?' said the Spider to the Fly . . . ," Sailor quoted, and I giggled until I snorted, even though we were in a museum.

Before we left I made sure to ask everyone who was staffing the exhibit, from security guards to ticket takers to the gift store operators, whether they knew a woman named Scarlet. A couple of people thought the name sounded familiar, but they had no information about her.

"Well, that was a fascinating exhibit, but I don't think it told us anything," I said on the way back to the parking lot. "Although . . . the catalog lists Parmelee Riesling as one of the curators of the exhibit."

"You know her?"

"Carlos introduced us. She's a clothing conservator at the Asian Art Museum, and Maya saw her name mentioned on Autumn Jennings's Web site. I should probably see what she can tell me about Autumn, and maybe about Scarlet as well." I shrugged. "Probably just another dead end."

"Don't get discouraged there, supersleuth. It's your first day out. You did a pretty handy job getting those dogs back home."

"We were a good team," I said, smiling. The ocean wind whipped my hair; here the elements were more primal than by the bay. The open sea beckoned and made itself known.

"And besides, if you think about it, the only thing that's happened to you directly is that a dog walker reacted oddly. You're not actually involved in Autumn's death, except that it freed you from a lawsuit. You could just walk away."

"I appear to have inherited her dog. Or Maya has, if I've played my cards right. Besides, I *saw* Autumn. She seemed so frightened . . . and alone. I feel compelled to help. And I think there's more to this: Don't forget, Autumn's name was in Aidan's satchel."

"That's right." He ran his hand through his hair, rubbed the back of his neck. "Okay, that's interesting."

"What does it mean? If someone's name is in that bag?"

"That they're into Aidan for something. Could be a lot of things, but usually it's something major."

"That's what I was afraid of." I gazed out at the golf course down the hill from the museum. A couple of old men scooted by in their electric cart. "I was wondering . . . What if . . . what if something were to happen to the satchel while Aidan was away?"

We headed toward the purple van, which loomed on the other side of a tiny Smart car. Sailor gave a low chuckle and shook his head.

"It's not that I don't like where your head's at, tiger,

but I am nowhere near strong enough yet to protect you if you burn Aidan's satchel. *Nowhere. Near.* And besides, we're supposed to be working with Aidan these days, not against him, remember?"

"I suppose you're right."

"I'm always right."

"Not always."

"Often enough to make it a habit."

"Sailor . . . What kind of danger do you suppose is coming?"

He shrugged. "Patience and I have been trying, but whatever—or *who*ever—it is, they're cloaked. But we'll face it together. You, me, Oscar, Aidan, Selena, Patience . . ."

Ugh. Patience.

". . . all the cousins . . ."

"I don't suppose we could confront the coming danger without your family and assorted 'cousins'?"

He smiled and ruffled my hair. "They're not that bad. They're sort of an acquired taste, I'll grant you. But then, so are you, my fine, fair witch. Now, this is precisely why we're on our way to the beach. Make hay while the sun shines, and all that."

We stopped at a corner store whose inventory suggested they were popular with folks heading to the beach for a picnic. In addition to thick deli sandwiches, assorted chips and cookies, and drinks to quench every thirst, the store sold sweatshirts and beach blankets, little plastic pails and shovels. Sailor unearthed a bottle of Anderson Valley Zinfandel and even remembered to purchase a corkscrew.

We parked at the lot across from the beach, where a sign indicated that dogs on leashes were allowed. Local ordinances would no doubt frown on a pig's mere presence on the beach, but I still insisted Oscar wear the hated leash. Still, all the cutbacks in the park department's budget meant no one official was around to enforce the rules.

Sailor had been right: Few people were braving the chill at the beach. The fog had rolled in, cold and damp, making it hard to remember it was June. The three of us ran along the water's edge just to get our blood pumping, Oscar squealing as he dashed in and out of the surf, but the icy Pacific made our feet numb. We used a few of Oscar's blankets to make a nice pallet on the beach, wrapped our coats around us, and ate our picnic while gazing out at the sea.

The cupcakes were delicious. Oscar mowed through half a dozen before I even noticed.

Sated, the three of us huddled together, lulled by the sight and sound of the crashing waves. A bee came buzzing by, buffeted by the ocean winds, and landed on the sleeve of my coat. She tip-tapped on her tiny feet until I lifted my arm and she alit, flying out toward the ocean.

I watched as she disappeared into the gray horizon, which blended so well with the overcast sky that there seemed to be no separation at all, just a never-ending stretch from the Pacific Ocean all the way up into the heavens.

Chapter 9

It was late afternoon by the time we got back to the Haight, where we found a small group clustered on the sidewalk in front of Aunt Cora's Closet. We parked around the corner in the driveway I rent for my vehicles and walked back to find Conrad, Bronwyn, and Bronwyn's boyfriend, Duke, gazing at the sign hanging in the window: *Closed for Inventory.*

"Duke and I had a late lunch down the street," said Bronwyn, "and thought we'd drop off a doggy bag for Conrad. This is *such* a shame. And I can't believe it about poor Autumn!"

"Did the police speak with you?" I asked.

"Yes, they asked a lot of questions about the scones and tea I brought her in the gift basket." Bronwyn paused, looking troubled. "Lily, you don't think . . . I mean, there couldn't have been something in there by accident somehow, could there?"

"No, of course not," I assured her. "You wouldn't

make a mistake like that. You've been mixing herbs for a long time and never had any problem."

"Listen to Lily," Duke said, concern for Bronwyn written all over his lined, sun-burnished face. Duke was a retired fisherman, but still enjoyed sailing. "She knows how careful you are."

"I make sure to buy from certified organic, non-GMO sources! Only the very best!" Bronwyn's expression showed her horror at the idea that she could have harmed someone.

"I know you do. Carlos says it's all standard procedure; they just have to rule out the obvious suspects. And sad to say that through me, you had motive, because of the lawsuit she was bringing against me and the shop."

"How long are they planning to keep the shop closed?" asked Conrad.

"Not more than a couple of days, I hope," I said.

"Ooooh, what's going on?" asked Sandra Schmidt as she approached our group.

"Nothing," Bronwyn and I said in unison.

Sandra's store, Peaceful Things, was right next door to Aunt Cora's Closet. It featured vaguely Haight-Ashbury-inspired items, like tie-dyed T-shirts and love beads and imported handmade carvings from Thailand and Nepal. Unfortunately, despite its name, I had never found the space particularly harmonious, probably because of Sandra herself. A nervous sort, she had a habit of standing too closely, speaking too intently, and rising on her tiptoes and dropping down again as though her energy had nowhere else to go.

"I thought maybe someone broke in and vandalized the place!" Sandra breathed out. *"Again!"*

Sandra was prone to exaggeration, but in this case she was right: It looked like a bomb had gone off inside my shop. The forensic team clearly hadn't held back—from the window we could see they'd not only searched Brownyn's herbal stand but had knocked over entire racks of clothes as well. I felt my temper rise, and I struggled to control it.

"We're doing inventory," I said.

"But then why are you all standing out here instead of inside, working?" Sandra asked.

None of your goldurned business, I felt like saying, but Sailor stepped in. "Because I swept Lily off for a romantic picnic at the beach," he supplied smoothly. "Bronwyn and I worked together to fool her into closing for inventory for a few days."

"Oh," said Sandra, looking disappointed. Apparently she'd been hoping for something more scandalous. "But I don't understand. If you're closed for inventory, why aren't you here working on inventory? And why's there such a mess?"

"Cupcake?" Sailor asked, holding out the pink box and lifting the lid. Only four cupcakes had escaped Oscar's clutches.

"Ooooh," Sandra said, peering into the box, distracted.

"Did you know they call these 'fairy cakes' in Great Britain?" Sailor said. I smiled at him, and he gave me a wink. "I highly recommend the white cake with sprinkles."

"Isn't that just too adorable!" She took the white cake topped with a generous dollop of pink frosting dusted with multicolored sprinkles and a little candy fairy perched on top.

"How have you been, Sandra?" I asked. "It's been a while."

Sandra dropped by Aunt Cora's Closet occasionally, and I ducked into her shop from time to time as well because it was important to be on good terms with one's neighbors. But she and I would never be true friends. Sandra was often unkind to Conrad, calling him my "pet hobo." Conrad ignored her, but I found it difficult to forgive such rudeness. And she was forever asking questions about things that were none of her business. And she had a fascination with literature such as the *Malleus Maleficarum*—a witch-hunting manual from the bad old "burning times"—which I simply couldn't get behind.

But still, we were neighbors, and as such, we all worked at getting along.

"To tell you the truth," Sandra said, her mouth full of cupcake, "I have news. I'm considering closing my shop. My sister has an antiques store in Carson City and I was thinking of joining her there. Rents and everything are just too expensive in San Francisco nowadays. And"— she cast a glance toward Conrad—"the Haight's gotten a bit too *urban* for my taste."

"Oh . . . um, Carson City sounds like fun," I said. "It's a small town?"

"Why, it's the *capital* of the state of Nevada!"

"Oh, that's right," I said, embarrassed. "I wasn't ever much good at naming the capitals."

"The capital of Wyoming is Cheyenne," said Conrad helpfully. "No one ever remembers Wyoming. Or Wisconsin, for that matter, which is Madison. Maybe it's a *W* thing? Washington's is Salem, of course."

"Dibs on you for partner next time we play Trivial Pursuit," said Sailor.

"*Dude*, you are very wise. I know all fifty capitals. And don't get me started on the state birds and flowers." He tapped his temple with his forefinger. "Mind like a steel trap."

"How come no one ever wants *me* as a partner for Trivial Pursuit?" I asked.

My friends laughed.

"Well, anyway, I suppose I should get back to the salt mines," said Sandra. "I'm just glad to hear that you didn't suffer a break-in. What with the way things are these days . . . I was worried."

"Let's be sure to get together before you go," I said. "I mean, if you do decide to make the big move. We could try the pub around the corner. My treat."

"Thank you. I'd like that," said Sandra, nodding at everybody before heading back into her shop.

After she left, I wondered aloud, "What do you suppose Sandra meant by 'too urban'? This is San Francisco, after all. What does she expect?"

"Dude, *urban* means full of people you don't want to associate with," said Conrad. "Like me."

"Oh," I said, realization dawning. Conrad's placid expression didn't change, but I felt bad for him. "I'm sorry, Conrad."

He shrugged. "Dude. Been called worse, and probably thought of as *much* worse. If it fazed me I guess I'd change my way of life."

I nodded. I supposed that was a pretty good way to approach such things.

"On the bright side," Bronwyn said as she left with Duke, "with Aunt Cora's Closet closed for 'inventory,' now's the perfect time to spend a night at the Rodchester House of Spirits!"

"Oh, hey, that reminds me," I said. "Bronwyn, how did the idea for this sleepover occur to you? You mentioned you saw a brochure somewhere. Was it at Autumn's store, by any chance?"

"Yes, as a matter of fact, it was. How did you know?"

"I noticed the brochure there. Did you and Autumn talk about it?"

"Well, let's see . . . I believe I mentioned I hadn't been there in quite some time, and Autumn said, 'If you do go, be careful because it can be dangerous.'"

"Dangerous? Did she mean physically, or in terms of spirits, or . . . ?"

"She didn't say. She seemed very tense, but I got the feeling that was her usual mode of interacting with the world. And as I said before, I thought she might be sick. Which, given what happened, she *was*. Poor soul. I felt sorry for her."

"Because she was sick?" I asked.

Bronwyn shook her head. "Because she seemed so afraid."

"Of what?"

"Of everything."

As Oscar, Sailor, and I climbed the rear stairs to my apartment, Sailor said, "What's all this about a sleepover at the Rodchester House of Spirits?"

"I sort of forgot to mention that."

"I'm afraid to ask."

"You *should* be afraid. Especially when I ask you to chaperone."

He let out an exasperated breath. "And you say *I'm*

acting out of character? Seems to me *you* prided yourself on being a solo act. Held yourself apart from others, did your own thing. Or did I imagine all that?"

"It's my new approach to life: I'm supposed to ask for help, remember?"

"All right, then. What do you need?"

"Come be our bodyguard?"

He let out a little groan. "I suppose I can't very well say no, now, can I?"

"Not really."

"When is this little shindig?"

"On Saturday. Unless I can somehow put a stop to it."

"Is this in lieu of our Mystery Date?"

"It *is* our Mystery Date." I had considered booking tickets to Alcatraz, the former federal penitentiary on an island in San Francisco Bay, but wasn't sure how much Sailor would enjoy it. Alcatraz was historical and fascinating, but the place had seen so much pain and sadness. Tortured souls roamed the forlorn island, and you never knew with psychics. Sometimes the spirits just wouldn't leave them alone, so that an experience others enjoyed could become harrowing.

"No offense to you or Bronwyn, Lily, but spending the evening with you and thirteen coven sisters isn't exactly my idea of a great date."

"Sounds *awesome* to me," said Oscar, rubbing his hands together. "Woo-hoo! I can't wait!"

"Oscar . . . ," I began, searching for words. It's tough to explain to a gobgoyle why he can't come on an overnight with a coven in a haunted house. "I'm sorry, but this isn't something for pigs."

He stared at me, wide-eyed.

"I doubt the Rodchester House is a pet-friendly place."

"I don't get it."

"You can't come," said Sailor bluntly.

"B-but I love the Rodchester House of Spirits! It's an *awesome* haunted house!"

"You've been there?"

"Sure. It's a major attraction in these parts. Haven't you taken the tour? Course, there's the normal tour, and then there's a *special* tour. Take my word for it: You want the special tour."

"I—no, I haven't been." Oscar had a way of throwing me. How on earth had he managed to go on a tour—a *special* tour—of the Rodchester House of Spirits? But then, he wasn't a standard witch's familiar; he had his own life, and sometimes he disappeared for hours or even days at a time. For all I knew, he was touring local attractions, taking in a play, and stopping off for a three-martini lunch at John's Grill with his gang of ersatz witches' familiars.

"Anyway, Oscar, the point is that the Welcome coven has arranged for an overnight stay, but the Rodchester House doesn't permit animals."

He scoffed and waved his oversized hand in my direction.

"I'm serious, Oscar."

"B-but the Laaaady, and all her coven sisters?" His eyes were huge, his tone tragic.

I looked to Sailor for help. He shrugged and splayed his hands out, helpless.

"I'm really sorry, Oscar," I said. "I'll make it up to you. How about mac 'n' cheese for dinner tonight? With fried okra?"

This was a new gobgoyle favorite. Okra was technically a vegetable, but since it was breaded and fried,

Oscar made an exception to his carbs-and-cheese-only rule.

"And fried green tomatoes, too?"

"Sure."

"Mm-kay," he mumbled; then he turned and dragged his talons into the kitchen. I could hear him grumbling under his breath about being kept out of all the fun stuff, and I felt bad.

"How much you want to bet he shows up anyway?" said Sailor.

"*No.*" I blinked. "Seriously?"

"Ten bucks says I'm right."

"But how would he get there?"

"How does he get anywhere? Besides, didn't you give him a travel cloak a while ago?"

"That's right. I did." Not that Oscar needed the cloak to travel. Sailor was right. I had no idea how Oscar managed to get himself anywhere, but manage he did. I sighed.

Sailor laid a heavy hand on the back of my neck and emitted a low chuckle. "Oscar can take care of himself. I *would* worry about Bronwyn and her coven, however."

"Why? Have you been to the Rodchester House? Is it dangerous? I mean, it strikes me as a bad idea, but I don't have anything concrete as justification. Merely a general feeling of dread."

He shook his head thoughtfully. "I haven't been there. I imagine you and I have that in common: We don't frequent haunted houses if we can help it."

"So it's really haunted?"

"I have no idea. But even if it wasn't to begin with, all those visitors fervently believing it is would create more than enough energy to stir things up. Thousands of tourists, day in and day out . . . Well, you do the math. Not to mention the Widow Rodchester was famous for hosting séances and inviting folks like Houdini to call on the dead. . . ."

"You mean she might have unwittingly invited someone into her home?"

"Someone, or some*thing*."

"It sounds like you know more about this place than you're letting on."

"As Oscar said, it's pretty well-known around here. I haven't been there, but most people I know have."

"And is it true that the Widow Rodchester kept building onto the house, hoping to appease the spirits?"

"That's what they say. But if you think about it, does it seem logical that she would attempt to appease the spirits by spending the money she made from selling the guns that killed them?"

"That sounded a little strange to me, too."

"I've also heard that Sally Rodchester was a frustrated architect who used her own house as her guinea pig. She was interested in spiritualism, but that wasn't unusual at the time. When her husband died, she inherited a huge fortune that allowed her to do pretty much whatever she wanted."

"So you don't think she was a little crazy, a prisoner of her own house?"

"Akin to what we were discussing at the Vintage Victoriana clothes show earlier: I think this is the sort of thing history usually says about independent women."

"That they're mad?"

"Yes. In your case, of course, it's true." His hands settled on my waist, his head bent toward mine, and he gave me a ghost of a smile. "Mad as a hatter."

Chapter 10

The next morning I called Maya.

"How's Loretta? Everything going okay?"

"She seems just fine. Mom took her in to the sewing loft with her today. I think it's fair to say that one would be hard-pressed to find a mellower dog. Still, I promised to drop by and take her for a walk later."

"I was thinking . . . one of Autumn's neighbors, the cupcake lady, said there was a dog park around the corner from the shop. Dog people know each other, right?"

"If they go to the same park at the same time, they'd probably at least recognize each other."

"I encountered the dog walker yesterday about now. If she keeps to a schedule . . ."

"Tell you what: Meet me at Mom's and we can go together."

"Really?"

"Sure. It just so happens I have an unexpected day off. And I think I need to check out this cupcake shop."

* * *

I headed out to Lucille's Loft to pick up Loretta. As I squeezed into a tight spot at the brick building near Potrero Hill, off Fifteenth, I rolled the phrase around in my mouth a few times, *Loretta's at Lucille's Loft*, smiling at the alliteration.

The loft was on the second floor of an old factory building that had been divided into several work spaces. Unlike many buildings in the city, which had been renovated and rehabbed within an inch of their lives, this building was true to its roots, featuring a creaky old freight elevator and ugly dropped acoustic ceilings in the hallways.

Inside the loft, though, old redbrick walls, huge multipaned windows, and tall, beamed ceilings more than made up for the lack of outward panache. A few women stood at huge worktables cutting cloth with crinkly patterns, while half a dozen others sat hunched over sewing machines. The floor was covered in thread and scraps, and one whole wall was lined with bolts of brightly colored retro-style cloth.

"Hello, Lily," Lucille called out, lifting her gaze but not moving from the worktable. She held a huge pair of shears in one hand and a bolt of fabric in the other. Her short-cropped, graying hair was dotted with bits of thread and fluff. No doubt it was a professional hazard. "Maya should be here any minute."

Apart from the gray hairs, a few extra pounds, and a handful of wrinkles, Lucille looked almost exactly like her daughter. Both were beautiful in an understated way; strong and steady. I wondered what it must be like for Maya to know what she would look like at her mother's age. Would it be comforting, or disconcerting? I took after my father more than my mother, which, given his character, was more than a little disturbing.

Several of the women glanced up and shouted hellos at me across the open floor. I recognized a few of the faces because Lucille preferred to hire and train women from the Haight women's shelter whenever she could. Aunt Cora's Closet donated professional clothes to the residents four times a year, in an event organized by Bronwyn's Welcome coven. A new wardrobe might seem rather low on the list of resources the shelter women needed, but in fact it wasn't. One of the many hurdles facing those trying to get back on their feet was the inability to dress properly for job interviews.

Besides, as we liked to say at Aunt Cora's Closet: Changing your clothes can help change your life. And the afternoon spent trying on garments was a rare, lighthearted event that helped women in difficult circumstances feel better about themselves.

"Where's Loretta?" I asked.

Lucille tilted her head toward the windows. I walked farther into the space and spied Loretta in a patch of sunlight, lying on a bed of scraps. The charms on her collar gleamed in the sun, but they didn't so much as tinkle since she remained motionless, save for a single lazy thump of her tail.

"Well, she certainly seems at home."

"She's a perfect workplace dog," said a woman named Beatriz, working at the nearest table. "Just perfect. Except, we might lose the loft soon."

"Lose the loft?" I repeated. "Why? What's going on?"

Lucille finished with the fabric she was cutting, straightened, and shook her head. "The owner wants to sell the building. He's been a great landlord so far but wants to move to Idaho or North Dakota or one of those. The new folks are planning on turning this building into expensive condos. 'Lofts' in the hipster sense of the word; essentially they'll be condos with brick walls and nice windows, but no decent parking or other amenities."

"I'm so sorry to hear that." In San Francisco these days, being evicted often meant having to relocate to a new town altogether. The city was becoming so expensive its demographics were changing, with immigrants and artists and artisans making way for tech folks who could pay many times as much to rent or buy an apartment. I thanked my lucky stars I had signed a ten-year lease when I moved into Aunt Cora's Closet.

"It's such a shame; we were just getting to a point where the business was in the black. Now . . ." She trailed off with a shrug, looked at the women hard at work, and dropped her voice. "I honestly don't know what we're going to do. It's true we don't need this much room, but even so I haven't been able to find a place I could even begin to afford. And you know these women don't have the ability to commute to outlying areas. Neither do I, for that matter."

Just then Maya arrived. Loretta lifted her big head and gave a welcoming, muffled *woof.*

"Wow, you've made a conquest," I said. "Loretta gave you two whole thumps of her tail, *and* a woof."

"I have a way with animals," Maya said with a smile. When she first met Oscar she had referred to him as "the other white meat," but over time her attitude had changed. As was the case for many who thought themselves immune to the charms of animals, sometimes it just took one or two special interactions to change their minds.

"So, which dog park are you going to?" asked Lucille.

"It's over off Buchanan, around the corner from a store called Vintage Visions Glad Rags."

"Checking out the competition?"

"Not really . . ." If Maya hadn't already told her mother what was going on, I didn't want to try to explain it all. This was a position I found myself in fairly often, given the way my life had developed. "But that's where we found Loretta."

"I just told Mom we were keeping Loretta for a friend for a few days," said Maya.

Lucille's intelligent eyes settled on me for a long moment; then she nodded in a sage, patient way that again reminded me of her daughter. "I see."

"C'mon, Loretta, let's go," I said, patting my thigh. The pup didn't move.

Maya took her key ring out of her pocket and tinkled it. Loretta lifted her head, then rolled onto her feet, stood, shook herself, then trotted over to the door.

"As I was saying," said Maya, arching one eyebrow. "A way with animals."

The dog park appeared to have once been a large lawn but now was a big brown space surrounded by a chain-link fence. A few oak trees and some patches of dusty ivy were the only things hardy enough to survive both the drought and numerous high-spirited canines.

An older couple sat on a wooden bench, and one woman stood under a tree with her head bent, reading on an electronic device. Half a dozen people stood around in a loose circle, chatting while their dogs played. Occasionally someone would throw a slobbery ball that had been dutifully dropped at their feet, but otherwise it was social hour for the humans as well as the pets.

As soon as I undid her leash, I expected Loretta to shoot out of the car and race toward the park and freedom, but she stood by our sides, a dignified old lady checking out the scene.

"Go on, now," I said softly. "Go play with your friends."

She looked up at me with her soulful brown eyes and gave a lackadaisical swish of her tail.

"Or not. Whatever floats your boat."

"I don't think Loretta's what you'd call a high-energy dog," said Maya. She gestured with her head. "Want to go infiltrate the group?"

We had stopped for coffee on the way over, and we clutched our cardboard cups as we moseyed around. Loretta followed a few feet behind, looking at the other dogs but making no move to leave our sides. Maya and I edged our way into the informal circle, nodding and trading hellos.

Before I could launch into my story, one of the young men said, "Hey, isn't that Loretta?"

"It is, yes. I take it you know her?"

"Sure. Where's Scarlet?"

"She's sick, right?" said a young woman with strawberry blond hair and freckles. She turned to her companion. "I told you so. Last time I saw her, she didn't look all that great, I gotta be honest. Didn't I say that?"

Both she and the bearded young man at her side looked familiar. When the man opened his mouth to speak, I realized I had seen them at the cupcake shop yesterday. They had been leaving just as Sailor and I arrived.

"Yeah, you did say that," he said to Freckles. Then

he turned to me. "Hey, didn't we see you at Renee's yesterday?"

"Yes, I was just thinking you looked familiar."

"Great cupcakes. Did you try the bourbon-and-bacon one?"

The mention of this culinary delight engendered a long and passionate discussion within the group, with individuals defending their personal favorites, from red velvet to something with the dubious moniker of Zucchini Surprise.

"Sorry," the young woman said. "Cupcakes are a favorite topic around here, as you can see. I'm Eleanor, and this is Cody. And that little ragamuffin there"—she pointed to an admittedly odd-looking hound that appeared to be a cross between a German shepherd and a spaniel, but with the stubby legs of a dachshund—"is Mr. Bojangles. He's a rescue."

"Nice to meet you. I'm Lily; this is Maya. And I guess you all know Loretta."

Loretta was leaning her considerable weight on Maya, who braced herself and petted her patiently.

The others went around the circle introducing themselves: George and Jessica and Ling and Graydon and Rolando, and their respective dogs: D.C. and Samantha and Jack and MacAllister and Sunshine.

"So, seriously," asked Cody, "is Scarlet okay?"

"To tell you the truth, I'm not sure," I said. I heard a bee buzzing nearby; it came and landed on my shoulder. "I saw her briefly yesterday, but the strangest thing happened: She left the dogs she was walking. Just dropped the leashes and took off."

Everyone in the group looked surprised.

"That doesn't sound like Scarlet," someone said, and the others all nodded.

"In what way?" Maya asked.

"She was pretty dependable. Came here with a bunch of dogs every day, right about now."

Without thinking about it, I put my hand up to my shoulder; the bee crawled onto it, and I released it into the wind. Graydon caught my eye and gave me a thumbs-up.

"She must really have been sick if she took off and left the dogs like that. I hope she's okay. I noticed the vintage place was closed, too," said Cody. "The store owner wasn't feeling well, either. Maybe there's something going around."

"Is that why you're taking care of Loretta?" asked Ling, a fiftyish woman with a ginger-colored Pekingese.

"Sort of . . . ," I began. The group started speculating about whether or not it was smart to get a flu shot. This being San Francisco, the discussion quickly morphed, with emotions running high, into a debate about requiring immunizations for school-aged children, and the perils of the pharmaceutical industry.

Maya and I exchanged looks.

"Soooo," I ventured as soon as the discussion died down a little, "does anyone know how to get in touch with Scarlet?"

Several shrugs and a flurry of shaking heads.

"Sorry," said the man who had introduced himself as Rolando. "We see each other here, but to tell you the truth I didn't even know anyone's name until today. I know the animals, mostly."

"Me, too," said Graydon with a laugh, and the others nodded in agreement.

"I know Scarlet from here, and I also saw her at the vintage store sometimes," said Eleanor. "Maybe she worked there part-time? I don't go in there very often, but Cody and I live down the block, the apartment building on the other side of the bank. So we walk by all the time."

"Usually on the way to the cupcake store, to be honest," said Cody with a smile.

"You mentioned that Autumn—the owner of the vintage store—seemed to be under the weather, too?"

Cody shrugged. "I mean, it's not like I know her that well or anything. I'm telling you, not to sound like a broken record, but in this neighborhood we all know each other from this dog park or that cupcake shop. Makes you think about what might bring urban neighbors together, right? A shared love of pets and frosting—that's the heart of the place."

Eleanor looked at Cody with affection shining in her light eyes. "That's beautiful. Who knew a computer programmer would have the soul of an artist?"

He grinned and shrugged. "I'm, like, totally a poet, and didn't even know it."

"And Autumn seemed ill?" I tried to bring the conversation back but realized that at this point everyone was starting to gaze at me warily. I tried to cast a bit of a reassuring spell to encourage them to feel comfortable speaking to me. I got the sense that here at the dog park the conversation tended to be a bit more organic and meandering.

"I guess," Cody said with a shrug, clearly wishing he hadn't said anything. "She just looked a little green around the gills, if you know what I mean. Or maybe, I dunno, last time I saw her she seemed angry with Renee, too, and left the shop without buying anything. I mean, who *does* that?"

"Right?" said Eleanor. "I can't imagine leaving that shop without a cupcake!"

"Do you remember what they were arguing about?" I asked.

He shook his head and threw the ball for Mr. Bojangles.

"Sorry if we're asking a lot of questions," said Maya, clearly noticing that the crowd was wearying of the inquisition. "It's just that . . . I don't know if you heard, but Autumn Jennings passed away yesterday."

"What?" Eleanor asked. Everyone looked stunned. "What happened?"

"I think you're right; she was sick," Maya said. "Lily and I went to talk with her and found her in pretty bad shape. We called the paramedics, and that's how we ended up taking care of Loretta. So we're here today to try to find out a little more about her. We thought maybe Scarlet could tell us something, or maybe take Loretta."

"I doubt she'd be able to offer Loretta a home," said Eleanor with a shake of her head. "I think she was having a hard time as it was, finding an affordable place to live in the city. A place for a dog as big as Loretta . . . ?"

"That's like the Holy Grail in this city," said Jessica, a young woman with long dreadlocks. "I had to do some fancy footwork to find a place that allowed my little beagle."

Everyone nodded in commiseration.

"I'd still love to talk to her," I said, handing my card out to everyone in the group. "If you happen to see her or hear from her, would you let me know?"

"I can't believe what you're saying, though, about Autumn," said Eleanor. "She's *dead*? What happened? What did she have? Do you think Cody's right, that Scarlet got the same thing?"

"Is it, like, ebola or bird flu or something?" asked the young woman with dreadlocks.

A few folks edged back, probably without meaning to. I realized I might start a neighborhood panic if I wasn't careful.

"I don't think so. I mean, I'm no expert and I don't really know what the doctors found, but it might have been something environmental. Perhaps . . . a poison of some sort. I think now they're focusing on trying to figure out whether it was accidental or on purpose."

"On purpose?" asked Eleanor. "You mean she might have killed herself?"

"I don't really—"

"She didn't seem all that happy, to tell you the truth. Her husband died a couple of years ago. No family, lived above her store . . ."

"She didn't have any relatives?"

"I was in the store once around Thanksgiving, and Scarlet was grousing about having to go visit her family in Missouri, and I remember Autumn telling her she was lucky to have a family to complain about," Eleanor said.

"That's really sad," said Rolando. "To think she might not have anyone to mourn her."

A moment of silence followed. As people do in times of stress, we turned to watch the antics of the dogs: Two were playing tug-of-war with what looked like an old sock; a young pup was bouncing around Loretta, trying to entice her to play; one dignified old pooch with a graying muzzle lay in a patch of shade, sniffing the air. I thought about how animals typify the teachings of Zen: enjoying the here and now, not asking for anything more. Living every moment.

"Well," said Ling. She called her dog and attached his leash to a teal rhinestone collar. "On that note, I'm going to go home and call my mother. Nice to meet you, Lily. If I see Scarlet I'll let her know you're looking for her."

"Thanks," I said, though if Scarlet knew I was looking for her, she'd be sure to run in the opposite direction. "If nothing else, maybe let her know about Autumn? If Scarlet's not feeling well, either, it's possible she needs medical attention."

"That's a sobering thought," murmured Cody.

"Aw, man, I hope she's okay," said Eleanor, looking troubled.

Most of the others followed Ling's lead, calling their dogs and heading home. Loretta had ventured all of three feet away from us and was currently enthralled with whatever scents she could pick up from the trunk of a nearby oak tree. Mr. Bojangles brought his ball back to Cody and Eleanor several times, hopping around excitedly, and Cody obediently picked it up and threw it clear across the park. Mr. Bojangles chased it, long tongue hanging out, ecstatic.

"Cody, you don't suppose . . . ," Eleanor began.

"No," said Cody with a firm shake of his head.

"What?" I urged. "Did something occur to you? About Scarlet, or Autumn?"

"It's just . . ."

"Oh, come on, Eleanor," Cody scoffed. "That's just a stupid rumor."

"I'd still like to hear it," I said.

"I have this, like, friend? And she was in Autumn's store once and overheard her on the phone saying she thought she was . . . *cursed*."

Chapter 11

"Lily knows a thing or two about curses," Maya said, her tone matter-of-fact. "She once helped a man who had a love curse on him."

"Really?" Eleanor asked, fixing her pale blue gaze on me. She was probably in her midtwenties, maybe pushing thirty, but with that fine hair and freckles it was easy to see what she must have looked like as a kindergartner. "You, like, know about things like that?"

"I don't know," I said, choosing my words carefully. "I think in that case the man was his own worst enemy, believing he would never find love and therefore sabotaging himself. He's involved with a very nice woman now."

"But you do believe there's such a thing as curses?" asked Eleanor. "Cody says I'm ridiculous, but I have to wonder . . ."

Cody rolled his eyes.

"What curse are we talking about?" I asked. I had brushed up on hereditary curses to try to help a man named Bartholomew Woolsey, who believed himself to be suffering under a curse laid upon a Puritan ancestor. But the truth was that such curses were extraordinarily rare. And in Bart's case, I still wasn't sure whether the curse had succeeded through magic, or whether Bart and his family had so believed in the curse that they'd manifested the results. That was the problem with curses, and with magic in general—it was very complicated.

"Well, not long ago, Autumn got hold of a trousseau for her shop. And according to what my friend said, she began to think it was cursed."

"A cursed trousseau?" I asked.

She nodded.

"Why would a trousseau have a curse attached to it?" asked Maya.

Cody made a dismissive noise and wandered off to play with Mr. Bojangles.

"He doesn't believe."

"But you do?"

Eleanor shrugged. "I'm not sure. But now that you tell me about poor Autumn, it makes a person wonder, right?"

"Do you know anything about the supposed curse?"

"The way I heard it, it had to do with this feud between a shoeshine boy and a rich guy, and then one of their fiancées died from a cursed trousseau. Or something like that. I looked it up online after my friend told me about it, but I forget the details."

"So you think the curse is still on the trousseau, and that's what killed Autumn?"

"It's possible, right? I mean, otherwise she, what, just got sick and keeled over? Right after buying it? That's sort of unusual, isn't it?"

"Unusual, yes," said Maya. "But I'm not sure I would

jump straight to a case of a cursed trousseau. More likely a case of bad seafood or lead poisoning or something. People die of all sorts of things, every day. Even seemingly healthy people keel right over from a heart attack, embolism, stroke . . ."

"I declare, Maya, you are a regular ray of sunshine."

She smiled. "I try. I'm just saying, people die and it's a tragedy, but it's hardly ever the fault of frilly corsets."

"My point exactly," said Cody, using a wet wipe to clean his hands as he rejoined our trio.

"It's pretty funny," Eleanor said. "You'll never meet anyone more cynical about the occult than Cody, but he works for the Rodchester House of Spirits, of all places!"

"The one in San Jose?" I asked. That was certainly a coincidence, and coincidences rarely boded well in my life.

"Yeah, have you been?" asked Eleanor.

"No, but I've been meaning to go," I said. Now, more than ever. "In fact, a friend of mine is having an overnight birthday party there in a couple of days."

"Really? Cool," said Cody. "It's a new thing we've been offering; we've already had several bookings. I'd love to hear how it goes."

"But I take it you don't really believe the house is haunted?"

He seemed to hesitate. "Well, obviously the sales team likes to exploit that idea; people seem excited by it. But, I dunno, I think it's an amazing place just as it is, a true architectural wonder; why do they have to come up with spooky stories about it? But I was raised not far from there by a pair of computer engineers who thought of it as a historic monument. Probably the acorn didn't fall far from the tree; I'm into computer science, too. So maybe I'm not the target audience."

"I noticed a brochure for the Rodchester House in Autumn's shop, as it happens."

"Yeah, I pass 'em out from time to time, leave some at the local shops. I gave one to Scarlet a few weeks ago; she wanted to try to get a job there, or at least volunteer. She was always looking out for interesting things like that."

"Do you think Scarlet believed the Rodchester House was haunted?" I wasn't sure why this would be pertinent, but it seemed important to know whether I was dealing with a believer or a skeptic.

"I have no idea. I mentioned I worked for them, and she got excited, asked me about maybe getting a job. I gave her the brochure, but like I told her, I'm not actually involved with the house per se. I'm just a computer guy: I maintain their Web site; that's about it."

"*And* he does some of the graphic design work—he put together those brochures, and a beautiful catalog of all the collections!" Eleanor said, holding his hand and beaming up at Cody.

It dawned on me that without his beard, he would look as young as she. Amazing how certain style choices can age a person; like looking back at high school graduation pictures from the 1950s and thinking everyone looked about forty years old.

"But the cool thing is he's not even on-site. He gets to work from home, and so do I," Eleanor added. "That way, we hardly ever have to be apart from each other, or Mr. Bojangles. Just our own nice little family."

"Speaking of work," said Cody, checking an old-fashioned wristwatch, "I really should be getting back.

Working from home means I get to set my own schedule, but it doesn't mean I don't have to show results."

I thanked them for their time and watched as they leashed their dog and walked away.

Loretta sniffed lazily at a scruffy bush, and I sipped my now nearly cold coffee.

"Do you think that much togetherness could really work for a couple?" Maya asked. "I mean, wouldn't it be hard for you and Sailor to work *and* live together?"

I choked on my swig of coffee and quickly dissolved into a full-fledged coughing fit. Maya patted me on the back ineffectually, but she couldn't hold back the chuckle.

"Sorry," she said, trying to stifle her smile. "I'm guessing this theme's a little . . . fraught?"

"I just hadn't really thought about it," I wheezed. "It would take a lot. On both our parts."

"It's not a *terrible* idea, you and Sailor moving in together," mused Maya as we headed back to the car. I considered putting Loretta's leash back on as law declared, but she was so mellow it was hard to imagine the necessity.

"I mean," Maya continued, "you two are pretty darned cute together."

"Yes, you mentioned that before." I tried to keep the images at bay, but they flooded my mind: waking up in Sailor's arms every morning, cuddling in bed, gazing at each other over steaming cups of coffee; him coming home at the end of the day as I was closing up shop, tending to the receipts and the cash in the register; locking the front door and climbing up to the apartment, fixing dinner together for us and Oscar; the sounds of Oscar's snores emanating from his cubby over the fridge while Sailor and I shared a last glass of wine . . .

Or, I supposed Sailor might not want to live in my apartment. I surely wouldn't want to live in his dreary place in Chinatown. So then would we have to look for rentals . . . ? As the dog park group had pointed out, finding a place to rent in San Francisco—especially with a pet pig—would be a challenge. I wouldn't shy away from using some magic to increase my chances, but it was still a long shot. And would I be willing to leave my terrace botanical garden behind and start again? *No.* There was no way I was going to move.

So that left Sailor moving in with me, into my apartment above the shop. And that would mean him being there. All the time.

Unlike some ex-boyfriends I could mention, Sailor wasn't thrown by my witchy ways, but what if he got tired of distinguishing my bags of cemetery dirt from garden soil, or the raw goat milk for new moon ceremonies from the milk for the cereal? Or what if the sometimes noxious smoke from my brewing got on his nerves? I wasn't about to hold back on my brewing and spellcasting, so if he dared to imply—

"So, did our trip to the dog park tell us anything?" asked Maya, interrupting my flight of fancy and bringing me back to the here and now.

At the sound of her voice, I tried to focus my mind on the matter at hand. Sailor and I were nowhere near ready to move in together, no matter the locale. I pushed it from my mind and turned my thoughts to Autumn and Scarlet, the Rodchester House of Spirits, and an allegedly cursed trousseau.

"I don't know. The idea that the trousseau might be cursed is new. Sailor and I both felt there was something off about those items, but as to whether there's an actual curse behind all this, that's something else altogether."

I unlocked the car, we climbed in, and I started driving across town.

"I'd like to look up this story about the shoeshine boy and the curse," I continued. "Eleanor mentioned it was pretty well-known."

"And by that you mean you'd like *me* to look up this story about the shoeshine boy and the curse?"

"I think you're becoming a mind reader yourself. You sure you're not psychic?" I teased. "Unfortunately, as you know, Aunt Cora's Closet is still closed, pending the forensic team's investigation, so we can't even use the computer."

"Bronwyn told me they'd made a huge mess. What a drag."

"This won't be the first time we've had to put the shop back together."

"That was sort of my point."

"Sorry. I know. We're a problem store. And I'm probably a problem boss. Want me to take you to your apartment, or back to the loft? Or somewhere else?"

"I take it Loretta's still hanging out with me?"

"If you don't mind, at least until we can settle this."

"Then let's go back to my folks' house. That way she has a yard so she can go outside. And I can use their computer and look up this alleged curse for you."

I headed south toward the Bayview. On the way, we stopped for take-out Thai food for lunch, to make up for the dinner we'd missed the evening we found Autumn. The van soon filled with the delectable scents of lemongrass and curry, making my mouth water.

As we drove, Maya noticed the show catalog I had picked up from the Legion of Honor. "Cool, did you check out this Vintage Victoriana show? I keep seeing the posters but haven't made it over yet."

"Sailor and I went yesterday."

"Really. Sailor's into vintage clothing shows, is he?"

"Sailor's been a little . . . surprising lately."

"In what ways?"

"He's more open to things than before. Haven't you noticed? It's probably all the work he's doing with Patience Blix."

"What I've noticed is that he seems like a much happier man than before. Still moody, but nothing like he was. I assumed it had to do with *you*."

By then, I felt on the verge of hyperventilating at all the relationship talk, so I just shrugged and concentrated on my driving.

Maya studied the catalog. "*Huh*, I recognize that name: Parmelee Riesling. It was on the Web when I first looked up Autumn Jennings, remember? It rings a bell because Parmelee's not a name you hear very often, and then it's paired with a last name that sounds like wine."

"I met her once, actually, with Carlos. She's a clothing conservator at the Asian Art Museum. I've been meaning to give her a call, see if she can tell me anything about Autumn, or maybe even Scarlet."

"Why would she know them?"

"I don't know that she would, but there was some paperwork at Autumn's store that suggested she lent some items to that show, and Scarlet volunteered there.

So there's a possible connection between the three. Maybe."

Maya rented a room not far from Aunt Cora's Closet, in the Haight, but her childhood home was a humble Victorian in the Bayview, dating from a time when a working-class family might have been able to afford to have a home built in San Francisco. Lucille's parents had owned the home since the thirties, and I knew Lucille had been raised here with several siblings, one of whom still lived in the home with her, as did Maya's oldest sister, her husband, and their two children. The result was a multigenerational, somewhat chaotic and crowded, loving home. I had been invited to a few holidays and cookouts in the yard, and it always smelled of pot roast or barbecue.

I found the home's cheerful bedlam charming, if a tad overwhelming. It wasn't exactly what I was used to, given my own strained relations to family. But it warmed my heart to be welcomed into such a cozy environment.

When we entered the house, Loretta seemed already very much at home. She trotted over to a little oval rug placed in front of the fireplace and lay down with a moan. All worn-out from her big outing at the dog park, I was guessing.

We said hello to a few family members, then served ourselves plates of Thai food. Then Maya sat down at a computer atop a little desk and logged on while I called the Asian Art Museum to ask Parmelee Riesling if I could come by to talk later in the afternoon.

"Listen to this," Maya said as I hung up the phone. "The society woman *'must have one or two velvet dresses which cannot cost less than $500 each; she must*

*possess thousands of dollars' worth of laces, in the shape
of flounces, to loop up over the skirts of dresses . . . ;
ball-dresses are frequently imported from Paris at a cost
of from $500 to $1,000. . . . Then there are traveling-
dresses in black silk, in pongee, in velour, in piqué,
which range in price from $75 to $175 . . . evening robes
in Swiss muslin, robes in linen for the garden and
croquet playing, dresses for horse races and for yacht
races . . . dresses for breakfast and for dinner, dresses for
receptions and for parties . . .'"*

"What are you reading?"

"It's from *Lights and Shadows of New York Life*, by
James McCabe, 1872. He's writing about what was considered proper for a high-society lady's trousseau. All
sorts of ball gowns and croquet attire, too?"

"For the wealthiest women, I suppose so. I get the
sense there were a lot of wardrobe changes, back in the
day. And as you know, I love old clothes, but it is amazing to think how constricting the clothes were, especially for the upper classes. Corsets that restricted one's
breathing, and you should have seen the narrow shoes
in the show; I swear their feet must have been bound to
have remained so slender. They weren't supposed to be
able to move easily; it was all about showing off their
husband's or father's wealth and social class."

"It gives such insight into the time and customs,
doesn't it? And here I always thought trousseaus were
all about lingerie, for some reason."

"They usually included lingerie, but also things like
bed linens and towels, all embroidered, of course. Often
the women in the family would spend years, all through
the girl's youth, sewing and embroidering. It was part of
how they showed their skill with needlework. And then

the linens would be monogrammed, once the young woman knew what her new name would be."

"Such a different time . . ." Maya trailed off, her fingers flying over the keyboard, the muted clacking of the keys joining the sound of a news program playing in the next room, and a rap beat emanating from a neighbor's house. "Okay, let's see what we can find about a cursed shoeshine boy."

It didn't take her long. She put "cursed trousseau" and "shoeshine boy" and "San Francisco legend" into the search engine, and up popped several references. I peeked over her shoulder as she scrolled through the first couple of hits.

"Well, first off, the 'boy' in question was actually a twenty-six-year-old man. The year was 1882, and a wealthy young man—a 'nob,' as in Nob Hill—used to frequent the shoeshine 'boy.' Says here the two had been friends as children; the shoeshine boy was educated on a charity fellowship. The wealthy fellow was named Jedediah Clark; the shoeshine man was Thomas Parr. Parr appears to have gone a little crazy with jealousy over Clark's intended—who was only fourteen years old, by the by. It says here that Parr sought out a practitioner of the 'dark arts' and cast a curse upon Clark's intended and any issue he might have had in the future."

"I'm betting this practitioner didn't have the proper license for such a thing."

"Excuse me?"

"Did you know there's such a thing as a necromancy license in San Francisco?"

"Are you serious?"

I nodded. "And get this: You need a license even if you're just going to *pretend* to be a necromancer, or soothsayer, or any number of other things. I wonder if Patience Blix has a license . . ."

Maya scrolled through a few more tales of the vindictive shoeshine boy, but the bones of the story remained the same.

"Okay, Thomas Parr and Jedediah Clark—and what was the name of the fiancée?"

Maya leaned toward the computer and read a name: "Beatrice Beech. They called her Bee. Can you imagine, being engaged at the age of fourteen?"

I let out a long breath and shook my head. "I really can't. But then, if you spend your childhood preparing your own trousseau, maybe that's all you want in life. What I can't imagine is why the fiancée was the one who was cursed—why not the nob?"

Maya shrugged. "Maybe going after the object of his affection hurt his pride or something like that?"

"Maybe. This is all a bit sketchy, but I think it's time to call in the SFPD about this trousseau."

Chapter 12

I phoned Carlos before leaving Maya's house, and he suggested we meet at El Valenciano in the Mission. El Valenciano had a bar and restaurant in the front, with a dimly lit dance floor at the back. I had seen it packed to the maximum on Saturday nights, but on a weekday afternoon it was mellow, the dance floor abandoned. Two guys sat hunched over drinks at the bar, and the bartender was leaning back against the counter, checking his phone.

"You want anything?" Carlos asked as we passed the bar. I had the sense he knew the owner of this place, as we'd met in the back before and he always made himself at home. I knew from experience they mixed a mean margarita, but it was a little early in the day.

"No, thanks. I'm fine," I said.

The bartender glanced up at us and gave Carlos a small nod; then his attention turned back to his messages. We walked through to the back, where Carlos pulled out a chair for me at a small round cocktail table in a shadowy corner of the empty dance floor.

"I take it you don't want anyone to see us together?"

"No sense rubbing anybody's nose in it. As I mentioned, I might not be Stinson's favorite person."

"But you found out something of interest?"

He nodded. My eyes were adjusting to the low light, but it was still dim, and Carlos's already dark eyes looked black and unreadable.

"Autumn Jennings died of arsenic poisoning."

"Arsenic? Seriously? That's just awful. Who uses arsenic in this day and age? I mean . . . isn't that something the Borgias used to use to rid themselves of political rivals, way back in the day?"

"Exactly. It's easy to trace with modern forensics—in fact, I heard someone dug up Napoléon's remains not long ago and they were able to perform tests on his hair, even after all this time—so people don't use it that much anymore."

"Huh."

"But it's still readily available."

"How so?"

"It's rat poison, essentially. And it's used in fireworks as well. I don't know the details, but sometimes workers in fireworks factories are accidentally poisoned. It's come up on the Chinatown beat from time to time."

"So someone put arsenic into Autumn's food? Who would do something like that?" Had she been a secret heiress of some kind? The vintage clothes business wasn't normally profitable enough to kill over. Her apartment over the store had some nice things, but it wasn't *that* posh. "Did she have a lot of enemies, do you know?"

He hesitated. "I don't feel all that comfortable talking

to you about this—not only would it not be a good idea anyway, but it's not even my case."

"I know, Carlos, but this case involves vintage clothes, and now I've been informed that some of Autumn's recent acquisitions might have been cursed. Besides, I'm implicated at some level, and so is Bronwyn." Which reminded me . . . "They didn't find anything suspicious in Bronwyn's scones, did they?"

He shook his head. "No. They haven't figured out how Jennings was exposed yet."

I slumped in relief.

"As far as the Autumn Jennings homicide investigation goes . . ." He trailed off.

"What?" I urged.

"It's really none of my business, since it's not my case. But it sounds like they're not convinced it was homicide. The medical examiner still hasn't made his ruling, and not all the tests are in."

"They think Autumn could have ingested the poison by accident?"

"It's possible. Back in the day people were accidentally exposed to all sorts of things. It's like lead poisoning; it could be caused by any number of things."

"So Inspectors Stinson and Ng think it was accidental? Do you agree?"

He shrugged again. "As I said, I'm not exactly bowled over by Stinson. I don't know Ng as well. I think it's possible they're searching for something that isn't there. It bothers me that they're sniffing around you, obviously."

"Thanks, Carlos," I said, feeling warm and fuzzy at the thought that this tough homicide cop cared about what happened to a rather sketchy witch.

"So, not that I believe in curses, but tell me how this would work. You're saying there's a cursed trousseau?"

"According to legend, two local men had a falling-out over a young woman, and somehow one of them managed to cast a curse, and the woman died."

"Seems more like a curse against the woman than the man."

"I suppose sometimes it's harder to be the one left behind than to be the one who passes."

Carlos stared at me for a long moment. Finally he cleared his throat and gave a swift nod. "I suppose you're right. So you're saying this woman may have died from a curse long ago, and now what? The curse is still working against people who acquire the trousseau?"

"No, I wouldn't think so. Normally curses don't work that way. I mean, there are hereditary curses, but those are usually passed down through a family bloodline. If the item held a demon or something like that..." I trailed off and shook my head. "But I touched a few of the pieces of the trousseau, and while I felt a lot of sadness there, I certainly didn't feel anything demonic."

"Always a plus."

"Indeed."

"And when was this?"

"What?"

"When did you feel the trousseau?"

I pondered lying and telling him it was the evening Maya and I first found Autumn Jennings in the upstairs apartment. But ... Carlos was a friend. He was a cop, but he was also a friend. Also, so much of my life required a certain obfuscation of the truth that I was trying to be more transparent whenever possible.

"I asked Sailor to go back with me, hoping he might be able to communicate with Autumn's spirit. In case she was lingering there."

"Why am I not surprised that Sailor was involved?"

"It wasn't his fault; I asked him to go."

"I have no trouble believing that. The two of you make quite a pair. Anyway, Jennings died at the hospital. So if a person believed in spirits . . . wouldn't she be lingering there?"

"Apparently not. I thought the same thing, but Sailor says a lot of times people return to their homes or some other locale that's important to them."

"Uh-huh." He passed a hand over a whiskery cheek, the scraping sound familiar and comforting to me. Then he started idly tracing designs on the tabletop with his finger.

I knew Carlos well enough by now to note the signs of him moving out of his comfort zone regarding all things supernatural. He was much more open-minded than the average person—much less the average cop—when it came to things like witchcraft and paranormal crime. But he was a still a tough urban homicide inspector. It wasn't easy for him.

"Let's go back for a moment to the breaking and entering."

"It wasn't breaking and entering. I had a key."

"Autumn Jennings gave you a key?"

"Sort of."

"I didn't realize you two were buddies. Would this be before or after she served you with legal papers?"

"I'm saying: She gave me the keys in a manner of speaking."

"What manner would that be?"

I was glad the lights were too low for him to see me blushing.

"In that when Maya and I found her, we were left to close up shop. And to take care of her dog, Loretta, I should mention."

"She has a dog named Loretta?"

I nodded. "Now, apparently, Maya or I have a dog named Loretta. Unless . . . you live alone, right?"

"Don't even think about it," Carlos interrupted. "I don't do pets."

I smiled. "I'll bet you'd be great with a big old dog. Carlos and Loretta, hanging out and watching the ball game . . ."

"I have enough trouble taking care of big old Carlos. Let's get back to the discussion of you letting yourself into crime scenes. You know how I feel about this. One of these days I'm going to wind up arresting you for some shenanigan like that."

"You're right; I should have asked you first. But there was no crime scene tape up—"

"No tape?"

I shook my head. "In fact, it didn't look as though the cops had been through there. At least, it looked nothing like my place. They did a number on Aunt Cora's Closet."

He swore under his breath.

"Was it something I said?" I asked.

"No, it's just . . . I guess they have a different way of doing things. But it sounds like they're hoping to declare this case an accident, or suicide. Still, they should have gone through her place with a fine-tooth comb, just in case there's, I dunno, an open container of rat poison on the kitchen counter or some such."

"You're suggesting she took the poison on purpose?"

"I'm not suggesting anything. But the inspectors on the case should be ruling out suicide as well as homicide, especially since we're talking a poison like arsenic. Though if this was homicide, most folks would have used something a lot more subtle and difficult to detect than arsenic. As you pointed out, that's old-school, Borgia-style murder."

We both sat back and pondered for a few moments.

"You know, Scarlet the dog walker was volunteering at an exhibit of historic dresses at the Legion of Honor, which was co-curated by Parmelee Riesling. Remember her?"

"The clothing conservator at the Asian Art Museum?"

"Precisely."

"How does Riesling fit into this?"

"I'm not saying she does, but she appears to have known Autumn and maybe Scarlet through the exhibit as well. And Riesling sure knows a lot about old clothing. I asked if I could drop by and chat with her this afternoon. Want to go? I mean, I know this isn't your case, and you probably have lots of better things to do on your day off."

He stood. "Let's go."

Parmelee Riesling rocked a severe pageboy haircut; she was several inches shorter than I, and on the stout side. Thick glasses gave her a slightly bug-eyed appearance. And she took herself very, very seriously.

"Who are you?" she asked when she opened the door.

"Lily Ivory. I called earlier? And this is Inspector Carlos Romero, remember?"

"Right. Insect-ridden trunk full of worthless items,

mostly merchant-class nineteenth century. Trunk itself was from Salem."

"That was us," said Carlos.

"And you were wearing a nice example of a sundress, North Carolina dye lot."

"Yep, worthless trunk, insect infested, indigo dye lot."

"Uh-huh." She reached out and pinched my skirt between her thumb and forefinger.

"Same period as the last dress I saw you in. Favorite era?"

"I guess so. I branch out from time to time, but I like this style."

Her magnified eyes looked me over, from head to toe, intently. After a moment she gave a quick nod. "Suits you."

"Um . . . thank you," I said. From such a critical sort, I took that as a high compliment.

She hadn't invited us in, so we still stood out in the corridor. Riesling's lab and offices were on the second floor of the museum, away from the crowd, but still public.

"We were hoping we could ask you about a woman named Autumn Jennings," said Carlos.

"What about her?"

"You bought some clothes from her?"

"From time to time."

"Could we maybe buy you a coffee and talk?"

She hesitated, checked over her shoulder. Then said, "How about a Manhattan?"

"Well . . . sure," I said, glancing at Carlos, who nodded. "Of course."

"I'm taking a break," she yelled behind her, then came out into the hall, muttering all the while. "We got in some trusses from the Heskett Collection. Nothing but moth-eaten junk. Hate that crap."

"Oh, sure. I know what you mean." I must have looked befuddled.

She frowned, homing in on my tone. "Surely you know the Heskett Collection? I thought you were in the vintage clothes business."

"I am, yes indeedy, ma'am," I said, my inner Texan coming out when faced with authority figures. Even though Parmelee was shorter than I, and probably not more than a decade or so older, I felt intimidated by her officiousness.

I could tell Carlos was smiling at my response.

"But I don't count myself an expert," I continued. "Not by any means."

"Jennings seems to know a lot. Can't get that woman to stop talking about the fabulous Missoni maxi sequin duster cardigan she acquired for a 'mere' thousand that she was going to turn around and sell for two. Or the Valentino wedding gown? Please, if that baby's authentic, it would go for twenty-five, thirty thousand, easy."

"I think Autumn was more up on things than I. Not to mention in a whole other league, pricewise," I said, thinking about Autumn's apartment over her shop. There were some nice furnishings, despite the dreary feel of the place. Still, if she was dealing with such valuable fashions, couldn't she have afforded nicer digs? Where could all her money have gone? "At Aunt Cora's Closet, I sell a lot of old sundresses."

We descended the broad sweep of stairs to the open lobby. Schoolkids on a field trip ran around, past the museum gift shop featuring an exhibition on India's maharajahs. I could feel little whispers on my bare arms, the sensations of confused spirits attached to items in the museum, no doubt wondering where they were and what the heck had happened. I wondered what it must feel like for a spirit to be bound to a Buddhist temple in Bangladesh, then find him- or herself here in San Francisco. A transplant, much like me.

We stepped outside the front doors of the museum, into a sunny afternoon.

"Was?" Parmelee demanded.

"Was what?" I asked.

"You used the past tense," she said. "You said Autumn Jennings 'was' more up on things than you."

Darn. I was wishing we were already ensconced in a dim bar, drinks in front of us. I didn't know how close she and Autumn were and I hated delivering news of someone's demise, though it seemed like something I should get used to, considering how my life was shaping up of late. I glanced at Carlos, hoping he would take control of this aspect of the conversation.

"I'm sorry to tell you this, Ms. Riesling," Carlos began.

She waved a hand in the air. "Oh, please, call me Parmelee."

"All right, then, Parmelee. I'm sorry to tell you this, but Autumn Jennings passed away."

She looked at him, startled. "Passed *away*?"

"Early yesterday morning."

"That's . . . I'm shocked. What happened? Car accident?"

"We're not sure yet," said Carlos. "But she was sick. We're afraid it might have been a poison of some sort."

"On purpose?"

"I'm sorry?"

"I mean do they think she was poisoned on purpose? In our line of work there are a lot of poisons."

"This is exactly the sort of thing we were hoping to talk with you about," said Carlos.

We descended the steps and crossed McAllister to a restaurant and bar called Soluna. A lush community garden thrived next door, the Federal Building stood on the next block, Hastings Law School was down the street, and the City Hall plaza sat directly in front of the museum. Nonetheless, it wasn't a great area and it bordered the Tenderloin, one of the more down-and-out areas of the city. San Francisco was so small, geographically speaking, that run-down neighborhoods sat cheek by jowl with posh ones. It was a startling reality check to walk out of a fine French restaurant and have to negotiate a soup kitchen line at Glide Memorial.

Inside, the restaurant was chic and dim, with heavy drapes keeping out most of the late-afternoon light, and extravagant light fixtures of amber glass that cast a very subtle golden glow throughout. It was quiet; the bar's official happy hour wouldn't commence for another hour.

"They fix a mean Manhattan," Parmelee said as she hoisted herself onto a tall barstool at the corner. I sat on one side; Carlos stood on the other, leaning against the bar. He ordered a beer, and I felt like something of a party pooper when I asked for club soda with lime. But I'd felt the need to keep my wits about me lately.

"So," said Carlos. "What kinds of poisons might a person in the old-clothes business be exposed to?"

"All sorts: carcinogens of all kinds, of course. Lead, mercury, cyanide . . ."

"Arsenic?" Carlos asked.

"Sure. Victorian ball gowns were full of the stuff."

Chapter 13

"Are we talking enough arsenic to kill a person?" Carlos asked.

"More than enough. Sometimes there were long-term effects—neuropathy, organ failure, that sort of thing. But in some cases the poisoning was acute."

"There was no mention of that in the Vintage Victoriana show," I said.

She made an impatient gesture. "That was a political decision—one of the directors thought if we mentioned it, the whole show would start revolving around that, and the focus would be taken off the fashion industry. But in my view it's more historical than political. But I stay out of those kinds of discussions."

"So, how did the poisonings occur, exactly?"

"There was a particular shade of green that was wildly popular during that time, made of the same thing as Paris green—which is, essentially, still used as rat poison. Mauve is a likely culprit as well. Some of those beautiful Victorian ball gowns were so laden with arsenic dust that the women would essentially let off clouds of poison as they were twirled around the dance floor."

"That's quite an image."

"Isn't it? Also, when a person sweats, the moisture further activates the poison, and the pores open, letting it access the bloodstream that much faster. That led to acute problems: dizziness, confusion, paranoia, numbness and tingling in hands and feet . . ."

"Didn't people realize what was going on?"

"Not for a while. I'm not sure the public health authorities were on top of things back then, if such a department even existed. We modern folks don't realize exactly how many safeguards are in place, keeping us from harm. We like to complain about government oversight, but without consumer protections, things like this can happen far too easily."

"Good point," I said.

"And besides, the colors were fashionable. And fashion often rules the day, as you should know. You ever see what corsets did to rib cages?"

"I thought I knew a fair amount about fashion, but that show was eye-opening. I couldn't believe the narrow shoes."

"Yup. People think foot binding was a Chinese thing, but women have been injured and maimed for the sake of fashion all over the world, in almost every era."

"I guess I deal mostly in wearable outmoded fashions. I have a few flapper dresses from the twenties, and one or two older items on the wall, but most of my stuff's from midcentury or more recent. I can't imagine putting myself, much less my customers, at risk for the love of a particular color."

"Besides ball gowns, several people—including children—lost their feet or legs after being poisoned by their beloved striped stockings. Arsenic dyes can eat right through skin and cripple a person."

"What a horrifying image," I said, thinking of the box full of stockings in Autumn Jennings's apartment.

"That's disturbing," said Carlos. "I have to admit, I do have a soft spot for lacy Victorian underthings."

"Get in line, pal," said Parmelee in a world-weary voice. "Anyway, the old white cotton stuff is fine. It was the dyed silks and satins that were the problem, so the wealthy folks got dinged on this one. And the poor slobs working in the factories that produced the products, of course."

The bartender set our drinks on the bar in front of us.

Parmelee took a sip of her Manhattan and smiled. "Now, that's a good drink. What was I saying? Oh, right. It wasn't just clothing. There was a case of a mother who gave her children a stuffed animal that they teethed on, killing them both like that." She snapped her fingers. "And wallpapers, too. William Morris factories were famous for poisoning their workers. A lot of the intricate Victorian wallpapers off-gassed and killed off whole families. Children were often the first to go, since they are lower to the ground and arsine gas is heavier than air. Even Napoléon was said to have died of arsenic poison; some say he was assassinated, but it was very possibly due to his luxurious accommodations on the isle of Elba."

"I read about that," said Carlos.

"And finally, it wasn't just arsenic. Those tall beaver hats were often made with mercury—hence the reference to 'mad hatters.'"

"I've always wondered about that expression," I said.

"Shoe polish was no walk in the park, either. Still isn't, though it's better than before."

"Shoe polish?"

"Cyanide poisoning. Nitrobenzene has gruesome effects on the central nervous system. It's also a carcinogen. I'm telling you, I could go on and on. There's loads of this stuff, even today. You know, every once in a while they'll find a trove of clothes laden with lead, or toys that kill—we're living in a global society and we have a hard enough time keeping control over our own products, much less the imported stuff."

She paused, shook her head, and downed a good portion of her drink. Then she fished out the cherry and popped it in her mouth.

"Do you happen to know a local story about a curse cast by a shoeshine boy?" I asked.

"This the one about the trousseau?"

"Yes—you've heard it?"

She made a dismissive gesture with her hand and signaled to the bartender for another drink.

"It's probably a bunch of hooey. Listen, I hear about curses all the time—I've dealt with the wrapping of *mummies*, for heaven's sake. Like I said, there are a lot of unknown poisons involved with old textiles. You don't know that? You should take some time to bone up, being in the business."

"As I was saying, my stuff is more recent. My inventory isn't as museum quality as Autumn Jennings's was."

"I wouldn't oversell her inventory. She sold me one or two items, lent a couple of things to the show at the Legion of Honor—that was it."

"She mentioned you on her Web site."

She rolled her eyes. Behind the thick lenses of her glasses it had a rather startling effect.

"She *tried* to sell me things all the time, liked to think of herself as a player in the field. I'm sorry to cast aspersions, particularly considering . . . what happened. But while she had a lot of old stuff, most of it wasn't museum quality. Maybe for a small-town museum or something; I mean, historic items are always interesting. But the textiles on exhibit in San Francisco or any other large city are world-class, Worth gowns and the like. And after all, how many nineteenth-century ball gowns can people gawk at?"

"Have you ever been to her store?" asked Carlos.

"Once. Usually people bring things to me, rather than the other way around, but I live not far from there and frankly I was hoping to get her off my back. She was . . . I don't want to use the word 'stalker,' but once that woman got an idea in her mind, she was hard to dissuade."

"And the idea she had in her mind was . . . ?" Carlos prompted her.

She shrugged. "Rents are skyrocketing in the city, as you probably know. No rent control for businesses. And I don't know why else; frankly, she wasn't a friend, so I didn't know the ins and outs of her finances. She mentioned the rent, is all. Glad my landlord's my father-in-law, or else I don't think I'd be able to live in the city on my salary, either."

"So you were saying you stopped by the store?"

She nodded, sipping her fresh drink. "She had a decent collection, especially for that sort of place. No offense."

"None taken."

"But there were . . . Again, far be it from me to talk

ill of the dead. But there may have been one or two issues with labeling." She gave me a significant look.

"Labeling?" Carlos asked.

"Labels are a big issue for haute couture vintage," I explained. "Designer labels, like Valentino or Louis Vuitton, can fetch thousands of dollars. Sometimes fraudulent labels are sewn into knock-offs, or genuine labels are taken out of ruined garments and attached to random items. A lot of customers don't know enough to be aware."

"You think Jennings was involved in fraud?" Carlos asked.

"I'm not saying anything," Parmelee said, holding her hands up. "All I'm saying is she was desperate for money, and a few items looked fishy to me. But it's a moot point now, right?"

Maybe. I thought of the labels I had seen behind the counter at Vintage Visions Glad Rags. Could Autumn's death have to do with something related to fraud?

"Anyway," continued Parmelee, "what Autumn really wanted me to look at was this allegedly cursed trousseau. She wanted me to buy it from her, thought she could get a good price for it."

"You saw the trousseau? Upstairs?"

"Yes. She hadn't put it out yet. It was quite a haul, linens and underthings and three ball gowns that were in great shape, never worn."

"Did you offer to buy them?"

She shook her head. "We have no use for them here at the Asian Art Museum, and that show out at the Legion of Honor fulfilled any local desire to see such things. She was pretty disappointed. Then she asked if

I could authenticate the items and put a good word in for her so she could sell them for opera or stage productions. But first I told her she would have to have them tested."

"For arsenic?"

She nodded. "Two of them, the green and the mauve, were particularly suspicious. I'm telling you, those are some killer colors."

"No, I will not break into Vintage Visions Glad Rags with you, Lily," Carlos said as we drove away from the Asian Art Museum. Parmelee had headed back to work, apparently unfazed by her two-Manhattan afternoon tea.

"I have keys," I pointed out. "Plus, I'm her dog sitter, and the poor woman's dead, so it really isn't breaking in, not if *you're* with me."

"The US legal system, through the lens of Lily Ivory. I'm afraid dog sitters don't get special exemptions. Besides, I've already meddled plenty in this case. You have any idea what sort of a fit Stinson would have if he heard I'd been trespassing on his crime scene?"

"As I told you, they're not treating it like a crime scene. Besides, you're a *cop*. I really don't see the problem."

"Hate to break it to you, Lily, but police officers don't get to just go wherever they feel like and do whatever they want."

"What's the point in being a cop, then?"

"Good question. I ask myself that every day."

We shared a smile.

"Fair enough," I said. "But where does this leave us, then?"

"Let's wait and see what the medical examiner declares. If it's homicide they'll investigate further."

"And if it's declared accidental?"

"Then, that's that."

"Really? Just like that?"

"Sometimes people screw up, Lily, even to the point of accidentally killing themselves or someone else. As someone who deals with botanicals you should know that—wasn't there something about a poisonous corsage not too long ago . . . ?"

"Yes, there was, as a matter of fact, but that didn't turn out to be an accident, either. I mean, I guess it sort of was, but there was a culprit at the base of it."

"And you think that's the case here? You think Autumn Jennings really fell under a curse?"

"Maybe."

"Even if I were going to try to open my mind to that idea, what could you possibly do about it? It was cast by someone a long time ago, who is long dead."

"True . . ."

"How about if I suggest they burn the trousseau? Would that make you happy?"

"I think they should test the whole kit and caboodle, just in case: the dresses and everything else. I saw some old stockings in a box, too. But a *curse* isn't that simple to deal with, Carlos. In fact, they're not simple at all. And then there's the whole weird Rodchester House of Spirits connection."

"Sorry—what Rodchester House of Spirits connection?"

"When Maya and I took Loretta to the dog park, we met this couple who knew Autumn, and the dog walker,

Scarlet. He works on the Web site for the House of Spirits and had mentioned it to Scarlet, and then Bronwyn saw a brochure at Autumn's store. Plus a friend of Bronwyn's arranged for an overnight birthday party there."

"That sounds like trouble."

"Exactly."

"But this is related to an arsenic death how, exactly?"

"I have no idea, but the dog walker was the one who served me with legal papers, and she turned and ran when she saw me the next day. Why would she do something like that?"

"Maybe she was scared of you."

"Why in the world would she be scared of *me*?"

He smiled and inclined his head. "*I'm* scared of you."

"That's what Sailor said. But I don't believe either of you."

"How *is* Sailor?"

"He's okay. Why are you asking?"

"Just a friendly inquiry. Say hi to him for me. Speaking of your dubious men friends, I hear Aidan Rhodes left town suddenly. You don't happen to know where he went?"

"Aidan? Is he in trouble?"

"Just like to know where he is," said Carlos, his eyes not leaving the road. "And . . . where he isn't."

"Carlos, what can you tell me, for real, about Aidan?"

"Not much," he said with a shake of his head. "Certainly nothing I can pin on him. I just know he's a player in this town, and I don't exactly know how, and that makes me nervous."

"What?" I let out a little nervous laugh. "Are you saying he's involved in organized crime or something?"

Please say no, Carlos.

"Here's an interesting factoid," said Carlos after a beat. "Did you know San Francisco is unique in that, as a major city, it has very little organized crime?"

"Didn't I hear something about criminal brotherhoods in Chinatown?"

"Yes, some of the tongs were the famous exception, but while they might have exerted some influence in Chinatown at different points in history, they don't have much pull in the city as a whole."

"So . . . are you saying Aidan is involved in organized crime?"

"I'm saying I like to know where he is. And where he isn't."

As much as I liked to think of Carlos as a friend, he was a cop first. So there was really no way to get him to spill the beans—about a crime, or a certain wickedly handsome witch—when he wasn't ready to do so.

"Aidan's afraid there's something . . . afoot lately."

"Afoot?"

"Some sort of supernatural threat brewing in San Francisco."

Carlos pulled to a stoplight and turned and gave me a look.

"Is this something I want to know about?"

"Just thought I should give you the heads-up. Unfortunately, as is often the case, I don't actually know enough to make any helpful suggestions. It's more a free-floating worry at the moment."

"Then we'll just have to cross that bridge when—and if—we come to it. In the meantime, back to this dog walker . . ."

"Scarlet."

"Right. So, Scarlet saw you and turned and ran. Anything else seem suspicious or out of the ordinary?"

"Well . . . she was volunteering at a clothes show at the Legion of Honor, so that was the connection to Parmelee. And the folks at the dog park said she was looking ill, too. I wish I could track her down, if only for the sake of her health."

He nodded. "Good point. If we're talking an accidental poisoning, and your dog walker was exposed at the same time as Jennings . . ."

"Autumn Jennings and Scarlet the dog walker were both pretty petite," I said. "Maybe they both tried on the ball gowns and managed to poison themselves."

"Why would they try them on?"

"That's half the fun in this business."

Carlos grunted. "A toxic trousseau. But would it have been that easy to poison themselves? Just by trying on a dress? Riesling mentioned sweat and exertion."

"Maybe that's where the curse comes in?" I suggested.

"But what does any of this have to do with Rodchester House of Spirits?"

"I have no idea."

"I'm confused."

"Join the club."

"What makes you think all these things are connected?"

I blew out a long sigh. "I guess you're right; maybe none of this is connected. It just seems like a whole lot going wrong all at once, and in my experience these coincidences do not bode well."

A long moment passed. Carlos drove along Fell Street toward the Haight. I watched the scenery: rows of Victorian houses on one side, the lush Golden Gate Park Panhandle on the other.

"I don't really believe in coincidences," Carlos said finally.

"I'm beginning to think that way myself."

Chapter 14

Out of habit Carlos pulled up to the front of Aunt Cora's Closet.

"I forgot," he said, "you have to go in the back, right?"

"No worries, I'll walk around. It's not worth you trying to make an illegal U-turn. Besides, just because you're a cop doesn't mean you can do whatever you want, whenever you want."

He gave me a smile.

"Lily," he said, just as I was climbing out, "I'll let you know what I find out about all of this. But in the meantime, be careful."

"Sounds like you don't think Autumn Jennings's death was an accident."

"We both know what I said, and it wasn't exactly that. It probably *was* an accidental poisoning, but . . . you're right that something about this feels a little hinky."

"I'm like a hinky magnet." I nodded. "Thanks. I'll be careful. And, hey, on the off chance that you get a call from the San Jose police on Saturday, would you mind vouching for me?"

"This the coven birthday party you mentioned?"

"That'd be the one."

He chuckled softly. "Tell Bronwyn happy birthday from me, and tell her to be careful, too."

"I will."

The sight of the *Closed for Inventory* sign and the chaos I knew lay beyond my shop's front door depressed me. But as tough as it was for me, I believed Oscar was the one suffering most from the current situation; though he slept most of the day away on his purple silk pillow, he really did enjoy his time in the shop: the squeals of shoppers when they spotted him, the petting, the peeks he attempted to steal under the curtains of the communal changing room.

He had plenty of books and movies in the apartment to keep him occupied. Not to mention snacks. Still—it didn't seem fair that I got to traipse around town all day while he was closed in.

On the other hand . . . as Sailor had pointed out, Oscar was more than able to get himself around, somehow, without being seen. Many's the time I had come home and found him gone, especially now that I had released him from servitude to Aidan. He stayed with me and acted as my familiar because he chose to, not because he was forced. So if every now and again he went gallivanting off somewhere, that was his right. And I had given him the travel cloak, of course, which he had the power to use to go wherever he wanted, apparently.

So I shouldn't feel too bad about not allowing him to accompany us to the Rodchester House of Spirits, I decided. I was almost sure about that one.

Sandra was standing outside her shop, bouncing up and down on her toes in apparent agitation, looking irate. With her was a tall man about forty years old, with a paunch and a mustache and a shock of black hair. Last time I had seen Khalil Singh was when I signed a ten-year lease on my store. Since then I hadn't heard a peep, but, then, I hadn't asked for anything, either. This was the sort of landlord-tenant relationship I could get behind.

"Everything okay?" I asked, addressing them both.

The man gave me a toothy grin, but Sandra scowled.

"Of course, of course, no problem," said Khalil in a lilting British-Indian accent. "May I introduce myself? I am Mr. Khalil Singh, Esquire. I own this beautiful building."

"Yes, I know. I'm Lily Ivory, one of your tenants—I own Aunt Cora's Closet, right here?"

"Oh, yes, of course! I thought you looked familiar."

It was actually sort of refreshing to be forgotten. I was used to sticking out in crowds and spent a lot of time trying to fit in and seem normal so I could pass unnoticed—which was why I had decided to settle in the Haight, traditional home to iconoclasts and free-thinkers of all stripes. I figured it was my best shot at floating under the "normal" radar.

It was odd to feel the other side of things, to be overlooked. *Perhaps I'm fitting in more,* I thought.

Out of the corner of my eye I noticed two women approach the door to Aunt Cora's Closet. One wore an honest-to-goddess big black pointy witch's hat, and the other some sort of black lace number. It was nowhere near Halloween, and even on Haight Street they seemed a little out of place.

"We're here for the head witch. Is that you?" asked the one with the purple eye shadow and some sort of gold chest plate.

Khalil turned his dark eyes on me. "Head witch?"

So much for fitting in.

"It's an honorary title," I said to Khalil. Then I turned to the women. "Give me just a minute, please. I'll be right with you."

Finally, I looked back to Sandra. "What's going on?"

"He's saying he won't let me out of my lease," she said in a whiny voice. "I want to go to Carson City!"

Khalil lifted his shoulders to his ears, splaying his hands in a "What can I do?" shrug.

"Surely it wouldn't be hard for you to rent this space, right here on Haight Street?" I said.

Another shrug. "I live up in Napa. I do not like to have to come down here all the time to show the place, run credit checks. I am no longer a young man. It is a full-time job, looking after all my properties."

"Oh, I see." *Must be tough, having all those properties.* "Do you mind my asking, how much time do you have left on your lease, Sandra?"

"Almost two years," she said, her voice scaling up. "How was I supposed to know how I would feel back when I signed it?"

"But signed it you did, and that is the way business works in this marvelous country of yours." He leaned toward me and winked. "Land of opportunity. Best country in the world! Long live the USA!"   .

"Um, yes . . . thank you," I said, unsure how to respond.

But something had been simmering in the back of my mind since Sandra first mentioned she was interested in moving out, and now it came to the fore. "Khalil, what if I were to buy out Sandra's lease? You already know me, so you wouldn't have to run another credit check or anything like that . . ."

His eyes gleamed and he actually rubbed his hands together, as in a cartoon. "Well, now, perhaps we could work something out. Would you like to rent this place?"

"I was thinking perhaps of taking over Sandra's lease, at her current rent." Last thing I wanted him to do, now that he had come south from Napa, was to decide to check the market rate. "And it would be for a good cause—I'd like to add an annex, for the new clothes made by my friend Lucille and her employees, and they could move in here and use it to produce their dresses."

Khalil looked dubious.

"It's a woman-owned business, and her employees are from the Haight Street women's shelter. It could be great publicity for you, at a time when people are vilifying landlords."

"That's because they're making everything into expensive loft spaces," muttered Sandra.

"But this place wouldn't qualify for that sort of thing," I said hastily, lest Khalil got any bright ideas. "No way to rezone it or get the permits to radically alter a historic building. Trust me on this: not worth the hassle and it wouldn't succeed anyway."

"I suppose that's true . . ." Khalil trailed off.

"Indeed." I started murmuring under my breath a little, just a quick charm to make him more open and amenable. I felt justified in doing so because this man didn't *need* to raise the rent, and I was a good tenant. And Lucille and her employees needed those jobs.

Khalil agreed to think about it. I bid farewell to him

and to Sandra and went to join the two women waiting for me.

The one in the hat had her arms crossed firmly over her chest, the picture of stubbornness. The other one was looking through the glass.

"That's a real mess in there," she said, as though I hadn't noticed.

"We're closed for inventory."

She raised one eyebrow. "Looks more like it's been ransacked."

"You wanted to see me?" I asked, not wanting to engage in this conversation.

"Yeah, Aidan says you're the head honcho for the interim."

"That's what he tells me."

They both looked me over, clearly unconvinced. As was the case whenever Aidan stopped by, I didn't want to simply say, "What can I help you with?" because of the implied obligation. It's a witch thing.

So instead I made a show of checking the time on my antique Tinker Bell watch.

"Indigo wants to allow men into our coven, even though there's an affiliated men's group already."

"Not *men*. Just man. One single man. Pablo is special."

"Just because you have the hots for him doesn't mean he's special."

"Also, don't you think it's time we moved beyond gender? I mean, who's to say what we are in our hearts? Is biology really destiny? What about all the trans-everything out there?"

"If *Men* and *Women* are good enough for every restroom sign in America, it's good enough for me."

"I was in the airport in . . . Chicago, I think? And I saw a restroom with a sign that didn't say *Men* or *Women*. It simply said: *Human*. I like that."

"There's something special about the femininity of the circle," the first one insisted, then turned to me. "*Tell* her."

I was supposed to weigh in on this eternal debate about inclusiveness and gender and equality? "I think—"

"We're a *feminine* circle," the one in the hat cut me off. "Feminine, as in the crone, the mother, and the daughter. Where in there does it say boyfriend?"

"You are being completely unreasonable! What about your friend Geronimo? You weren't so picky when we were talking about *him*—"

"Geronimo was totally different! If your boy toy goes trans, then we'll talk. But as long as he's got what he's got between his legs—"

"Hold it!" I finally yelled.

"Hey, there's a pig in there."

I could see Oscar inside, standing at the door, even though I'd closed the door to the back and told him to stay off the shop floor. Still, the police tape was down so maybe they'd finished. I hoped so.

"You've got a *pig*?" The woman in black started laughing, and the other joined in. "Cute little fella!"

I unlocked the front door and Oscar came out, his little hooves clacking on the sidewalk as he hopped around in excitement. The two witches were enthralled.

With tempers somewhat defused, I tried again.

"I'm not trying to pass the buck here," I said, "but isn't this issue best resolved by the decision of the coven?"

"The vote was evenly divided," said Indigo.

"Don't you have thirteen for the coven?"

"Fern dropped out. She went faerie last year and we haven't replaced her."

"Which is why Pablo should be allowed to be our thirteenth. He's willing to do the apprenticeship."

"Okay," I said in a commanding voice, fearing yet another ratcheting up of the argument. I tried to sound like Aidan. "Let me consult my, er, crystal ball and the satchel and I'll give you my decision tomorrow."

"The *satchel*?" said Indigo in an awed whisper.

"Why the satchel?" asked the other, clearly afraid.

"I, um . . ."

"You know what?" said Indigo, backing away. "Never mind. I mean, why mess with tradition, right? We'll leave things as they are—my kid sister has been asking about maybe joining the circle, so we'll just do that. Pablo can join the men's drumming circle."

"Yeah. Great, great. Thanks. That's perfect. Thanks a lot, Lily. Bye, piggy."

Oscar snorted loudly as the two women walked down the sidewalk.

I glanced down at Oscar; he looked up at me. "I guess I just resolved another witchy conflict. Problem is, I don't know what I did."

He snorted again.

Since the police tape was down, and Oscar had already violated the scene, I led the way into the store through the front entrance, locking the door behind us.

On the glass display counter was an envelope addressed to me. Inside was a note from Inspector Stinson.

Thank you for your cooperation. Please accept our apologies for any inconvenience you might have suffered. The scene is hereby released.

I picked up the phone and dialed the number at the bottom of the letter.

"Stinson," a man's voice answered.

"Hello, Inspector. This is Lily Ivory, from Aunt Cora's Closet. On Haight Street."

"Yes, hello, Ms. Ivory. Did you see we released the scene?"

"I did, yes. So, that means we're off the hook?"

There was a pause. I could hear police station noises behind him: phones ringing, someone yelling, the sound of a printer spitting out a document. "I believe the case has been closed. Thank you for your cooperation, and I apologize for any inconvenience."

As I surveyed the mess, I fought the urge to request city-funded housekeeping services to put the place back in order. But I did have one pertinent question for the inspector.

"Was Autumn Jennings's death ruled accidental?"

"It is no longer considered a homicide," Stinson said in a curt tone. "I can't discuss it any further at the moment, until her relatives are notified."

"Oh, okay. Thank you for telling me."

"Speaking of relatives, would you have any idea how to get in contact with Jennings's family? Her maiden name was Autumn Clark, if that rings a bell?"

"Not really. As I said, I barely knew her. I've heard she didn't have much family." Clark. Wasn't that the name of the family cursed by the shoeshine boy? On the other hand, it wasn't an unusual name. . . .

"Where did you hear about her family?" Stinson demanded.

"At the dog park. I seem to have inherited Autumn's dog. I don't suppose—"

"Have a nice evening, Ms. Ivory."

"You, too."

As soon as I hung up, I realized Oscar had shifted into his natural form and was looming over me from the top of a tall walnut display cabinet. He was doing his gargoyle impression.

"Wait just a *goldurned* minute," he said, his voice a strident growl. "You've inherited her *dog*?"

"We'll try to find a better place for Loretta, somewhere with a yard," I said. "I'm hoping Maya's parents will decide they're in love. But I feel ultimately responsible for placing her somewhere if they can't take her."

"Why *you*? Just take her back to where you found her, let 'er be someone else's problem."

"Oscar, you don't mean that."

He shrugged. "Or you could drop her off in Golden Gate Park, let her make her own way in this world, toughen her up a little."

"Now, just how do you think you would feel if I did the same for you?"

He waved one oversized hand and grimaced, which was his way of smiling. Soon his bony shoulders began to shake as he started to cackle, quietly at first, and then raucously. I was going to assume he was pondering the hilarity of the idea that he wouldn't be able to make his own way in Golden Gate Park. Oscar was tough. His breed was probably like cockroaches: They would be living on this earth long after the rest of us had made it uninhabitable for humans.

"My point is, Loretta's a perfectly nice dog. She deserves a home."

Oscar harrumphed.

"Anyway, I guess we should start cleaning up the

store," I said, my voice unconvincing even to my own ears.

"But . . . what about *dinner*?" Oscar asked, outraged.

"You're right," I said with a smile. "Let's go upstairs and fix some dinner, and then afterward we can start cleaning up."

"Or tomorrow."

I sighed. "There's always tomorrow."

Chapter 15

Oscar was right; by the time we'd made dinner, eaten, and done the dishes, we were both plumb tuckered out. Oscar absolutely needed to find out whodunit in the book he was reading, and I was pondering a hot bath. Tomorrow sounded like a better option to tackle the mess on the shop floor.

Besides, that way I could call on friends for help. I sat on the edge of my bed and phoned Bronwyn and Maya, asking if they would be free to come in tomorrow to get the place in order, and maybe even open for business depending on how long it took us. They both agreed; Maya said she would bring Loretta.

As I hung up, my gaze settled on Aidan's satchel, which sat on the bed beside me. I stroked the soft leather, pondering the bag's significance—and more importantly, why Aidan had left it with me. Had he, indeed, merely needed someone to take over his bureaucratic duties while he was out of town? And what was so important to keep him away from San Francisco? It

wasn't as though he went out of town often. . . . I didn't
approve of keeping people's markers and forcing them to
do one's bidding. That sounded way too much like what
Carlos would call organized crime. But if we were dealing with a supernatural threat, then maybe Aidan was
simply doing what was necessary to keep everyone safe.

I felt a headache coming on. I should have brewed
willow bark tea after dinner.

My eyes alighted on the note the woman had written
earlier when she came into Aunt Cora's Closet, asking
for help with the mayor. The missive was long and
involved and made references to prior events I had no
way of knowing anything about. It seemed like an ongo-
ing story. I had promised to call the mayor on her
behalf . . . but I had no idea why, or what to say. Also, it
was after hours.

Still . . . what good was having the mayor's private
number if a witch was afraid to use it?

Mind made up, I opened the bag and pulled out the
mayor's card, then dialed the number scribbled in pencil on the back.

"What is it?" answered a man's voice I recognized
from press conferences. But when speaking in public
his tone was forever patient, ready with a quick joke or
folksy story. Now it was terse and impatient.

"I'm sorry to disturb you," I began. "I needed to
talk to you about—"

"Tomorrow, at your new office. Six?"

"Sure. I—"

He hung up.

I stared at the phone for a long moment. That was . . .
odd. He didn't ask who I was, much less what I was
calling about. And he said we'd meet at "your new

office"—did he mean Aidan's place in the recently rebuilt wax museum on Fisherman's Wharf? Didn't he notice he wasn't actually speaking to Aidan?

What in the Sam Hill?

I guessed my questions would be answered tomorrow when I met the mayor face-to-face. Maybe I really was moving up in the world, from vintage clothes dealer to someone with the mayor's ear. I made a mental note to mention the streetlight in front of the store was out when we spoke.

I was about to dig through the satchel a little more when I heard someone let him- or herself in to the store downstairs. Heavy boots thudded on the stairs leading to my apartment, and I was enveloped by the scent of roses. *Sailor.*

I ran to meet him at the door.

He paused; his dark eyes swept over me; a smile played on his lips. I resisted the urge to throw myself in his arms like the heroine of the novel I was reading.

"Hi," I finally said, feeling oddly shy.

His smile broadened. He placed his helmet on the chair by the door and stepped toward me.

"Hi, yourself. C'mere." We shared a long, luxurious kiss. Then he lifted his head and said, "Don't distract me, now. Aren't we due to meet a man about a curse?"

"Oh! I plumb forgot!"

"Grab your coat and hat, madam. It's cold out there."

Pier 39 is the sort of tourist extravaganza that locals avoid like the plague. Nearby Fisherman's Wharf at least had a legitimate history, with historic restaurants like Alioto's, the sourdough bread factory, old fishing docks, and big steaming vats where crabs were cooked on the sidewalks by hawkers. But Pier 39 had been developed specifically for tourists, so it was crowded with tchotchke shops and chain seafood restaurants, and though it was built on an old pier, there wasn't much left of the historic structure to be savored. Still, it had its enjoyable aspects: There was a nice aquarium featuring the life of the San Francisco Bay; sea lions entertained visitors with their incessant barking and antics as they pushed each other off the adjoining docks; the carousel featured San Francisco scenes and sent merry music to vie with the calls of the sea lions; and street performers juggled and danced and made people laugh.

Sailor glanced down at me as we walked along.

"You're smiling," he said. "You like it here?"

"It's gaudy and silly, but I like tourists. Always have."

He chuckled. "I don't think there are a lot of locals who would agree with you on that one. San Francisco's a tourist mecca, but that doesn't mean we have to like it."

"It's their vibrations—don't you feel it? They're upbeat and open, excited and . . ."

"Exhausted?" Sailor suggested as a harried-looking woman dragged a screaming child toward the restroom.

I had to laugh. "Yes, exhausted, too, of course. Look—there's the sign for the mirror maze, upstairs."

I stepped on the first step, and it made a tinkling sound. So did the second. Only then did I realize the stair risers were black and white, made to look like piano keys.

"What's this?" I asked.

"You don't know the musical stairs?" Sailor asked. "It's like in that old movie with Tom Hanks . . . which I'm going to assume you never saw."

I shook my head.

"We really are going to have to work on your pop

culture education, now that you're a proud recipient of your GED."

Sailor hopped onto the stairs and starting jumping from one step to another, creating a simple rendition of a song, with only a few missteps: "The Yellow Rose of Texas."

A semicircle of tourists formed around us almost immediately. They laughed and clapped when he finished, and a couple of kids rushed onto the steps to make noise. I reached into my pocket and threw Sailor some coins.

He caught a quarter, then jumped off the staircase to land at my feet.

"Don't throw coins, milady," he said, breathing heavily. "Throw kisses."

I laughed and gave him a quick kiss.

The tourists, thinking they were witnessing an act, tried to press a few dollars into his hand, but he begged off.

Show over, Sailor and I climbed the tinkling piano steps and made our way to the mirror maze, bought two tickets, and entered. The effect was disconcerting, definitely off-putting, but Sailor walked smoothly through the labyrinth, as though he had a map in his head.

"You're good at this," I said. "Is it related to the mirror thing I witnessed you doing at Autumn's place?"

"No, nothing so complicated." He pointed. "Look at the floor. There's a tell."

Then I saw what he was saying: The edge of the mirror at the floor left a little line, which wasn't there on the real path.

"Still, I'm impressed. I find it a little . . . alarming," I said as I headed right into a never-ending reflection of myself. "Where do you suppose this guy is?"

"If you didn't set a particular meeting place, it's up to him to find us. That's the way shakedowns usually go."

Just then we heard someone behind us, panting and complaining. A man ran toward us, around a corner of the maze.

"*Jeez,*" he said, leaning over and putting his hands on his knees as though trying to catch his breath. "What is it with youse two? Usually I catch up to folks in the first turnaround."

"My friend Sailor's pretty skilled with mazes."

"Yeah, I can see that," he said, looking Sailor up and down. "Look, I never said you could bring somebody. I dunno this guy."

"You don't know me, either."

"Ya got me there." Jamie was small and wiry, with a rather rodentlike face, but it was the way he carried himself that really put me in mind of a weasel. "Anyway, you got the money?"

"Yes. But first we have a few questions."

He rolled his eyes. "Here we go . . ."

"What were you doing for Autumn Jennings?"

Confusion entered his eyes, and then they narrowed. "*Waaaiiiit* a gol-danged minute. *You're* supposed ta be Autumn Jennings."

"There was a change in plans," I said.

"This is what I was just saying about trusting people." He shook his head as though lamenting the fall in morals in today's society.

"Anyway, we're here now, and I think I have something you want." I waved the manila envelope under his nose. "A lot of money. Even has your name on it. I mean, you are Jamie, right?"

"Yeah," he said with obvious reluctance.

"And now I want some answers."

"Awright, awright. But let's get out of here. Had clam chowder for dinner, and these mirrors are makin' me nauseated."

We exited and went around to the side of the pier, where we leaned against weather-beaten gray rails. Here we could hear the lapping of the water against the pilings, the incessant barking of the sea lions, and the far-off music from a street performer playing Stevie Wonder songs on a keyboard. A few couples strolled by, but most of the tourists remained on the main part of the pier.

"Why would Autumn seek you out?" I asked.

He shrugged. "Why does anyone seek me out? She wanted a curse removed."

"Too late," said Sailor.

"Why?" Jamie asked. He looked from one to the other of us.

"She passed away two days ago."

"What—seriously? *Damn*. That's one thing about this business—there's a real issue with timing. You don't get to someone in time . . ." He trailed off, shaking his head.

"I don't understand," I said. "You're saying she keeled over just like that, simply from touching a cursed item? I felt some of those items in the trousseau myself, and they were definitely sad, but they didn't feel . . . *evil*, or anything along those lines."

"What are you talking about, a cursed trousseau?"

"You were the one who just said she was cursed."

"It's got nothin' to do with *clothes*. What, are you talking about that store of hers? She runs a vintage clothes store, right? But none of this had nothing to do with that. I mean, not directly."

"So what does it have to do with?"

"It had to do with her family."

"I heard she didn't have any family."

"Yeah, well, that was partly my point. She used to. Plenty. But they all died off. Her father came from a big family; everybody died young. And then in her generation, everybody died young, too. Including her kid, I guess. Always sad when a kid gets it, am I right?"

I nodded.

"And her husband died a coupla years ago, too. So she figured maybe she was cursed, like maybe something was following her around."

"But it wasn't related to a trousseau, then?"

"She mentioned something about that, but I got the impression she thought the trousseau was historic, like from her family. Maybe her great-grandma's or something. Doesn't really matter; this was a hereditary curse."

"That actually makes more sense," I said to myself as much as to the men. "It's not the clothes that are cursed, but the bloodline."

"And what were you promising to do for her?" asked Sailor.

"Hey, I got skills. As do you, I can tell. I got a nose for this kind of thing. You're a seer?"

"What I'm seeing right now," said Sailor, "is that you were planning on taking Autumn Jennings's money and giving her nothing in return."

"Well, now, that's not exactly true. What I do is I go back through the documents and try to see where the trouble began. Then, I got a girl out in the Avenues, Russian, they're good at this sort of thing. She does a whole cleansing-type deal. Real convincing. I mean, the cleansing's legit and all, but she does a whole show . . . you sorta gotta be there. Anyway, she goes a long way toward convincing someone the curse is lifted, and as you probably know . . ."

"The belief in the curse—or the cure—is as powerful as the actual curse."

He nodded his rodentlike head. "Exactly."

I studied him for a moment. "So you're basically the go-between for someone who thinks they're cursed and this Russian woman in the Avenues."

"Basically."

"And for this you charge two thousand dollars?"

"What I got"—he laid his finger on the side of his nose—"people are willing to pay for. And not for nothin', but sometimes the more they pay, the more they believe in the cure, if you catch my drift."

I nodded. The sad truth was that he was right. As a general rule, the more someone invested in something—in this culture it tended to be monetary—the more they valued it. It was true for cars and jewels, and magic as well.

The wind kicked the salt off the bay, enveloping us in the night breezes. I thought about all the happy—and exhausted—tourists, the couples headed out to crab dinners and hopping onto the carousel for another ride. Autumn would never take another ride, would never have another night out. All of us would eventually cross that bridge from the lives we knew now to the beyond, of course, but Autumn's life, tragically, had been cut short. And no matter what Stinson and Ng thought, I wasn't buying the accidental death theory. There were simply too many coincidences and loose ends and people acting strangely.

"All right," I said, blowing out a breath. "You don't happen to know a young woman named Scarlet, do you? She was an associate of Autumn's?"

He shook his head. "As should be obvious by now, I never met Autumn before. We talked on the telephone, is all."

"Which begs the question: How did a nice vintage clothes dealer get mixed up with the likes of you?"

"Hey, I'm a legitimate businessman."

"Whatever. How'd she find you? Yellow pages?"

"Nah, through her neighbor, the cupcake lady."

"Renee?"

He nodded.

"Is Renee Baker a friend of yours?"

There was a pause. "I wouldn't say 'friend.' I help her out from time to time, so she refers people to me. Like that."

It was on the tip of my tongue to ask what he helped her with, but it really wasn't any of my business. People found support and solace and insight where they could, whether through religion or exercise or psychics or weaselly ersatz curse lifters like Jamie.

Still, I couldn't quite let it go . . .

"Are you licensed to lift curses?"

"Excuse me?"

I took a copy of the licensure for fortune-telling out of my bag and handed it to him.

"I wouldn't call myself a necromancer, much less a fortune-teller," Jamie hedged, looking at the regulations in his hand like they were about to jump up and bite him.

"Keep reading," I said.

"'*The telling of fortunes, forecasting of futures, or reading the past, by means of any occult, psychic power,*' yada yada yada . . ." He handed the paper back to me. "I don't do none of that hocus-pocus."

"You didn't read the second paragraph," I said, reading aloud: "'*It shall also include effecting spells, charms, or incantations, or placing or* removing curses.'"

"Lemme see that," he said, taking the paper back. He started mumbling: "'. . . *or advising the taking or administering of what are commonly called love powders or potions in order . . . to get or recover property, stop bad luck, give good luck, put bad luck on a person or animal . . .* '" He looked up at me. "*Dang.*"

"This is what I'm telling you. You're not licensed, you're breaking the law. You need to attend to the necessary paperwork," I said, feeling like a bureaucrat. "Don't make me go looking through the satchel for your name."

He looked from me to Sailor. When he spoke, his voice was edged with awe. "What's she doing with the *satchel*?"

Sailor shrugged and crossed his arms over his chest. With his heavy-lidded stare he sent out very subtle yet distinct warning pulses, wafting through the air right alongside the bay breezes.

Jamie's already sloping shoulders slumped further. He folded the paper several times and put it in his pocket. "A'right. I'll take care of it."

"See that you do."

Chapter 16

The next morning Sailor helped me to put right some of the heavier items on the shop floor but then had to leave for an appointment. We made arrangements to have lunch together.

Just as he was leaving, Bronwyn and Duke arrived with bagels and cream cheese, Conrad in tow, offering his services. I put on a mix of Nina Simone, Édith Piaf, and Spearhead—Conrad's current favorite—while Bronwyn brewed a pot of coffee, and we got to work sweeping and picking up, with Oscar somehow sleeping through it all, snoring contentedly on his bed.

Twenty minutes later, Maya arrived with Loretta.

Maya placed the dog's little rug in the area behind the counter, and after sniffing lazily at a few racks of clothing she plopped down. Oscar awoke with a snort and nosed at her, his little hooves clopping on the wooden floors as he circled her a few times, but Loretta just gave him a few thumps of her tail, closed her eyes, let out a long sigh, and went to sleep.

"I don't think even you, Oscar, can work up much animosity toward such an easygoing animal," I said with a chuckle.

"Mom and I took Loretta to the vet yesterday to have her checked out," said Maya as she started smoothing and folding a bunch of scarves that had been shoved into a heap on one of the shelves. "Tell you the truth, part of me wondered whether her lack of energy had something to do with . . . whatever happened to Autumn Jennings. I mean, who knows whether a dog could be poisoned by the same things we can? I know they eat putrid, disgusting things, but . . ."

"You're right," I said. "Arsenic's probably a whole different ball game."

"Arsenic?" asked Bronwyn.

I nodded. "The police think Autumn Jennings was poisoned by arsenic."

"Sounds like something the Borgias did to each other," said Maya.

"That's what *I* said." I picked up a couple of silky slips that had been knocked off their hangers. We'd tied their spaghetti straps together with blue ribbon to keep them from slipping off, but the result wasn't foolproof.

"I've read that arsenic was so popular back in the day it was referred to as 'inheritance powder,' or 'revenge powder,'" said Bronwyn, as she finished sweeping the floor around her herbal stand. The forensics team had taken samples from most of her jars, resulting in a lot of dried herbs and teas scattered here and there but no major damage. "More than one servant punished an unfair master by adding a little to the gravy. Imagine living your life knowing that the people who prepared your food might be ready to off you at any moment!"

Maya nodded thoughtfully and moved on to the parasols, rehanging a few on some fishing line in the front window, while placing the others in a huge pressed-metal urn. "I really should learn to cook, I suppose."

"In Autumn's case," I continued, "they think it was an accidental poisoning."

"How does one become 'accidentally' poisoned by arsenic in this day and age?" asked Duke. He was washing the front window, which the police hadn't bothered, but Duke was always self-conscious that his big callused fisherman's hands would snag the old fabric of the clothes, so he often made himself useful in other ways. He was a pleasant, easygoing presence in the store, and he made Bronwyn happy, and that was more than enough for me.

"According to Parmelee Riesling, a clothing conservator, it's not all that uncommon for people dealing with really old clothes. Many dyes in the nineteenth century contained poisonous ingredients or other toxic by-products of production."

"Such as arsenic?"

I nodded. "It was used to create a special shade of green. Apparently William Morris was famous not only for his intricate wallpaper designs, but also for poisoning a lot of workers with dyes."

"That's horrible," said Maya. "So the workers were sacrificed for the sake of beauty?"

"It wouldn't be the first time, sorry to say. But in this case it wasn't just those *making* the clothes, but those who *wore* them. As women danced in their ball gowns, their pores opened and sweat activated the dyes, allowing arsenic to enter their bloodstream. Or sometimes the arsenic leached out and wafted around the dance floor in clouds of poison dust."

Bronwyn stood, placing a flapper dress on its hanger, and blinked in shock. "What a terrible image. I prefer to think of it all as beautiful back then."

"Only for the wealthy people at the top," said Maya. "As a general rule, my people didn't live in quite such a pretty bubble. But as far as Loretta goes: The vet gave her a clean bill of health. I guess she's just lazy."

"Let's say mellow," said Bronwyn, going over to stroke Loretta's neck. "It sounds nicer. Anyway, that's a positive trait in a store mascot."

Oscar snorted.

"She means for Autumn Jennings's store, Oscar, not here," said Maya. "We've got more than enough mascot in you."

I was beginning to wonder whether my friends might be getting clued in to Oscar's true self. I knew people talked to pets like people, but Maya and Bronwyn and even Conrad had started talking to Oscar as though they expected him to understand. Which he did, of course.

"We're not open yet, Sandra," said Bronwyn as our neighbor sailed in, ignoring the *Closed* sign.

"Oh, do you mind terribly? I wanted to tell you something important . . . ," she said, standing in the middle of the store and rising on her tiptoes. Her gaze fell on the bagels on the counter.

"Please help yourself to a bagel, Sandra," I said. Oscar grunted again, I imagined in protest at losing part of his after-breakfast snack to someone of whom he was not fond. "What did you want to tell us?"

"What?" she said, distracted as she read the labels

from the three different kinds of cream cheese: veggie, jalapeño, and plain.

"You said you had something important to tell us?" I reminded her.

"Oh! Yes," she said as she slathered a sesame bagel with plain cream cheese. "The landlord said he agrees, and it would work for you to take over my lease."

"Really?"

Her eyes widened and she spoke around a bite of bagel. "Don't say you've changed your mind! I've already made plans! Carson City is waiting!"

Everyone in the store—with the exception of Loretta—turned to stare at me.

"What's going on, Lily?" asked Bronwyn.

"Well, as you all know, Sandra's moving out of Peaceful Things."

"My sister has a charming little antiques store in Carson City, and I think I'd like to live in a *different* sort of environment. I'll leave this neighborhood, such as it is"—Sandra gave a significant glance in Conrad's direction—"to those of you who can really enjoy it."

"Sandra and I share a landlord," I continued, "and I spoke with him yesterday about the possibility of taking over Sandra's lease on the space she uses for Peaceful Things. Maya's mother is getting kicked out of her loft. . . . I haven't talked with her about it yet, but I was thinking maybe we could open Aunt Cora's Annex. Or maybe call it Lucille's Loft, right here next door."

"I think that's a great idea," said Maya. "I'll bet Mom would love that. Can she afford to rent it?"

"We'll work out the money. Aunt Cora's Closet has been doing really well lately. We could figure out some sort of share of the profits from the new dresses or something. I was thinking she could have her sewing room there, but also use the front part of the space for her creations. And that way we could free up some space here; I could have my little kitchen-gadget corner without being so crowded."

"Wonderful idea!" said Bronwyn.

"Why don't I give Lucille a call right now?" I said. "I'd hate for her to think I was arranging her life and future without even letting her know. I didn't mean to be controlling; it's just that the opportunity arose . . ."

"I think it's great, Lily," said Maya. "Just give her a call; she hasn't been able to sleep lately, trying to work out where she was going to move. I'm betting she'll love the idea."

And happily, she did.

With all of us working together, it didn't take long to put things to right in the shop. Bronwyn's herbal stand had taken the brunt of the storm, but we were able to arrange a few racks and rehang dresses and tidy up enough to open the store by noon.

Our first customer was none other than Renee Baker, who arrived with a pink bakery box in her hands.

"I see you have two *more* handsome men in your realm." She smiled and winked at Duke, who nodded, and Conrad, who blushed. "Lily, how in the *world* do you do it?"

I introduced Renee to the gang, and the gang to Renee.

"Dude," Conrad said, eyes widening as Renee opened the box, revealing the frosted delicacies within. "I'm not embarrassed to admit, I'm a big fan of the cupcake."

"Try this one," she said, handing him one with white

frosting and sprinkles. "I have a way of knowing who will like which cupcake."

"Lily's like that with clothes," said Bronwyn. "She's quite gifted."

Renee looked around the store, then back at me. "Why, this place is lovely! And neat as a pin!"

"You should have seen it this morning," muttered Maya.

"Yes, I fear the police did a number on us," said Bronwyn. "I made poor Autumn—may the goddess show her the light—some scones a few days ago, so the officials were suspicious of my herbs and they tore this place apart. Can you imagine?"

"Well, that's odd," Renee said, perusing a rack of 1980s velour loungewear and polyester jogging suits. These sold well, amazingly enough, but they were nothing compared to the caliber of the clothes in Autumn's store. "They've left Autumn's place virtually untouched. Why do you suppose that would be?"

"I have no idea," I said. "The other day you mentioned the police came into your store and talked to you about what might have happened to Autumn, right?"

"They did come in; of course they did. An officer and a lady."

"I believe they're both inspectors."

"Right. The fellow liked my lemon chiffon, and the lady preferred chocolate, as many ladies do." Another wink in Conrad's direction. Luckily he was distracted by the cupcake he was eating. Conrad wasn't typically what one might call "smooth with the ladies."

"And you told them about the trousseau upstairs? About Autumn trying on the dresses?"

"I can't recall whether I went into those particulars.

They just asked me about enemies, family, suspicious people hanging around. That sort of thing."

"And were you able to give them any ideas?"

"Oh, no, not really. I didn't go in the shop that often; all I could tell them was that Autumn didn't have any family, and her husband passed away a couple of years ago." Renee held up a fitted jacket that was clearly too small for her, so I steered her toward a display of 1960s outerwear that would better suit her figure. "You really do have fun things here. So different from Autumn's inventory!"

"Dude, that was the best cupcake I've ever had in my life," said Conrad, sitting on one of the velvet benches near the dressing rooms, a serene look on his face.

"Have another!"

"Dude, I couldn't. Well . . . maybe one more." He chose a lavender one this time.

"You know, the cupcake business is doing *so well*. Everyone said when I started that I would never make it, but things are going great. I'm even thinking about seeing whether I could expand into the Vintage Visions space. Would you be interested in the merchandise?"

My hands, busy rearranging the carved talismans in the glass display case, stilled.

"Oh, Lily was just talking about expanding Aunt Cora's Closet!" said Bronwyn. Then realization dawned: "Of course, luckily our neighbor is simply moving, not . . ."

"Dead," Maya supplied the word she was looking for.

"Are you . . . in charge of Autumn's estate, Renee?" I asked.

"What? Oh. No, no, of course not. It just seemed ser-endipitous that the space should open up just like that, and I've been thinking I needed to expand . . ."

Maya and Bronwyn and I exchanged looks.

"Oh, I'm sorry," said Renee, clearly picking up on the tension. "Too soon?"

"A little," Maya said softly.

"Was she a friend of yours? I thought you barely knew her."

"We didn't, not really," I said. "Still and all, it's a tragedy, her passing away so quickly."

"Of course it was. And so unexpected. She wasn't very old! I'm just . . . Well, you know how real estate is around here. If you don't jump on something right away, the opportunity passes. There have already been folks poking around, looking in the windows. . . ."

Speaking of peeking into windows . . .

"Do you happen to know Eleanor and Cody . . . I don't know their last names," I said. "They have a cute dog named Mr. Bojangles."

"I don't recall. . . ."

"They're a young couple, twentysomethings. They were there the first morning I met you in your store— Cody has a big bushy beard?"

"What is *with* that style? I don't care for it at all."

"Agree with you there," said Bronwyn. The two took a moment to swap their least favorite current styles, sagging pants and bushy beards and muttonchops topping the list.

"So do you like the skinny jeans that are replacing the sagging pants?" Maya asked.

"Not really. They're usually paired with the strange facial hair! And ear plugs!" The two dissolved into laughter.

"I think this dress would suit you, Renee," I said, holding up a loose gauzy dress with a tropical theme. Its vibrations were confident but very sweet and mellow; there was something of an edge to Renee that made me want to help her relax. Her vibrations reminded me a little of Sandra Schmidt, our soon-to-be-gone retail neighbor.

"So," I said, hoping to get the conversation back on track. "You don't know him? The young man with the beard? I think he and his wife live in the neighborhood. He mentioned he frequents your shop."

"Hate to tell you, but there are a lot of people coming in and out of the shop. *Everyone* loves cupcakes. Why are you asking about him?"

"No reason in particular. Maya and I met them at the dog park, and Cody mentioned he maintains the Web site for the Rodchester House of Spirits."

"*Oooh*, the Rodchester House of Spirits!" cooed Bronwyn. "I just can't wait!"

"Wait for what?" asked Renee.

"I'm having a sleepover there tomorrow night. Can you imagine?"

Renee looked troubled.

"Are you all right?" I asked.

"Yes, of course," she said, shaking herself a little. "That place just gives me the creeps, somehow."

"Me, too," said Maya.

"You've been?"

"Hasn't everybody?"

"I think it's gorgeous," said Bronwyn. "And remember—spirits aren't here to bother us; they're part of the mystical veils that surround us, cloaking us in their warmth and knowledge. Tell them, Lily."

"What about demons?" Maya piped up. When I first met Maya she didn't believe in my abilities with the craft, much less ghosts and demons. Since then she'd seen a lot and had been on a pretty steep learning curve.

Renee blanched, and Bronwyn pursed her lips together.

"You think there might be *demons* in Rodchester House?" asked Renee.

"No, of course not," I said. "In fact, we don't know that there's anything at all paranormal in Rodchester House."

"I think there's something there, but I don't know what," Renee said. "I consulted a mage a few months ago, and he said there was no such thing as demons."

I sincerely hoped the "mage" she was referring to wasn't the dubious Jamie. I was trying to think of a way to frame my question so it wouldn't sound too pushy when Renee offered: "I went to see him to inquire about the next steps to take for the success of my business."

"Do you know a man named Jamie?"

"He has a beard, like the other fellow?"

"No, he's a lot older than Cody, probably in his thirties or forties. Not very tall . . ." It was on the tip of my tongue to say: "claims to resolve curses." But again, though my friends backed me up in my magical endeavors, sometimes they were best left protected. "Sort of a Jersey tough-guy accent? He had some business with Autumn Jennings, and he mentioned you had given her his name."

Renee was flipping through a set of psychedelic '60s muumuus and appeared not to hear me.

"Renee?"

Finally she paused and turned toward me. The others

were chatting among themselves, absorbed in their respective tasks, not paying us any attention.

So no one else saw what I did: Renee went from smiling, Anglophile cupcake lady to something else entirely. Her normally warm, sparkling eyes narrowed; they were as cold as ice.

"He shouldn't have told you that," Renee said.

Then she smiled again and resumed her former attitude, holding a hot-pink-and-orange maxi dress in front of her.

"You there, young man," she said to Conrad. "What do you think of this on me? Do you suppose I could pull it off?"

The phone rang. Still shaken by my interaction with Renee, I crossed over to the counter and answered absently: "Aunt Cora's Closet, Lily speaking."

It was Sam Spade. My "investigator."

"Couldn't find anything on the phone number you gave me; it's a burner cell phone. Therefore, no name associated with it. Sorry. But I ran that plate for you and got a hit. Motorcycle's registered to a fellow named Brad Goldman, works at the David Gallery off Union Square."

"Is that an art gallery?"

"They'd probably say yes, but what it really is, is like a spa for guys."

"A men's salon?"

"I guess. I mean, what's with that? Barbershop's not good enough for people anymore?"

"I don't know what this world's coming to," I said. Sam never got my jokes, but that didn't prevent me from making them. In fact, if anything, it spurred me on for my own amusement.

"Anyway, I tracked Brad Goldman down there and he's working ten to five today. Since I went there in person, that'll cost extra."

"That's fine." Sam was fairly new to the investigations business and still did everything as though he had a catalog of services by his side, with a list of costs. He wasn't what you'd call a natural detective, and I kept expecting to hear that he'd returned to his former career as a financial analyst. But so far he was hanging in there, and he had contacts that came in useful from time to time.

I wrote down the name and address of the David Gallery.

By the time we hung up, Renee had decided on the muumuu and Maya was already wrapping it up for her and placing it in one of our recycled bags with *Aunt Cora's Closet* emblazoned on the side.

"Thanks again for the cupcakes," said Maya. "Lily can't stop talking about them."

"Oh, you're welcome! It's great advertising! Maybe I'll be moving into this neighborhood next, one never knows! There could be Renee's bakeries all *over* this city!"

Maya smiled broadly. "One can only hope."

"Aren't you a *dear*!" Renee said. "Bronwyn, Duke, Conrad, you have been such loves!"

Only then did I realize that Oscar hadn't shown his snout the entire time Renee was in the store. Was he that put out by Loretta, or could there really be something problematic with the cupcake lady?

Unfortunately I didn't have time to track Oscar down and confront him. Not long after Renee left, Sailor stopped by to take me to lunch.

I turned to Bronwyn and Maya. "Mind if I sneak out?"

"Oh, please, go and enjoy!" said Bronwyn. "We have more than enough help at the store at the moment."

"Thanks." It was sunny and nice out, but I grabbed a peacoat and scarf just in case.

"Hungry?" Sailor asked.

"Getting there," I said, feeling guilty that I'd eaten a bagel and half a cupcake already today. "But on the way to lunch, we need to see a man about a motorcycle."

He let out a little groan and held his hands out for the keys. "In that case, I'm driving."

"Sometimes I think you just love me for my Mustang."

"It is a great car."

Chapter 17

David's Gallery was full of trendy young men getting not only haircuts but also facials and other spa treatments.

"I don't want to sound hopelessly behind the times," I said in a quiet voice, "but I've never seen such a thing. Have you?"

"Beats the heck out of me," Sailor said.

"On the other hand, you could probably use a facial," I said. "Or perhaps a manicure . . . ?"

"You just do your investigating so we can get to lunch. I'm hungry."

I asked the receptionist, a young tattooed man wearing blue eyeliner and a plaid lumberjack shirt that hugged his thin shoulders, for Brad Goldman.

"Brad!" he yelled over his shoulder, then turned back to his smartphone.

A young man trotted out from the back, then came to a stop and put his hands on his hips.

"You're not my one o'clock," he said. His own blond

hair had been buzzed very close to his skull, and I made out what looked like a tattoo of a horse on the side of his head. He had clear blue eyes and a rather chubby face that gave him a pleasant, boyish look.

"No, we're not. We're actually here to ask you about your motorcycle."

His expression instantly became interested. "Did you find it? Where is it? And who are you?"

"I'm Lily Ivory, and this is Sailor. We don't know where your bike is, but we're looking for a woman we saw riding it. Her name's Scarlet?"

His eyes widened and he stepped back.

"What about her?"

"We're trying to track her down."

"I dunno where she is. The truth is she begged me to borrow my bike, said she was late for her dog-walking gig. But she never came back. She bugged off with my bike."

"The black Ducati?"

He nodded and swallowed so hard I could hear the gulp.

"And you haven't heard from her?"

He shook his head. His lip trembled and his eyes filled with tears. "I really don't understand. She took my *bike*, man. I mean . . . I thought we were in love, you know? Like, she was the one."

"So Scarlet's your girlfriend?" I asked.

"*Was* my girlfriend, I'm guessing."

"Women are complicated," Sailor said.

"Man, you're totally right," Brad said slowly. "I mean . . . why would she do this to me?"

"You still love her?"

Brad nodded.

"Then stand by her," counseled Sailor. "She probably has an explanation, as far-fetched as it might be."

"I guess you're right," said Brad. "Besides, she wasn't feeling all that great. Maybe she just, like, went to bed or something."

"Where does she live?"

"She's not there; landlady said she left. And she's sure not at my place."

"Could you give me her address anyway?"

"Who are you, again?"

I placed my hand on his arm. I can't sway everyone easily, but Brad's open countenance had given me the idea he might be amenable.

"We're looking for her. She left all the dogs she was caring for, and we need to make sure we get them back to their homes. Surely she would want that?"

"She just left them? Man, that's weird." He shook his head but wrote down her full name, address, and the telephone number I already had on the back of an appointment card and handed it to me.

"Her last name's Funk?" I asked.

He nodded. *No wonder she went by just the one name.*

"How did Scarlet know Autumn Jennings? Do you know?"

"Autumn's the woman who runs the secondhand clothes store?"

I nodded.

"They met when Scarlet volunteered at the Legion of Honor. Then Scarlet did some odd jobs for her at the shop. She's from Missouri; man, it's been tough for her, trying to get by in San Francisco. But she's tough, you know. Tough but sweet. I think it's a midwestern thing, don't you? I think we San Franciscans are sort of soft."

The air in the salon was scented with the lavender from the foot soaks and facial scrubs. *He might be right,* I thought.

"Did she have any connection to the Rodchester House of Spirits, do you know?"

"Why are you asking?"

"I'm going down there on Saturday for a party. Someone mentioned she might have looked for a job there, so I was just wondering . . ."

He was shaking his head, a blank look in his eyes. "Still, that's totally weird that she left the dogs. She really liked them. But like I said, she wasn't really feeling herself lately."

"Wasn't feeling well, how?"

He shrugged. "I don't know. Sort of weak, and a little confused."

"Do you happen to know if Scarlet might have a dress from Autumn Jennings's vintage clothes store?"

He wouldn't meet my eyes. "I really don't know anything about that."

"What about some fake couture labels?"

He shrugged and shook his head.

"And no other idea where we might find her," I persisted, "if she's not at home?"

He shrugged. "Ah, man, my one o'clock's here. Hey, if you find Scarlet, tell her I love her and want her back. And I want my bike back, too."

"Will do," said Sailor.

"Especially the bike. I mean, seriously. I didn't report it to the cops or anything, but I need it, man."

"Of course," I said, pulling out one of my business cards. "Brad, if you do talk to Scarlet, tell her Autumn Jennings died from a poison and that Scarlet might have been exposed herself. Even if she's not willing to talk to me, she might need medical care."

"What are you *talking* about?"

"Autumn Jennings, from Vintage Visions Glad Rags, passed away suddenly, a couple of days ago. She had been exposed to a poison, and I fear that Scarlet might be as well."

"Um . . ." He looked down at the business card. "Yeah, sure thing. I'll let her know if I see her."

Sailor and I left the salon. Outside I breathed deeply to clear my lungs of the scent of hair products. The sidewalks were bustling with tourists and locals who flocked to Union Square for the high-end shopping: A huge Neiman Marcus dominated one corner, and a massive Macy's famous for holiday window displays took up another block. Smaller boutiques featured Cartier, Gucci, Balenciaga, and the like.

"He was lying toward the end, when you asked him about the dress labels," said Sailor. "I saw mock orange."

"Excuse me?"

"Mock orange is a flower, and a traditional symbol of lying. Sometimes I see Pinocchio." At my amused look, Sailor continued. "You wanted me to tell you more about the way things work for me, so there you go."

"I think it's cute that you see flowers and children's characters."

"I take what I can get." He shrugged. "Anyway, I'll bet Scarlet *did* take something from Autumn's shop— or maybe Autumn gave it to her; it really doesn't matter at this point."

"Except that if it's one of the poisonous dresses, she might be in danger."

"Speaking of poison, I'm ready to name mine. I'm

hungry," Sailor said as we negotiated the crowded side-walk in front of the St. Francis Hotel. "I know a nice little restaurant in walking distance; that way we don't have to move the car."

"Perfect," I said. Even with my parking charm, find-ing a spot near Union Square was near impossible, so we had parked in the expensive underground garage beneath the plaza. "Where?"

"Belden Place."

"Where's that?"

"You don't know it? It's the French Quarter."

"There's a *French* Quarter in San Francisco?"

"It doesn't hold a candle to a place like New Or-leans, of course, but yes. There's a little alley full of restaurants, and a few little shops."

"Where?"

"Tucked between Union Square and Chinatown."

"I declare, this town never ceases to amaze me."

"I still don't know how I didn't even realize this was here. I'm not *that* new to town," I said as I sipped my glass of rosé at an outdoor table under a big red um-brella. "I'm poleaxed, is what."

"You don't get out much."

"Don't tell that to Maya and Bronwyn. They'd say I'm never at the store anymore."

"Let me rephrase: You don't get out much for things like long lunches at sidewalk cafés. Unless you're meet-ing your old boyfriend, that is."

Sailor had spotted me in North Beach having lunch with an ex-beau not long ago, and though he claimed he trusted me, I could tell it still rankled since he kept bringing it up.

"Very funny."

"But seriously, you're never in the shop because you're too busy running around chasing murderers."

Just then a waiter walked by and gave me an odd look.

"Mostly buying old clothes, I'd say."

"I'm going to start calling you Nancy Drew. And before you ask, Nancy's a very smart sleuth, the protagonist of an extraordinarily popular series of books for young adults."

"I've heard of Nancy Drew," I said, with just a slight defensive note in my voice. "And Sherlock Holmes, too. Oscar loves mysteries, and we trade."

Sailor smiled. "Has he talked you into letting him come for Bronwyn's sleepover yet?"

I shook my head.

"Mark my words: He'll find a way. He's a resourceful little critter."

"Don't I know it."

The waiter arrived and took our order for lunch; he sported a thick French accent and told us he was from Lyon and adored San Francisco.

My mind cast back to my chat with Carlos, about the lack of organized crime in San Francisco. Why had the French never had organized crime? I wondered. Perhaps they did, but since they'd never had any really good movies made about it, I didn't realize. Or, I thought as I dug into my delectable appetizer of duck pâté, most likely they were distracted with delicious food, excellent wine—and chocolate.

Just as Sailor and I started in on our shared dessert—a chocolate extravaganza—a man approached our table, his hat literally in his hands.

"Excuse me. I'm so sorry to interrupt," he said. And then he launched into what he needed from me: another intervention with the mayor's office. He had a file tucked under his arm. I asked him to leave the information with me and promised him I would see what I could do.

After he left, I shook my head and polished off the rosé. "I know you probably wouldn't agree with me, but I sure hope Aidan comes home soon. I don't think I can take much more of this."

Sailor nodded but didn't say anything.

"What do you think's going on? Why would he have left me in charge?"

"I think he's got something planned for you," Sailor said carefully.

"Something, as in . . . ?"

"I believe he's testing the waters, seeing how folks react to you, and you to them. You know he's been wanting you to combine forces and work with him."

"You were in on that discussion as well. And do you think that would be the worst option? Say what you will about Aidan, he's helped me out in the past. When the chips are down, he weighs in on the right side of things."

"He weighs in on *Aidan's* side of things," said Sailor. "But that being said . . . I suppose it depends what he's sensing. I know he's feeling something coming. I've been hoping my aunt Renna or Patience could tell me more from their end, but the threat is still unclear. So in the meantime, working with Aidan appears to be our best option."

"'Our'?"

"Where you go, I go."

"Even if Aidan's involved?"

"*Especially* if Aidan's involved."

"Speaking of Aidan, another thing he abandoned to me was Selena's training sessions. She's coming by tonight to watch me brew. We're working on control."

"That's good. Her metal magic is rare and could come in handy. Be sure to have her polish some silver things while she's at your place."

"I don't see how I could avoid it. That girl's like a polishing machine, with a one-track mind. It's a little scary."

"Witches are scary. One of these days you'll have to cop to that."

"Oh, I don't know . . . I've known a few psychics who scared the scalded haints out of me."

Sailor chuckled. "I guess we're a scary lot."

"Speaking of which, are you up for Bronwyn's birthday bash tomorrow?"

"I'm going. As to whether I'm 'up' for a night with a coven in a haunted house, that's harder to say. Especially . . ."

"What?"

He shrugged. "I've got a lot of love for the Wiccans out there, but you have to admit: This is one wacky coven."

I smiled. "You are a prince among men, Sailor—you know that?"

"All I care about is that *you* know that," he said as he paid the bill.

"Thank you for lunch. This was a rare treat."

"You're most welcome. Now that we're getting in the habit of taking time out for picnics and lunch, I might be spoiled for real life. But alas, I've got training with Patience this afternoon."

I tried to stop myself from asking but didn't succeed.

"So, what does Patience think of you joining us for the overnight at Rodchester House?"

"Are we back to that?"

"No," I lied. I toyed with my dessert fork. "All right, a little bit."

"The training is going well. My powers are coming back—I can feel them; I have more control, more abilities to touch base with the beyond and to interpret the signs. I need these abilities in order to make a living, among other things, Lily. Not to mention to help keep tabs on you, make sure you're safe." He reached out and placed his hand over mine on top of the small café table. "You're going to need me, you know, if you're going to work with Aidan to keep the magical forces in this town in check."

I let out a shaky breath. "Maybe that's what I'm afraid of."

He gave me a crooked smile. "Of the magical forces, or of needing me?"

"Both. But mostly . . . of needing you."

"I know," he said softly, tossing his napkin atop the table. "But you'll get used to it. And I will reiterate: You have absolutely nothing to worry about with me and Patience. Nothing. To. Worry. About."

I rose and took his arm, and we walked toward Union Square.

"I'll go check out Scarlet's last known address; it's not far from where I'm headed this afternoon anyway," said Sailor.

"Brad said she already moved out."

"Mock orange, remember? I'm not ready to trust Brad."

I nodded. "Okay, thanks. Sailor, did you notice anything . . . off about Renee?"

"The cupcake lady? Not particularly. But neither was I looking for anything. Why?"

"I was wondering whether she might be involved in this whole affair, somehow."

"The *cupcake* lady?"

"I grant that her association with cupcakes makes it a harder notion to accept. But just because she's a baker doesn't mean she can't also be powerful. After all, how many vintage clothes dealers would you think were superpowerful witches?"

He grinned. "Superpowerful? Aren't we getting a little big for our britches?"

I nodded, acceding to his point. "But remember yesterday the little weasel—"

"Jamie?"

I nodded. "Jamie said Renee had recommended him to Autumn. Why would a cupcake baker know anything about lifting curses?"

"Maybe she had use for his services at some point. That would be no more sinister than going to Patience for a crystal ball reading or to my aunt Renna for Tarot. I know that you don't engage in magic in exchange for money, Lily, but some of us who are very close to you do."

"True. But today when I asked her about it . . . she gave me a funny look."

"What kind of funny look?"

"Sort of . . . blank, funny. Almost like you look when you've made contact with the beyond. Sort of spooky."

"And yet in my case you're willing to give me the benefit of the doubt."

"Well, you're a special case."

"A funny look after you ask her about her association with a fellow like Jamie, in front of a group of strangers, might have been due more to embarrassment than anything more. Or . . ."

"Or . . . ?"

"Far be it from me to disregard your witchy intuition. I suppose at the very least it indicates that we should be careful around her. But for now, do you think you can stay out of trouble until tomorrow?"

"I'll do my darnedest."

Chapter 18

Back at Aunt Cora's Closet, Maya told me the afternoon had been mellow, with just a few customers in and out. Duke and Conrad had stayed, and they'd decided to order pizza for dinner—with an extra one for Oscar, sans pepperoni.

I begged off dinner, citing the huge leisurely French lunch I had shared with Sailor. Plus I was nervous about my appointment with the mayor at Aidan's office, so I wanted to get there early.

First things first: I went upstairs to my apartment, closed the door, and asked Oscar for some advice.

His eyes grew huge. "You're meeting the *mayor*? Wow. You go, mistress! You mind asking him about a coupla parking tickets . . . ?"

"How in tarnation did you manage to rack up parking tickets?"

He shrugged. "Sometimes you think you're gonna be, like, ten minutes, and then one thing leads to another, and you totally forget how much time you've got left on the meter."

"No, I understand *that*, but . . . oh, never mind. I don't want to be late. Do I look all right?"

He scrunched up his muzzle and made a funny kind of grimace-slash-shrug.

"You think I should change?"

"The mayor's a little . . . *traditional*. What about a nice suit of some sort?"

"The only suit I have is from the nineteen forties. Do you think that will do?"

"Sure! Put it on and I'll tell you what I think."

When I emerged from the bedroom he suggested softening up the brown outfit with the addition of an Hermès scarf in tones of gold, sage green, and rust. Then he told me to try pinning my hair up in a messy bun on top of my head: "It says formal but not stuffy, if you know what I'm saying," Oscar said.

I stood back and checked my reflection in the mirror.

"That's not bad," I said. "Not bad at all. I'm impressed, Oscar."

"Why do you sound so surprised? I hang around in the shop every day; I pick things up."

"You sleep fifty-five minutes out of every hour."

"I'm a quick study. I get it from my father's side: Goblins are smart. Everyone knows this. Here, a few bangles at the wrist and you're good to go."

Oscar. Gobgoyle sidekick and fashion consultant.

"Okay, any actual advice for my meeting the mayor, beyond wardrobe?"

"Don't mention eels."

"Eels."

"Or seesaws."

"Why on earth would I mention eels *or* seesaws?"

"Exactly." He shook his big head. "Good luck. And don't forget to ask about those parking tickets!"

As I neared Fisherman's Wharf, I realized I was absurdly early. I didn't want to cool my heels in Aidan's office for a full hour and a half. It wouldn't be much of a detour to pass by Vintage Visions. Maybe I'd stop in next door for a cupcake and try to suss out what was my overactive imagination from what was real.

I drove down the street, but Renee's cupcake store was closed. Along with the permanent closing of Vintage Visions Glad Rags, it made the whole street seem a little sad.

Then I saw Mrs. Morgan across the street, trying to make it down the long flight of wooden stairs with Colonel Mustard's leash in one hand and a walker in the other.

I double-parked and rushed out to help her.

"Mrs. Morgan, are you all right? May I help you?"

"Oh! Would you? It's good for me to take Colonel Mustard to the park, but these stairs are daunting. It seems counterintuitive, but going up is so much easier than down, isn't it? I was better about getting out before, but now that Mr. Morgan has passed . . ."

I took the dog's leash and the walker from her hands. Once she could hold on to the rail she seemed able to make it down without a problem.

"Why don't I drive you around the corner to the park?" I offered. "Then you only have to walk in one direction."

"Oh, would you? That would be lovely."

I helped Mrs. Morgan into the passenger side, and Colonel Mustard hopped into the backseat. We arrived at the park in about twenty seconds. I helped Mrs. Morgan out and onto a nearby bench, while Colonel Mustard clambered off to play with a rambunctious black Lab.

"It's too bad the cupcake store's closed," said Mrs. Morgan. "I would have treated you as a thank-you!"

"*Mmm*, too bad. I could have gone for another Chocolate Suicide."

"Have you tried the rosemary-orange? That's my favorite."

"Yes, I remember."

"You do?"

"From the other day," I said. "When I brought you one from Renee."

"Oh, I forget things sometimes," she said, waving it off but giving off a little whiff of embarrassment.

I was forgetful enough as it was; I couldn't imagine how I might be when I got to be Mrs. Morgan's age. A forgetful witch could be a handful. . . .

I had hoped to spot Cody and Eleanor at the dog park, but though there were a few people with their pets, the only person I recognized from the other day was Rolando. But then, it was a different time of day, and most people stuck more or less to their daily schedules. We laughed as Rolando threw the ball for his dog and Colonel Mustard ran after it, trying to beat him to it. Then they both picked up a stick, each carrying one end of it. Fast canine friends.

"Do you happen to know a young man who comes here sometimes, with a big beard?" I asked Mrs. Morgan. "His name's Cody?"

"I'm no good with names, either, child. Forget them

just like everything else, I'm sorry to tell you. Is he a friend of yours?"

"No, I just know him from here. And I saw him once at the cupcake shop. But I wanted to ask him some questions about the Rodchester House of Spirits. Do you happen to know it?"

"I went there many years ago. But I know Autumn was talking about it recently, and she and Renee had something of a feud going about it."

"A feud?"

"That's too strong a word, probably," she said. "They argued, is all."

"What about?"

"I'm sure I don't know. But I believe Renee donated the cupcakes to an event down at the Rodchester House. She and Scarlet went down there."

"Scarlet? As in dog walker Scarlet?"

"Yes, I told you she was always looking for odd jobs."

I thought over what I had learned from Mrs. Morgan as I drove toward Fisherman's Wharf.

Renee had acted like she hardly knew Scarlet. She certainly hadn't mentioned driving down to San Jose with her. That trip took an hour; it wasn't as though it could have slipped her mind. They must have spoken. They *knew* each other.

So what was I thinking? That they had worked together to kill Autumn with a cursed trousseau? For what possible reason?

I had no patience for parking like a cowan today, so I used my parking charm to free up a spot and squeezed my Mustang in between two huge SUVs half a block from the newly reconstructed wax museum. This was my first time back since I had been instrumental in burning down the old one. Not that it had been my intent, but I was implicated. They had rebuilt it awfully quickly, but then I supposed they were motivated; it held pride of place right there on Jefferson, the main street of the tourist mecca of Fisherman's Wharf.

Sitting in the enclosed ticket booth was Clarinda, a young woman who dressed like a Queen of the Dead. Clarinda had been injured in the disaster that closed the old museum. Apparently she'd recovered and had gotten her old job back.

"Hi!" I said, pleased to see her even though she'd never given me so much as a smile and always pretended as if she didn't know me.

This time was no different. She looked bored out of her mind and put the battered paperback she was reading facedown on the counter, then looked up at me languidly.

"How many?"

"Just me. But I don't need a ticket; I'm letting myself into Aidan's office."

"Yeah, real funny, lady."

"I'm serious."

"Look, I got work to do. Besides, Aidan's not even here."

"That's why I have his keys," I said, holding up the ring and tinkling it.

Her eyes grew huge. "For real?"

"I have the satchel, too."

She waved me through. "It's behind the Great Entertainers exhibit."

The new wax museum was sleek, with lots of chrome and glass surfaces. It didn't look much like the old place, but it was nonetheless difficult to hold at bay the memory of the wax figures liquefying, their features slipping and pooling, the scent and sensation of burning hot wax on my feet as we made our escape. I shuddered. What would make someone like Aidan, who had resources, want to have his office here?

Perhaps he gained strength from the wax figures. Poppet magic was a whole supernatural world I was barely getting to know.

There, behind sculptures of Louis Armstrong and Barbra Streisand, I could barely make out a door. Aidan's office, I was sure. He had cast a glamour over it; it didn't make the door invisible, exactly, but most people wouldn't notice it. You had to be sensitive, and you had to be looking for it.

As I slipped the key in the lock I hoped I wouldn't be greeted by Noctemus, Aidan's pure white longhaired cat. We weren't fond of each other.

Gathering strength, I pushed in the door. Aidan's office was done in what I liked to think of as Late Victorian Gentleman Fortune-Teller. The floor was covered in a plush oriental rug in shades of deep red, sapphire blue, ochre, and green. Heavy red velvet drapes, edged in gold fringe and tassels, covered the windows, leaving the place dimly lit by hand-blown sconces that lent a subtle, orangey light to the room. Two walls were covered in floor-to-ceiling bookcases filled with a library that focused on the magical world; many were leather bound and ancient, with scribblings in the margins written by mages and academics. Although a lot of this information was now available on the Internet, there were some nuggets that were available only in this sort of collection. I hadn't cared much when the original wax museum burned down, but I had winced at the thought of Aidan's library going up in smoke. Somehow he had pieced it back together over the last few months.

No sign of a feline nearby. As Aidan's familiar, Noctemus would have accompanied him on his trip, unless he had a reason for her to stay.

I tilted my head and perused a few titles on the shelves, and my gaze landed on a big book titled *The Rodchester Mystery. Hmm.* I took it out. Perhaps some bedtime reading for yours truly?

A huge mahogany desk dominated the room. The vast surface was clean save for a lamp, a blotter, and a manila envelope with the mayor's name printed on it. I lifted it; I felt something inside, though not a stack of money. Something with dimension, like a metal or ceramic object. I thought back to the envelope for Jamie I'd found in Autumn's bedroom. Was this the standard for bribes and shakedowns these days? I wondered.

There was an upholstered chair for visitors. A globe, an hourglass, a crystal ball, a black mirror for scrying. The signs of a practitioner on display.

I checked the clock on the bookcase: five fifteen. The mayor wasn't scheduled to arrive for another forty-five minutes.

I was alone in Aidan's office.

Alone in Aidan's office. Probably there weren't a lot of people who could utter those words truthfully. I could rummage through his desk drawers if I wanted, or peek in the closet. I had broken into Aidan's office at the Ferry Building once, but I'd never been invited in.

Why would he trust me so implicitly? I was a snoop; surely he knew that.

But then . . . he probably didn't keep any real secrets

here. Certainly not if he knew I was going to have access to the place.

I slipped into Aidan's leather chair behind his desk. The weight of responsibility fell on my shoulders, a tangible burden. It was all well and good to complain about bureaucracy, to tease and joke about Aidan being the witchy godfather of the city. But now . . .

Not for the first time, I wondered where Aidan actually lived and tried to imagine his everyday experiences. Did he have a personal life? Anyone he cared about? He always seemed so elegant, but I knew for a fact that his image was, in large part, due to the glamour he cast over himself to hide the scars of a demonic battle, years ago.

Did he ever do anything normal, like sitting around in his pajamas, eating ice cream straight from the carton and binge-watching TV dramas?

Not that I would ever do such a thing . . . at least not very often. What would Sailor think about something like that, if we lived together?

Best not to allow myself to go down that mental road. Besides, thinking of Sailor and Aidan in the same moment made my mind want to explode.

So I got up and opened a little half door behind the desk. It led to a six-sided chamber. This was Aidan's vision chamber, a special room set up to encourage the opening of the portals and the ability to connect to the energy through the ages and to see through the veils. Tiny nooks held a series of magical objects: crystals, pyramids, and black mirrors.

Essentially, the room helped focus and coalesce power. And it worked. Aidan and I had once combined our energies in the old version of this hexagonal room, and we ended up melting his light fixtures and door hardware.

I caressed my medicine bag, took a deep breath, and closed myself in.

Shutting my eyes, I concentrated on opening myself to the forces extant in the tiny chamber; I could already feel the whispers along my skin, the tingling on the back of my neck, what felt like the marching of an army of ants along my spine.

When I opened my eyes, I saw the horizon beyond the Golden Gate Bridge; it was covered in dark clouds. The coming storm.

Was this what Aidan had been seeing that had so disturbed him?

As I watched, the clouds came together. Thunder and lightning shook me to my core. The rain came in a torrent, but it turned to blood as it poured into a bottle that reminded me of a massive version of the lacrimatory from the Vintage Victoriana exhibit: covered in gold and silver filigree, but shaped like an almond rather than a long tube.

I saw thread being drawn through a pearl, sand pouring through an hourglass. A crown of parsley, a cup of snakes. Ashes. And a phrase: *coincidentia oppositorum*.

A loud knock on the door roused me from my vision.

Startled, I felt my heart pound and I wondered how long I had been in the chamber. Aidan was right; something was coming. I wasn't sure how to interpret what I had seen, but I knew I needed to be sure Selena was safe. And me, and my friends . . . and this city. Suddenly claustrophobic, I yanked open the door, almost panicked that it would be locked. But it opened easily and I stumbled out.

The knocking was on the outer office door. I glanced at the clock: six on the dot.

I opened the door. The mayor was standing there with a blindfold on.

He held out his hands.

I placed the letters from the two people who had approached me for help with the mayor in his palms. He put them into his breast pocket, then held his hand out again. I put the manila envelope into it.

Finally, he said, "That it?"

"Yes," I said.

He turned and walked away, still blindfolded.

Chapter 19

Well, if that don't beat all, I thought as I headed out to my car. Had I just bribed the mayor of San Francisco? And if so . . . with what?

I felt sort of larcenous and clueless at the same time, like a bumbling drug dealer.

Why would Aidan have gone and left me without a clue? Again, the thought occurred: He would probably find this hysterically funny. I hoped to heck he wasn't somehow watching all of this on some sort of punk-the-witch supernatural camcorder.

By the time I got back to the Haight and let myself into Aunt Cora's Closet, I found Bronwyn and Duke cleaning up after their pizza feast. Conrad had just left to claim his favorite sleeping spot in Golden Gate Park, and Maya had taken Loretta home.

My erstwhile ward, Selena, sat on the floor, industriously shining all of the silver jewelry she had taken out of the display cabinet. She looked up at me with rather empty, frightening-looking eyes in a pinched face. At fourteen years old, Selena was still young and awkward, and she was remarkably powerful. She reminded me a little of myself at that age: gawky, out of control, miserable. At least those last two traits I could be instrumental in addressing. We were working on finding positive ways for her to direct her magic, and that, in turn, was helping her to be more confident and—dare I say it?—happier. Even though she was still painfully thin, I thought she was beginning to fill out. Bronwyn and I were forever foisting food on her.

Selena still had a hard time with humans but was capable of great kindness when it came to animals; Maya had helped her find a volunteer position at the local no-kill shelter, where she went twice a week to help socialize the cast-off cats and dogs. Her smiles, though still rare, were usually reserved for the animals.

"Did you meet Loretta?" I asked her.

She nodded and handed me a shiny silver charm in the shape of a bee.

"I found this in your junk box. It was ugly but I cleaned it and shone it up for her," Selena said. "For Loretta's collar."

"Aren't you just a sweetheart? What made you think of that?"

"Because she has those charms on her collar. This will add to them."

And as I knew, Selena had imbued the silver with a little of her special power. The jewelry she cleaned flew off the shelves, as people just felt a little better when they put it on. The energy was subtle but powerful.

"Thank you, Selena. Why a bee?"

She shrugged. "Loretta reminds me of bees. I like bees."

"Me, too," I said and gave her a little hug. She immediately stiffened, as always, and she didn't hug me back, but she accepted it.

"Oh, Lily, Sailor called," said Bronwyn. "He said to tell you, 'There was no sign of scarlet funk.' I'm sure it must be some sort of lover's code. . . . I do hope everything's all right between you two? No . . . health issues?"

"Everything's fine," I said with a smile. "He's referring to a person. Thanks for letting me know."

After seeing Bronwyn and Duke off, Selena and I locked up, turned out the lights in the shop, and retired upstairs to my apartment. Selena's grandmother owned a *botanica* on Mission Street, and though she was skilled as an apothecary owner, she wasn't capable of helping her granddaughter learn to harness her special abilities. So Selena had started spending a night or two every week with me so we could study. She and Oscar had something of a love-hate relationship, and I had to sell him on her coming over by promising a movie and popcorn with *lots* of butter after we were finished brewing.

"I don't see why *I* can't go to the Rodchester House of Spirits for the overnight tomorrow," Selena said as we climbed the stairs, her tone sullen.

"That's what *I* said," Oscar grunted. Selena was one of the select few that Oscar transformed around whenever we were alone. The two of them were quite the pair; if they weren't trying to hex each other, they were peas in a pod.

"It's for grown-ups," I said as I opened the door to the apartment. "Besides, they say it's a haunted house. Do you like haunted houses?"

Her eyes grew huge, but she just shrugged. I was willing to bet she, like Sailor and me and other magical folks

I knew, didn't intentionally subject herself to haunted venues.

"I'd like to be with the coven," she said.

The Welcome coven, true to their name, had welcomed Selena wholeheartedly into their fold. The only problem was that she couldn't control her powers enough to join them when they cast the circle or drew down the moon; this was, in part, where I came in. Our coaching sessions were geared toward helping Selena learn to control her abilities and curb her anger, which, at least in part, fed those powers. I felt just a teensy bit out of my league since I was still working on these particular aspects of my own personality, but I did the best that I could, and I called my own grandmother for advice with ever-increasing frequency.

Selena would be a powerful witch one day; it was imperative that she remain on the just, humane path.

"Tonight we're going to work on a general protection brew, and we'll mix some sprite dust."

Selena nodded solemnly. She did most things with sober seriousness. If there was one thing I most wanted for my young apprentice, aside from keeping her safe, it was showing her that she could—and should—experience joy.

"You want to join us, Oscar?"

"Nah," he said, grabbing his book and making himself comfortable on the couch. "What time's popcorn?"

"After we brew. Aren't you still stuffed with pizza?"

"That was *half an hour* ago!"

I had to smile at the outrage in his voice. "Why don't you have an apple? Pink Lady, your favorite."

"We got any cheese and crackers?"

"Help yourself."

"What's first?" Selena asked as she grabbed the

basket I used to gather my herbs. I took my sickle-shaped *boline* out of the drawer, and we went out to my garden terrace.

"First, the protection herbs: I favor cinquefoil, black cohosh, mullein, and mugwort." With each herb I showed her where to cut for the health of the plant and to optimize the clipping's potential. Then I traded the *boline* for a small spade and showed her how to dig. "As for roots, I like galangal and ginger. Always tell the plant what you are after before disturbing the earth, and then thank it with a coin and a dollop of unpasteurized goat's milk."

She let out a snort of laughter. "Seriously?"

It was so rare that Selena was amused by anything, I tried to talk myself out of reacting with impatience. Still. The girl was capable of making metal shine light upon her and had witnessed someone destroy himself by twisting a poppet made of wax. But thanking root-stock was going too far?

I forced myself to answer with a gentle: "This is how I learned to do things. Maybe not all of it makes sense, but as a system it has worked for me, and for my grandmother before me, and her grandmother before her. Are you sure you want to laugh at that?"

She shook her head and adopted her humorless mien once again.

I showed her how to wash the herbs with rainwater I kept in a small cistern, and then to pat them dry in the moonlight while chanting a simple charm of thanks. Then we brought them into the kitchen and readied the cauldron, filling it halfway with springwater. We crushed several of the herbs with the ancient stone mortar and pestle Graciela had given me and started chanting while we added the others whole, one by one, along with the roots. I added another dollop of milk, several strings of spiderwebs, and three quail eggs.

Selena stirred the brew deosil. When she joined me in the chanting, I could feel the pull of her energy. She was strong but not centered. But as she continued to stir and chant, I could feel her powers focus and calm.

"Take out the spoon now."

She did as I said. The brew continued to stir on its own.

"You see?" I asked. "We did it right. It's creating its own energy now."

"And that's it? Just like that? It will protect people now?"

"Not quite like that. It needs to brew for a while. The heat transforms things, just like in cooking. The ingredients must transmute from raw to cooked; they combine to form something entirely new. The fire creates steam, and the steam helps make the magic."

"Whoa," she said quietly.

I was pleased that she was impressed, not so much for my ego but because she was being introduced to the wonders of what we could accomplish. We witches were a special breed, and she was on the brink of joining our sisterhood. But no matter how much innate talent she might possess, without study and practice she would never fulfill her potential. Or worse: It would be turned toward the negative.

While the concoction brewed, we went back out to the terrace and gathered club moss and lily pollen, then the tiny petals from the *Achillea millefolium*. We brought these into the kitchen and I had Selena grind them together with the mortar and pestle. To this I added a dash of cemetery dirt, red sandalwood powder, and a few shavings of mica.

We put the mix into a small casserole dish and I popped it in the preheated oven.

"What's the sprite dust for?" Selena asked.

"I'm not sure," I said. "But my Book of Shadows suggested it, and I'm not one to question my Book of Shadows."

"I wish I could see the book," she said.

"Someday soon," I replied. "When you're ready."

"When will that be?"

"I don't know, sugar pie. Seeing the future isn't one of my skills. But I think we'll know when it happens. All in good time, as they say. Now, you smell that?"

She wrinkled her nose and nodded.

"I'm sorry to say there's a good deal of stinkiness in brewing," I said with a laugh. "But are you ready for the next step? This is the exciting stage."

Selena gazed at me wide-eyed, then nodded. Oscar hopped up off the couch and bounded over to the kitchen.

"Oooh, I love this part! This is *awesome*!" he said.

I held my hand over the steaming cauldron, and using my ceremonial knife, my athame, I cut a tiny X in the palm of my hand. Then I let the blood drip into the cauldron: one, two, three drops.

There was a muffled *kaboom*, and steam surged out of the cauldron and coalesced under the ceiling. I looked up to see the amorphous face I knew would be there, looking down at me. Made of steam, it was there one moment, gone the next.

My guiding spirit. The Ashen Witch.

"Didja see that?" Oscar asked, excited. He was always thrilled when I called on the Ashen Witch. "That

was *awesome*! Mistress, is it time for movies and popcorn now?"

"Why don't you and Selena pick out the movie you'd
like? I want to pack for tomorrow, and then I'll pop
popcorn and join you."

"Okay, c'mon, Selena. Mistress?"

"Yes?"

"What am I supposed to do tomorrow while you're
gone? Why don't I just come with you, and that way
you don't have to worry about me?"

"Why would I worry about you? You're fine on your
own. I made you your favorite, mac 'n' cheese. All you
have to do is heat it up, and you can read or watch movies like any other night."

He harrumphed. "I can't watch movies *every* night.
What if you need me? I like to be useful."

"You could always do laundry," I suggested as I
took the sprite dust out of the oven and put it to cool
on a baker's rack. "There's always plenty of laundry."

He gazed at me for a long time, let out a long-suffering
sigh, then turned to Selena and shook his head.

"She just doesn't *get* me."

Selena shrugged, trailed him into the living room,
and suggested we watch *The Lord of the Rings*. This
engendered a long argument over whether the adapta-
tion held a candle to the original books. I was going to
stay out of this one.

I had worried about the Welcome coven sisters from
the moment I heard about the overnight, and now, with
the connection to Autumn, Renee, and Scarlet . . . my
worries seemed justified. I just hoped that my brew
and dust, and Sailor's presence along with mine, would
be enough to make sure the coven was safe. And who

knew? Maybe we would find the answer of how, and why, Autumn died.

First I aired out my sleeping bag; then I packed an overnight pack with pajamas and toiletries, along with salts, my athame, a few sprigs of vinca, and a length of sorcerer's rope. Just in case.

Once the liquid in the cauldron cooled, I filled two widemouthed mason jars full of protection brew and packed these along with salts, extra herbs, and the sprite dust in my woven shopping bag.

"Have either of you ever heard of a game called Clue?" I asked as I brought out the popcorn and heated oil in a deep pan.

Selena shook her head.

"I got no clue," Oscar said, then cackled.

"What?"

"What, what?"

"Seriously, you haven't heard of it?" I repeated. "It's a board game, I think."

Oscar blinked at me. "What, is this the start of a joke?"

"Why?" I asked as I poured the kernels into the pan and placed the lid on tightly.

"What are you *talking* about?" Selena asked. She was as pathetically out of touch as I was, but she had a shorter fuse.

"*Everybody* knows that game. It's like asking if I've ever heard of Monopoly."

"Oh! I've heard of that one!" I said, as pleased as a child winning a prize.

"Me, too!" Selena chimed in.

"*Everyone's* heard of that one," Oscar said, bottle-glass green eyes wide, with the exaggerated patience he used when trying to teach me something. "What did you two *do* when you were kids?"

"Learned how to brew, how not to accidentally burn down the school or cause my obnoxious classmates head injuries, and how to call on my guiding spirit in order to influence reality."

Selena nodded.

"Ah," Oscar conceded. "Well done, both of you."

I called Bronwyn and asked her if she had the game Clue. She did, so I asked her to bring it along for the overnight at the Rodchester House of Spirits. I didn't expect it would provide me with any clues, despite the name, but I was tired of being clueless.

When the popcorn was done popping, I poured plenty of melted butter over the top and sprinkled it with salt, and the three of us settled in to watch the movie.

Oscar had a point: It wasn't as good as the book, but we enjoyed it nonetheless.

Chapter 20

The next morning was busy, with folks stopping by who'd been disappointed to see Aunt Cora's Closet closed for the last couple of days. Bronwyn and I planned to leave early, but Maya and Loretta would stay and close the shop at the usual hour. Conrad was around for backup. Given the way my life was these days, I didn't like to leave anyone alone at the shop.

Selena's grandmother came to pick her up at ten. The girl stood stiffly while Bronwyn and I imposed good-bye hugs on her, and Maya shook her hand. The only overt affection Selena showed was for Loretta, who thumped her tail.

"We're allowed into the Rodchester House at six," Bronwyn explained when she left at noon to get her things together. "But there's a lot of traffic between here and San Jose, so I'd like to leave early. As long as we're all there by eight, though, we're fine. Thank you for letting us use the shop van, Lily! That way a bunch of us can go down together, Wendy and Starr and Winona and Averna. . . . Oh! I'm so excited!"

I had to smile at her enthusiasm, despite my trepidation. "I'm glad you can use the van. It's more fun to go as a group."

"Exactly! But at least you're coming with Sailor. Will Oscar be all right on his own?"

"He'll be fine." I ignored the imploring look in his pink piggy eyes. "I do believe he might do a little laundry with all his spare time."

When we approached Rodchester House, there was a young man standing at the old iron gates who checked a clipboard for our names, then instructed us to pull up the curved drive, past the mansion, and up to the left, where we could park "next to the purple van."

"Thanks," I said.

"Are you night security?" asked Sailor, leaning over me to speak through the driver's side window.

"Yeah, I'm on till nine. But there's a caretaker on the grounds, in the cottage."

"And what happens after nine?"

"We lock these gates. After all, here at the Rodchester House of Spirits, you can check *in* . . . ," he said, then lowered his voice to a sinister note, *"but you can't check out!"*

Sailor gave him a heavy-lidded look.

"Aw, I'm just kidding," he said with a nervous chuckle. "The back gate's modern and has a car-activated trigger, so you can leave, but you won't be able to come back in past eight at night."

"But no security on the grounds other than the caretaker?"

The guard looked as though he was searching for an answer. "Um . . ." He shrugged. "There's always 911. You're that worried, maybe you shouldn't be spending the night."

"Just wanted to know what the situation was," said Sailor.

"Honestly," said the guard, "every once in a while some of the college kids get drunk and dare each other to break in, but other than that we don't usually have much trouble. You wanna know what I think? People are too scared, afraid the widow's ghost'll come after them or something."

"Okay, thanks," said Sailor. I pulled slowly through the gates.

I had read about the Rodchester House of Spirits last night in the book I'd cadged from Aidan's office. It was full of photos, but the stories and pictures didn't do the mansion justice. In person it was much more impressive: a multistoried Queen Anne Victorian, painted a cheery yellow with maroon trim. There were turrets and spires, miles of pointy roofs, balconies, and gables. It was massive, more suited to a boarding school or a grand hotel than to the home of a lonely widow.

I didn't often "read" buildings from the outside, and even within them didn't feel things the way I did with clothes. But still, there was something forlorn about this house. It was grand and rich, and yet it seemed . . . so very sad.

But perhaps my imagination was running away with me, stoked as it was with the stories of the lonely Widow Rodchester searching for spirits at night and toiling away at her architectural drawings by day, seeking something she would never find in life: peace.

The ornate entry was framed by two mature palm trees, and the drive lined with formal manicured hedges. What I could see of the extensive gardens included mature trees, gravel walks, and topiary and statuary.

We drove around to the left and found the purple van. We didn't have to look any farther. As soon as we pulled up we were met by Bronwyn and her "wacky" coven.

"Oh, my goddess," she gushed, clapping her hands together under her chin. "We're all set up in the ballroom! There are *forty* bedrooms in the house, but we're in the *ballroom* so we can all be together; isn't that amazing? Oh, this place has forty-*seven* fireplaces and ten *thousand* windows! Can you believe this? We have the run of the place!"

The group gathered around and helped us to unpack, though we hadn't brought all that much: just sleeping bags and a small pack each, plus my shopping bag full of protection brew, the sprite dust, and some packs of herbs and stones. Just in case. Bronwyn had assured me the coven had snacks and dessert—and cocktails— covered.

"Too bad Oscar couldn't come!" said Val, one of the coven sisters.

"He really wanted to, but I made him mac 'n' cheese, so he's okay."

They laughed.

"So, really? We have the run of the whole mansion, and the grounds?"

"As long as we obey the signs," put in Wendy. Wendy was the head barista at Coffee to the People, and she was also one of the high priestesses of the Welcome coven. She liked to shop in Aunt Cora's Closet for vintage lingerie—slips, camisoles, garters, and the like—which she then wore as outerwear to complement her combat boots and tattoos and Bettie Page haircut. Despite her distinctive style—or perhaps because of it?—she was extremely practical and levelheaded, and I knew her to be one of the more law-abiding of the bunch. "Or else they reserve the right to send us out into the night."

"Well, then, by all means, let's obey the signs."

"And also velvet ropes," added Wendy. "We 'must respect the velvet ropes.' They have surveillance cameras as well, so they're pretty strict. There's still more than enough house to check out. This place is huge, as you can see." Her eyes swept over Sailor.

"Hey, he's not staying, too, is he?"

Her objection reminded me of the discussion I'd had with the squabbling witches yesterday.

"He won't be participating in the circle," Bronwyn said. "Sailor's here as our bodyguard."

"A psychic bodyguard?"

"Only the best for the Welcome coven," Sailor said with a slight shrug. "I like to think I can see 'em comin' and goin'."

"It's just in case," I said. "I wasn't sure . . . I don't know, haunted houses make me a little nervous. So Sailor and I wanted to make sure Bronwyn's birthday bash was just good, safe fun."

Wendy studied Sailor for another moment, then nodded slowly and said, "That's cool. Thanks."

"Well, now, let's all go inside and get you settled," said Bronwyn. "We were just having a quick arrival ceremony in this lovely grove of trees—which was where the Widow Rodchester used to sit and contemplate, apparently—but we're losing the light, so let's go inside! They don't use the actual front door here, except for very special occasions. And since we're practically like family already, we just use the side door!"

She looped her arm through mine and led me to the side entrance.

"According to Clyde, the front door was used maybe half a dozen times in all the years Sally Rodchester lived here. Can you imagine? In fact, she tried to use a different door every day and asked the servants to do so as well. They say when the bell tolled at midnight, she would take a different route to the Russet Room for her séances. Every night she would consult the spirits in her special séance room and then in the morning she would come out to the grove to analyze what the spirits had told her."

"And what sorts of things did they tell her?"

"Oh . . . all sorts of things! But mostly what to build next."

We passed through the small oak door. Inside, the hallway was cramped, low ceilinged, and lined with tongue-and-groove paneling painted a creamy white. Bronwyn, an intricate floor plan of the house in hand, led our group left, then right, this way and that. Up a few stairs, down some more. We passed myriad doors and windows, staircases, and narrow passages. "Labyrinthine" was the word that came to mind.

"I've always liked the servants' quarters in old homes, don't you?" Bronwyn asked as she led the way. She'd been here all of an hour but already seemed prepared to lead a tour. "The upstairs is quite grand, as you'll see, with paneling and stained glass windows and fine furniture, but if you asked me, the best parts of *Masterpiece Theatre* take place among the servants, in the basement service rooms and the kitchens. And speaking of which, there are *six* kitchens in the Rod-chester House."

"You already seem quite at home," I said. "And honestly, you have the run of the place?"

"Well . . ."

"As I was saying, and reminding my coven sisters, there are pretty strict rules," said Wendy, behind me. "All the velvet-rope places are off-limits, and of course any locked door. We're pretty much restricted to the regular tourist areas, though we get to check them out at our leisure, which, I'll admit, is pretty darned cool."

"They made us practically sign away our firstborn when we arrived," said Winona, another one of the group's high priestesses. The coven had several leaders, as any self-respecting nonhierarchical group would. Only recently had I learned that Winona, in addition to practicing witchcraft, was a very well-regarded paralegal in a high-powered law firm with offices in a high-rise on Market Street. Starr was a bookkeeper, and Kendall was a surgical nurse. We witchy women were to be found everywhere these days, it seemed.

We continued through the maze of hallways and chambers and past a second kitchen. Then we mounted a staircase made of very shallow steps and emerged in a broad wood-paneled hallway. There was a thick oriental runner on the polished inlaid oak floors, beautiful amber sconces glowing along the wall, and a row of stained glass windows overlooking the garden.

"Isn't it lovely?" asked Bronwyn. "This is a side hall, and right down here we take a left, and then we come upon the *ballroom*. I have to say, I'm glad to have the map in hand; I think it would be awfully easy to get lost in here, don't you?"

"I don't suppose it could go too badly," said Starr. "There are security cameras, and Clyde says they'll be watching."

"And Clyde is . . . ?" I asked as we headed down the hallway toward the ballroom.

"Clyde's the caretaker. He lives in a cottage on the grounds, so he'll be around if we need— Oh, here he is now!"

I was glad she pointed him out to me as a real person. Otherwise, I might have assumed he was a ghost. Not that he appeared to be floating or misty or fading in and out, but the fiftyish man sported an honest-to-goddess walrus mustache, and his portly physique was encased in an old-fashioned brocade waistcoat. I wondered what the well-coiffed boys at the David Gallery would make of him: I reckoned they'd either love his look—and therefore try to emulate it—or make fun of it.

"These are the rest of your folks?" he asked. He had a decided limp as he walked toward us.

"Yes, Clyde," answered Bronwyn. "The last two stragglers! Let me introduce Lily Ivory, and this is Sailor . . ."

"Just Sailor," he said as he stepped forward and put out his hand. "Nice to meet you, Clyde."

Clyde looked Sailor up and down. "Don't tell me they're lettin' menfolk into the covens these days?"

"That appears to be a matter of some contention," I murmured.

"Our dear Sailor isn't one of the *sisters*," said Bronwyn. "He's a protector. And so's Lily, in this instance. She won't be taking part in the circle. But they're both here as friends of the coven."

"Glad to hear it," Clyde said with a broad wink toward

Sailor. "Keep 'em in line, eh, Sailor? That way I don't have to get out of bed, come get you to quiet down with the giggling. I know how girls get."

"So, I take it the idea of the coven activities doesn't bother you?" I said, ignoring Clyde's blatant sexism.

"I've been caretaker to this house for several years now," said Clyde. "Our dear departed Mrs. Rodchester was quite a spiritualist herself, you know. She was a medium, I believe. Used her planchette—an early form of the Ouija board—every evening in the séance room to communicate with her husband and other friendly spirits. I do believe she'd be pleased as punch to welcome the likes of the Welcome coven."

"That's very accommodating."

"You know, we just started this overnight program and got lots of requests from people wanting to have bachelorette parties, that sort of thing. But I choose carefully—I don't like the idea of people staying here, hoping to be scared out of their wits or to scare their friends. Seems . . . disrespectful, don't you think?"

"I agree," I said. "I think that's a good way to approach this."

"Anyway, Bronwyn's got all the paperwork in the ballroom. You'll need to sign a release, if you don't mind—it's an insurance thing. And the girls can give you the floor plan map and inform you of all the rules. Remember: Always use the buddy system, and ring the bell if lost or anything goes wrong." He gestured toward a tasseled strip of heavy cloth hanging at the end of the hallway; I had seen several as we walked through the corridors. An old-fashioned bell pull, I gathered.

"We'll fill them in on everything," said Wendy.

"Good. I'm about to retire for the evening, now that you're all here. Just one thing I forgot to say: No sneaking around looking for the wine cellar."

The coven sisters looked at one another. Finally, Starr said: "There's a wine cellar?"

"There was, once," said Clyde. "If you didn't know, though, I probably shouldn't have mentioned it. But it comes up sometimes. It's in the architectural records. But one day Mrs. Rodchester went down there and she saw . . ."

Several of the women leaned forward.

"A *hand*print."

"A handprint?" repeated Wendy, clearly unimpressed.

"Now, that print was likely from one of the workers, but it scared her good and proper," said Clyde. "Took it as a sign. She had her boys seal it over, and no one's found it since. But some folks like to look for it."

"*Ooooh,*" said a few in the group, cracking jokes about old wine and haunted cellars.

"But I'm telling you, you don't have to go into any off-limits areas to get a sense of the spirits in this house. That's why we're called the House of Spirits. I'm not gonna deny there are"—he paused and seemed to be searching for the word—"*entities* here in this house, but that's why you're here—am I right?"

The coven sisters nodded. Clyde cast a rather nervous glance toward Sailor, who now stood in the corner with his arms crossed over his chest, glowering, reminding me of the man I'd first met in a dim bar. I imagined he didn't enjoy the idea of Clyde putting ideas of spirits in the heads of the coven members. Either that, or he just didn't like Clyde. Sailor would have made a terrible diplomat; he didn't hide his feelings.

"All righty, then. I'm going to take off," Clyde said, apparently anxious to go home, yet simultaneously loath to leave us alone. "Call me if anything goes drastically wrong, or you need anything. Except for hauntings—I do *not* want to be awakened because you get spooked by something otherworldly. Understood?"

We all nodded our agreement and bid him farewell, telling him we'd see him in the morning.

Bronwyn led us down the hall to the left and into the ballroom. A massive pipe organ occupied one wall, and on the opposite was a colossal fireplace. Three huge crystal chandeliers hung from the peak of a beamed cathedral ceiling. The green-and-red embossed wallpaper was old-fashioned and ornate, making me think of what Parmelee had told me about the William Morris poisoned wallpaper. On the floor were thick rugs but no period furniture, and overnight cases and sleeping bags were lined up at the base of the wall. Sailor and I dropped our bags with the others.

"They say there were no nails used in this room," said Bronwyn. "Just glue and wood pegs."

"Was that an occult thing?" Sailor asked, running his fingers lightly along the joinery of the wood finishes.

"They say it was for the acoustics, but who really knows?" Bronwyn answered. "Apparently the Widow Rodchester never entertained, so why would she have built a ballroom in the first place? Perhaps it was for the spirits! Oh, that reminds me, they were very specific about which bathroom we can use—apparently there's a little bit of a plumbing issue, moaning pipes, if you can imagine in such a place as this."

She and Starr looked at each other and said in unison, "Or so they say!"

"Maybe it's not the pipes at all," piped up Winona, "but something . . . *else*."

And then they burst into laughter.

A large folding table had been covered with a decidedly modern vinyl tablecloth and topped with the kind of smorgasbord I was accustomed to seeing when attending any coven function: from cookies to brownies to chips and dips. Crowning the spread, on a cut-glass cake plate, was a triple-tiered cake with pink icing that was listing radically to one side, so it had to be held up by a couple of strategically placed chopsticks.

"Had a little problem in the transportation end," explained Sylvie, another coven sister.

Bronwyn waved this off. "I think it's about the most gorgeous thing I've ever seen! I almost asked for cupcakes, but I think I ate my fill the other day. And this is homemade!"

On another folding table sat a large punch bowl and several bottles. This was, evidently, the cocktail area.

"We have the fixings for mojitos, whiskey whatever, and punch," said Wendy.

"What's in the punch?"

Several women looked at one another, grinned, and said at the same time, "Midnight margaritas!"

And then they all started repeating lines from yet another movie I had never seen.

"You haven't seen *Practical Magic*?" one of the women said, aghast. All conversation stopped as a coven of thirteen stared at me.

"Now, now," said Bronwyn. "We all know Lily's a little different. She's never even played Clue!"

I knew Bronwyn was just playing, and trying to make me feel included, but I could feel my cheeks burn. My childhood was somewhat stunted by the trauma of being shunned and "different."

Sailor, standing back against the wall near the door, caught my eye from across the room crowded with coven sisters. He gave me a slow, slight smile.

"Now, you two!" said Bronwyn. "I declare, y'all are just a pair!"

Wendy smiled. "Lily's accent's rubbing off on you, Bron. But she's right, Lily and Sailor. You know, there are forty bedrooms in this place. Maybe you ought to retire to one . . ."

"Very funny," said Bronwyn. "They're our protection tonight, remember? Speaking of which—do you really think we need protection? I'm no expert, but all the vibes here feel very warm and supportive to me. I love it! And isn't Clyde a lovely man?"

"You think *everyone's* lovely, Bronwyn," said Wendy.

"Well, sure, just about. I mean, not everyone, but most people are awfully likable."

"You're incorrigible." Wendy smiled and gave Bronwyn a quick hug. Though I respected Wendy, I had never felt close to her, so it was nice to see this side of the sometimes prickly barista. "I'd say our average age is hovering around forty-five. I haven't been a *girl* for some time. And yet he calls us 'girls' having a 'sleepover'?"

"But, so do *I*," said Bronwyn, as though truly confused as to Wendy's point.

"Yes, but . . ." Wendy glanced at me and Starr. "A little help here?"

"I agree Clyde has a little work to do on the whole woman thing," I said. "But at least he's open-minded about the work of the coven."

"True enough," said Starr. "And that's rare. This way there'll be no negativity for the circle!"

"Oh, Lily, I forgot to tell you," said Bronwyn. "As a special treat, we're allowed to call down the moon in the Russet Room."

"What's the Russet Room?"

"That's the séance room."

"Ah. This is where the Widow Rodchester communed with spirits every night?"

"The very one!"

Sailor was already locating the room on his map.

"All right," I said. "Let's take care of those waivers and have something to eat. Then Sailor and I will do a quick walk-through just to see what we're dealing with before you cast your circle. I know it's a tourist attraction and this is all fun and games, but . . . we want to keep it that way."

Chapter 21

Sailor led the way.

We walked in silence; back out through the formal entry hall, down one corridor, up another. I peeked into open rooms as we passed. Everything on this main floor was marked by the opulence of the Victorian era: rich, dark woods gleaming with French polish; heavy velvet and brocade drapes bordering intricate leaded and stained windows; Tiffany lamps hanging from the ceiling and studding the paneled walls. The fabrics were embellished with tassels and fringe, the furniture with knobs and stiles and curlicues.

Sailor would pause and check the map now and then at the junctions of hallways and foyers and parlors.

"You're good at reading that floor plan," I said.

"I like maps. No GPS for me. I need to be able to orient myself."

"Yet another of the reasons I like you. Do you feel anything?" I asked as we walked down one hall and around another. We went up one staircase that circled

back down, depositing us at the base of the stairs we had
just mounted, leading nowhere.

"The question, in a place like this, is what to feel
and what to ignore. It's jammed with sensations."

I heard a muffled banging. "Do you hear that?"

"Hammers."

"What?"

"According to what I've read, Sally Rodchester em-
ployed thirteen carpenters, twenty-four hours a day, for
thirty-eight years to build this place. They didn't put
down their tools until the moment she died." He turned
down a corridor, then opened a strange little door that
looked like a cupboard. We had to step over a foot-tall
threshold, but the portal opened onto a different section
of the house. "One or two are still on the job."

"Do you think all the coven sisters can hear it?
Or . . . is it just us?"

"Between the chatting and the margaritas, I'm sure
they'll hear only what they want to hear."

"Now you sound like the very sweet and sexist Clyde."

"We both know the Welcome coven is here for the
goodwill, not the icky stuff. Let's just make sure they
don't have to deal with any less welcoming than they are."

We walked down a broad hallway, and Sailor stopped
short in front of a huge mirror built into the wall. The
back was flaking slightly, as antique mirrors tended to
do, and the border was cracked in a few places.

"Now, this is interesting . . . ," he said, looking into
the mirror and then glancing behind us. Over and over.

"What is it?" I asked.

Sailor took me gently by the upper arms and posi-
tioned me in front of the mirror.

"Tell me what you see in the mirror."

"A very handsome man. Brooding and intense, but with a heart of go—"

"Cute. What do you see besides us. Anything else?"

I shook my head, wondering what I was supposed to see—or not. "All I see is the wall behind us, and an empty hat rack."

"Is there a crack in the wall?"

"No. Why?"

"I see a big crack in the plaster. And something that looks like a worker's smock hanging on the rack."

I craned my neck to look at the wall and the empty rack, then back in the mirror. What I saw reflected the here and now.

"Does that happen to you a lot? That you have visions in mirrors?"

"Not a lot, no. But it's something I've been working on. As you know, mirrors can be powerful. This is the only one I've seen in this house so far."

"You're right, I haven't noticed any others."

"If Sally Rodchester was a spiritualist, she might have avoided mirrors for that very reason. Too many issues with spirit portals, the backward world, that sort of thing. And right this moment, there's a worker standing behind us."

I whirled around but saw nothing but air.

Sailor chuckled slightly. "Don't let him spook you. He's just checking on the place. He put his heart and soul into this building."

"Quite literally?"

Sailor nodded. "I suppose you could say that. Okay, let's check on the Russet Room before the sisters draw down the moon. How much time do we have?"

I checked his watch. "They planned on midnight mountain time, which is ten o'clock here."

He gave me a questioning look.

"Bronwyn was born in that time zone. It's her birthday, so it's a thing. Apparently the staff even agreed to ring Mrs. Rodchester's tower bell to mark the occasion. Anyway, it's all margaritas and games until then."

"I didn't think covens formed the circle after drinking."

"They don't, not usually. It's sort of a special occasion. A birthday circle."

We passed through a second kitchen and a series of pantries. For a woman who lived alone and didn't entertain, the Widow Rodchester had quite the extensive party facilities. Sailor showed me a second-story door that opened to the outside with no stairs, another that opened onto a wall. Several windows led from one interior room to another, or were blocked by walls.

I started counting: thirteen panels in the ceiling of the dining room, thirteen lights in the chandelier, thirteen panes in the spiderweb-patterned windows, thirteen jewels studding the glass. We walked up a stairway with thirteen steps and down a corridor with thirteen sconces.

"There's someone in that corner, floating up near the ceiling," Sailor said quietly, maneuvering himself so he stood between me and the shadowy corner.

I didn't see anything . . . but I could feel the shiver, a feeling like a puff of cold air on the back of my neck.

"Keep walking," said Sailor.

"What was it?" I asked quietly when we reached the end of the hallway.

"Hard to say. A random occurrence, I think, nothing to worry about. An old house like this hosts all sorts of energy. Everything from residual memory in the walls to the occasional sentient spirit. I get a sense that woman may be one of the housekeepers; this house seems to have a way of keeping people around. She won't bother anybody."

"Oh. Good, then." I kept walking, but my nerves made me chatty. "Hey, remember when we went through the Paramount Theater after hours? That was fun."

He glared at me over his shoulder. "That wasn't 'fun.' You practically got me killed."

"Not really. I mean . . . Okay, maybe it did go wrong. But I was thinking about how you went with me and helped me even though you didn't even *like* me."

He muttered something.

"Sorry—what did you say?"

"I said I liked you."

"You did?"

"Of course I did." He paused and turned to me. "Why else do you think I went with you?"

"I thought Aidan forced you to go."

"He *told* me to go, but like I said, theaters are jammed with ghosts. They give me the creeps. I wouldn't have gone, but I knew you'd go without me if I refused. And I was worried about you."

"You were? Why didn't you say anything? You were always so . . . grumpy."

"I was smitten."

I had to smile. "*Smitten?* Seriously?"

He shrugged and looked away, as though embarrassed.

"You sure didn't *act* smitten."

"Yeah, well, you didn't exactly fit in to where I saw my life going. I may be a psychic, but I don't seem able to predict my own future. And you—you scared the hell out of me."

Sailor stopped suddenly outside a door. He cocked his head, waited for a moment, then consulted the floor plan in his hand.

"What's in there?"

"Something . . ." He glanced at his wristwatch and swore under his breath. "I don't want to get into this without enough time. The sisters are going to want to go call the moon soon. Let's go babysit the coven and then come back and check this out."

"Um . . . okay. What did you see? Or did you feel something?"

Sailor was already headed back the way we came. I trotted along to keep up with his long strides; he still held the map, and I feared I'd lose my way without it. Clearly something was on his mind. He was distracted; determined.

"Sailor?" I tried again. "Hold up a minute! What did you sense? Something dangerous?"

He stopped and turned to me. Lifted his hand and cupped my cheek. Gave me a half smile. "Not dangerous. I don't think. I'd rather not say more until we can come back and check it out properly. But it has to do with something I felt in Autumn Jennings's apartment."

The Welcome coven stood in a circle in the Russet Room, preparing to draw down the moon.

Sailor was guarding the door on the outside, and I looked down on the group from one of the odd interior windows that led from one space to another; it overlooked the room from a story up. On our quick walkthrough of the house we hadn't encountered the ghost of the Widow Rodchester, but I imagined if she was lurking she would approve of tonight's activities. From all accounts she spent every evening in this very room, conducting séances, calling on spirits, receiving messages. The bell in her tower used to toll, signaling midnight, while she tried to communicate with the beyond. I would think a well-intentioned coven drawing down the moon would be right up her alley.

Then again, she had lived a solitary life. And integral to the magic of the coven was the sense of community and connection.

My very favorite part of the ceremony was when they started to link hands, one after the other, touching their clasped hands to their hearts. It was a touching, bonding gesture. It linked them to one another and to the long line of powerful women who had walked Mother Earth throughout the ages.

As I watched, part of me wished I could join the circle. I had done so in the past, but only on specific occasions when I needed the strength of the coven behind me for going up against demons and the like. But although I had been learning to ask for help and rely on my friends, in general my brewing was a solitary affair. Notwithstanding Oscar and now, on occasion, Selena.

But coven magic was special. As I felt the hum arise from the circle, I realized I could never be a full member of this sisterhood. And I accepted that.

The coven moved through the stages of the circle, with first one priestess, Wendy, then another, Starr, taking the lead, invoking the Lord and Lady of the Woods, Quan Am, the Corn Mother, and Hulda. They called on several goddesses from different cultural traditions; it was an equal-opportunity belief system. Finally, Bronwyn moved to the middle of the circle and the women invoked the Mother, the Daughter, and the Crone, beseeching them to bestow their blessings through the light of the moon. Then Bronwyn went around the circle to receive a private blessing from each member, one by one.

As they bowed their heads in a final moment of worship, thanking the calm strength of the moon, as women have done throughout millennia, the bell of Mrs. Rodchester's tower began to toll.

And then Starr screamed.

Chapter 22

The door flung open and Sailor rushed into the room.

"Over there!" Starr exclaimed, pointing. "Did you see it?"

Sailor ran toward a pair of shutters that opened onto a kitchen the floor below. There were no stairs. The shutters were ajar.

"I saw someone, or some*thing*!"

"I saw it, too!"

"What was it?"

A cacophony arose from the group as the women milled around, gasping and exclaiming. I ran down the narrow stairwell and joined them in the room. By the time I arrived they were giggling with excitement and nerves, everyone talking at once.

"Was it a *spirit* of some sort?"

"More like a demon! It was so ugly, covered in scales, with a long snout . . ."

Sailor and I exchanged glances.

"And big ears, like a bat!"

"About how big was this creature, would you say?" I asked.

"I don't know, exactly; I just caught a glimpse—but not as big as we are."

"With green scales and a snout and long ears?"

"Big ears, and eyes that glowed green!"

"Yep, that'd be a common house demon," said Sailor in a grave tone. I gaped at him. When he met my eyes, I could see he was fighting to keep a straight face.

"A *house demon*?" said Wendy.

"Harmless little critter, by and large," he continued. "But he can be . . . mischievous, I guess is the best word. I think he was attracted by the energy of the coven. If I were you I'd go back to the ballroom and stay there for the rest of the night, just so you don't scare up anything else."

"Well," said Bronwyn, holding her hand over her heart. "This is the best birthday *ever*! If this doesn't call for a cocktail, I don't know what does!"

I encircled the entire ballroom with salt and sprinkled the protection brew at the four compass points: east, west, north, south. Then I lit a white candle and uttered a charm.

"Do you think that'll do it?" Starr asked Sailor.

He nodded. "Your average house demon won't cross the threshold of a protected room. No worries."

"Use the buddy system for the bathroom," I said. "And here, take the pouch of sprite dust when you go, just in case."

"Sprite dust?"

"It's helpful. Sometimes." It made spirits think of a

person as a sprite, and therefore they kept their distance. But I didn't think it was worth going into a long explanation. The dust was probably overkill, since we hadn't actually encountered anything particularly troubling in this bizarre house, but it couldn't hurt.

Then Sailor and I headed back to the strange door that had attracted Sailor's attention. As we traversed the house, I expected Oscar to show himself, but there was no sign of him.

"I can't believe he disobeyed me," I muttered.

"Really? You can't?" Sailor said in a sardonic tone.

"He does hate to be left out. Where do you suppose he is?"

"Probably exploring. It's a fascinating place. Given all I'm feeling, I can only imagine Oscar is sensing even more. It's sort of like a dog's sense of smell—Oscar can pick up on things way beyond human perception."

Since Oscar hated being compared to a dog, at Sailor's last comment I thought he might pop out of somewhere and surprise us, but all remained quiet. We climbed the steps to the third floor, and Sailor paused in front of the door that had caught his attention during our earlier exploration.

"What do you think is in there?" I whispered.

"One way to find out." Sailor reached out slowly, gripped the doorknob, and turned. The door opened onto a narrow stairway leading up into blackness.

"Do you suppose we're allowed to go up there?" I whispered.

"There's no velvet rope."

"True."

"There's something up there. And it's not on the

regular tour, so maybe there'll be less scattered energy and it'll be easier to tease out whatever it is. Want to wait for me here?"

"No, of course not. I'm your girl Friday, remember?"

He nodded and led the way up the stairs into the attic.

The roof was steeply slanted, so we could easily stand in the middle but had to crouch along the sides. The attic was dimly lit by the moonlight coming through several dormer windows. It was jammed with old furniture, cardboard boxes, and sheet-shrouded forms that looked, to my all-too-vivid imagination, like human-shaped creatures.

Sailor walked around the perimeter, pushing past an old armoire and a dusty globe.

"There's definitely something here. . . ." He sat cross-legged on the floor. "I'm going to take a moment."

"Of course. Sure."

I watched him. It bothered me, to tell the truth, to watch Sailor go into a trance. It took him away from me, however briefly. This was a part of his experience that I would never understand, something I could never be part of, rather like the sisterhood of the coven. On the other hand, my brewing was like that as well, a private, guarded thing. I supposed it was all right for each of us to keep part of our journey to ourselves. Alone didn't have to mean lonely, after all.

Still, it rankled that *Patience*, of all people, shared this with him.

I realized the banging sounds of the hammers had stopped. Silence enveloped us, broken only by the buzzing of an insect.

A honeybee flew by.

"Call me crazy," said Sailor finally, standing. "But this feels a lot like something I was feeling at Jennings's place."

"Are you saying Autumn Jennings was here? Or . . . *is* here?"

He shook his head and started pulling sheets off the cloaked items.

He revealed a couple of upholstered chairs and a dressmaker's dummy. And then a large black steamer trunk.

"This is it," he said.

"This is what?"

"This trunk holds the sense of the clothes we felt upstairs at Autumn's place." He opened the lid. The trunk was empty. "Come and feel."

I laid my hands on the shredded silk and threadbare velvet of the lining. Closing my eyes, I concentrated on sensing the vibrations of the fabric.

Sailor was right.

"But how . . . ?" I began.

"I guess that's the question," said Sailor. "What connection did Autumn have with the Rodchester House?"

"I don't know about Autumn, but Scarlet volunteered here once. And I was told Renee donated cupcakes for the event as well."

The bee buzzed lazily past me again. I held my hand out, and it landed.

"A little unusual to see a bee at night, isn't it?" asked Sailor. He was already moving toward the dormer window to see if he could get it open. It was stiff, but with effort he managed to lift the sash a few inches.

I held my hand out through the opening, and the bee tapped a little on my palm, then flew off.

"I've heard bees communicate through dance," Sailor said, his voice thoughtful. "Is she trying to tell you something?"

"I think it's possible," I said, realization dawning. Selena had mentioned bees the other day as well, when she gave Loretta a bee charm for her collar. "I wonder . . . Apparently the name of the woman who owned this trousseau, the woman who died because of the curse, was nicknamed Bee."

"And what do you think she's trying to tell you?"

"I have no idea. But . . . this reminds me of something I meant to ask you about: I had a vision that included a thread being pulled through a pearl, and a crown of parsley, a cup of snakes, and a phrase: *coincidentia oppositorum*. Any idea what that all means?"

"Since when did you start having visions?"

"I don't normally. But I was in Aidan's vision chamber and they came surprisingly easily."

"What were you doing in Aidan's vision chamber?"

"Waiting for the mayor."

Sailor looked at me for so long I started to feel defensive and was about to assert my right to be in Aidan's office whenever I darned well wanted to when he nodded.

"Okay. The thing about visions, in my experience, is that they can mean different things to different people— the symbols are incredibly personal. To some, a rose is about beauty, or love; to others, the thorns indicate danger."

"That makes sense. But I can't think what a pearl being threaded might mean."

"The pearl can be the world, the globe. The thread is

the energy that runs through its axis, the special energy that your kind tap into."

"My kind?"

He nodded. "A crown of parsley is female, the cup of snakes male. The *coincidentia oppositorum* is all about the primordial forces of male and female coming together, the All-Mother and All-Father."

"Seriously?"

"As I said, it's usually a personal interpretation. But that phrase was pretty specific."

"True. So . . . what does it all mean?"

He shrugged. "Beats me."

I chuckled. "Okay, back to the bee, or the young woman named Bee: Isn't this your area? Why isn't she talking to *you*, if she's hanging around?"

"These things don't work according to the rules you and I live by, as you know," said Sailor. "She might be sending you a sign because she knows you're the most likely to be able to help her. Or it might not be her at all, but something altogether different."

"Like what?"

"Your guiding spirit, letting you know you're on the right path." He shrugged. "Or knowing you, you could be manifesting it, somehow, because you have bees on the brain. There are a few things we could try, next time a bee comes by, to see if we can communicate. But for now, let's head back to the coven."

I started down the stairs, with Sailor following close behind.

"That's a disturbing thought," I said. "If I start manifesting everything on my brain—"

A man stood on the landing, glowering at us.

Chapter 23

I screamed. Just a little. More like an undignified squeak, really.

Then I realized it was Clyde, the caretaker. His hair stuck out from the side of his head slightly, as though we had gotten him out of bed.

"The attics are *off*-limits," he groused. "Don't make me send you and your friends home."

"Sorry," I said. "It didn't explicitly say so, and there was no velvet rope . . ."

He swore under his breath. "This is what I told the higher-ups when they came up with this harebrained scheme: that we needed to test it out. You never know what tourists will come up with. Listen here: The attics and basements and outbuildings are *all* off-limits, you got that? You kids have one hundred and sixty rooms in the regular house to look through, and you go up into the *attic*?"

"We apologize," I said.

Sailor just held the man's gaze until Clyde looked away.

"How did you know we were here?" I asked.

"You tripped an alarm."

"I really am sorry we got you out of bed. The truth is," I ventured, considering the respect the caretaker had shown for witchcraft and spiritualism, "Sailor is a talented psychic. He was feeling for spirits."

His rheumy eyes lit up. "Really?"

Sailor gave a slight inclination of his head.

"*Huh*. You feel stuff here? Like . . ." His eyes rolled upward. "Up in the attic?"

"Maybe," said Sailor. Mr. Cooperative.

"Could I ask you something?" I ventured. "There's a steamer trunk up there that looks like it used to have something in it. Was it recently emptied out?"

If possible, Clyde looked even more disgruntled.

"Yes. It's a shame, a real shame. People have no respect for this place. The only consolation is that what goes around, comes around. They won't be sleeping well at night, I'm sure about that."

"What happened?"

"There was a volunteer workday; that's all we can think of. That's the last time that section of the attic was opened as far as anyone knows. But we still haven't figured out how they managed to get all the stuff out of the house without being noticed."

"What kinds of things were in the trunk, do you know?"

"It was a trousseau. A *cursed* trousseau."

When I informed him that I might well know where the stolen trousseau had ended up, Clyde invited us to one of the kitchens still in use by the staff.

"The trousseau was acquired by the Widow Rodchester not long before her death, in the late 1920s," explained Clyde. "She purchased it in a lot, along with some other items, from a spiritualist dealer she knew in San Francisco."

He set steaming mugs of tea in front of us, then joined us at the large farmer's table.

"According to legend, the trousseau was never put to use because the young fiancée died on the eve of her wedding. Her intended always believed he had been cursed by a shoeshine man. Here's an interesting factoid: He included his lacrimatory in the trousseau. Some say that's why there was so much power there, though I don't know if that's true."

"A lacrimatory? I just learned what that was the other day," I said.

Clyde nodded. "Sort of an interesting mourning ritual, don't you think?"

"Very. And you have no idea how the trousseau was taken from the attic?" I asked. "You think it was one of the volunteers?"

He shrugged. "A lot of people go in and out on volunteer workdays. Those volunteers are good people, usually architecture students, that sort of thing. And it took a while to figure it out, even. It wasn't until we were moving things around up there and we realized it wasn't heavy enough. We opened it and saw the clothes had been taken. It was always chock-full of ball gowns and lingerie and linens, back when."

"Do you happen to know if a woman named Renee Baker was here on that day? She makes cupcakes . . . ?"

"Oh, I do remember some wonderful cupcakes! But I don't know who brought them."

"How about a young woman, named Scarlet?"

"I really don't recall names. Like I said, the administration didn't want to file a police report. They're very careful about what kind of press Rodchester House gets. Hauntings, creepy things like that? No problem. But any real-world issues, like backed-up plumbing or stolen items, they'd prefer to keep it on the down low."

"Was there a list of volunteers? Would it be possible for us to check for their names?"

"I don't know . . . I suppose I could look them up, if you'd like. A Renee Baker, you said?"

"And Scarlet Funk."

He grumbled about what he did for the guests of Rodchester House. Not that I didn't see his point; he had probably worked all day, it was now after midnight, and some stranger was asking him to look something up on the computer. But to my surprise, he agreed.

"We use an old pantry as the office. It's just around the corner—be right back."

"Thank you so much. And again, sorry we trespassed."

"S'okay," he said as he shuffled out. "Be right back."

I took another sip of my tea.

Moments later, we heard the sound of a body crashing to the floor.

We rushed out to find Clyde sprawled on the floor in the corridor.

I knelt beside him—there was blood on the back of his head, but he was conscious and swearing a blue streak.

Sailor ran down the hall and disappeared around the corner.

"Clyde, what happened? Are you all right? Don't move; I'll call 911."

"No! No, please don't call anyone. Remember what I was just saying about the administration? They hate this sort of press. I could lose my job."

"But you're hurt," I began.

"I've had much worse, believe you me. I'm an old farm boy; I know what a concussion feels like. This was just a little knock; I'd have gone after him myself except I lost my footing, twisted my bum ankle, went down like a sack of potatoes."

"At least let me take you to the hospital," I suggested. "We'll say it was an accident."

"You should go follow after your friend, see if he needs help. Don't bother about me."

I *was* worried about Sailor, but I felt torn.

"Didn't you say there were cameras? Is security watching?"

He made a disgusted noise. "You're looking at 'security.' And the cameras are there, but they're not turned on. Too expensive. They're just there to make people think they're being watched."

That was no help.

"Go on, then," Clyde urged. "Honestly, girlie, I'm fine. Go help your friend."

I heard a far-off banging and thumping, and a muffled noise that sounded like a shout. I ran down the hall in the direction Sailor had gone, stroking my medicine bag and mumbling a charm under my breath.

The hallway ended in a T. *Which direction should I go?*

I felt, rather than saw, a spirit beckoning me left. Maybe it was my imagination, but I followed my intuition. I ran down around the corner and thought I heard another noise, closer now. I felt cold puffs of air, hints of someone nearby, watching.

I ran through a solarium, a parlor, a library. Endless hallways.

Rounding a corner, I found an exterior door standing wide-open. There was another shout. Outside, I found Sailor crumpled on the gravel drive.

Oscar was chasing someone across the dark yard. The shadowy figure jumped onto a motorcycle and raced away seconds before Oscar caught up. He continued to run after it, but the machine zipped out of reach.

By the time I reached Sailor, he was already sitting up, swearing, holding a hand over his eye.

"What happened?"

"Why is it I always wind up wounded when I'm near you?"

"Are you okay?" I couldn't see well in the dark of night. The moonlight gave everything a silvery, monochromatic quality.

"I'll be fine," he said, sounding angry. "Feel like an ass, though. He jumped me, knocked me good, then managed to lay me low long enough to get away. I'm lucky Oscar showed up, after all."

I looked around, but my familiar was nowhere to be seen. I wondered whether he was still chasing after the motorcycle.

I helped Sailor stand, and he put one arm around my shoulders as we walked back toward the house. He winced and held his side, as though his ribs hurt.

Just as we were approaching, the Welcome coven poured out of the door like so many bees from a hive. With them was Clyde, who was limping but was being helped by Winona.

They were all talking at once.

"Oh, my goddess!" exclaimed Bronwyn. "What in the *world*? We saw you fighting from the ballroom windows, but it took us forever to find the right door to come out and help!"

"Who *was* that?" asked Starr.

"What's going on? Are you hurt?"

"Wow, I guess we really did need a bodyguard," said Wendy. "Are you all right? Hey, Kendall's a nurse; let her take a look at you."

"Should we call the police?"

"Hey, Sailor, if you're psychic, how come you didn't see this happening?"

"He and Lily did say they had a bad feeling about tonight, to be fair. . . ."

"I think I saw the house demon again! Such a spooky, ugly little thing!"

"How about I invite the whole coven back to my place, and we get ourselves settled down?" Clyde asked. "I've got a first-aid kit, the whole shebang."

"I tell you what, Bronwyn," I said once we were all sitting in Clyde's comfortable sitting room in the care-taker's cottage. Kendall was attending to the men's wounds, and Wendy passed around a flask. I took a good swig. "You throw a heck of a birthday party."

"It could have been Scarlet," I said around a yawn as I drove us home the next day. By the time we bid fare-well to Clyde, we'd managed to get only a few hours of sleep before morning. "Maybe she's not sick at all. Maybe that's just a cover-up, and she came down here on Brad's motorcycle and attacked us."

"Attacked *me*."

"You and Clyde. I meant 'us' in the sense of the royal 'we.'"

He reached out and tugged my ponytail. "Princess Witch?"

"How are you feeling?" I asked. I knew he had a headache and his eye throbbed, but so far he had refused to take anything for it. I was pretty sure it was because he wanted to stay sharp, just in case something else happened in the Rodchester House of Spirits.

He shrugged. "I'll survive. My ego's taken something of a beating, though."

"Don't be ridiculous. *I'm* the one who put you in harm's way, after all. And you went running after that assailant like you were Superman."

"Anyway, there is no way Scarlet was the one who attacked me. Whoever I was fighting was a man," said Sailor.

"Did he have a beard?"

"No. But with all due respect to some truly amazing women I've known in my life, it would have taken a heck of a woman to fight like that. I thought you said Scarlet was small."

"True."

"A petite woman with enough martial arts training could take me down, but we were grappling old-fashioned-style. Also, in that kind of situation I would have felt if it had been a woman."

"Psychically, women feel different?"

"Well, yes, but in this case I was referring to feeling other things. Girlie things."

I had to smile. "Girlie things?"

"I'm telling you, we were rolling around on the ground together."

"Ah. Gotcha."

"Even if not, I'd hate to think I couldn't smell the difference. You women have a certain scent about you."

"I doubt ne'er-do-wells put on perfume when they go for a brawl."

"I'm not talking perfume."

"Oh. Back to the point: When Scarlet first served me with papers, there was someone waiting for her on the bike."

"Are you thinking boyfriend Brad?" said Sailor.

"I guess. But why would Brad come all the way to the Rodchester House of Spirits to attack us? And how would he even know we would be here?"

"You mentioned it when we met with him."

"I did?"

He nodded.

"*Huh.* Okay. My bad. But clearly Brad's not the only person who rides a motorcycle. And what reason would he have to attack us?"

"Maybe he didn't want us to discover Scarlet had stolen the trousseau."

"I suppose. Speaking of which, I wonder how she managed *that* trick."

"Or," said Sailor, "it could be someone who was hired to harass us. Or most likely, someone completely unrelated. Brad's not the only person who rides a motorcycle, after all. Lots of people do, for the same reason as me."

"Because you look hot in your motorcycle gear?"

"Because of great gas mileage, easy parking, and lane splitting. As Clyde said, kids break in from time to time and dare each other to go into Rodchester House.

It could have been some kid hopped up on something, then just trying to get away."

"Possibly. I'm still suspicious of Brad, though. And you thought he was lying, remember?"

"Tell you what. When we get back to the city I'll go have a little chat with Brad. I got in a few good hits so he should have some bruises, and I'll use a little Vulcan mind control on him."

I stared at him.

"Sorry—forgot you wouldn't get the reference. I'll see if I can read anything from him, get a sense from him, at least."

A head popped up in my rearview mirror.

I shrieked and swerved, and a bag of leftover cookies went flying.

"Oscar! *Hell's bells*, you scared me!"

Sailor chuckled. "Sorry. I saw him when I put the bags in the back. I thought you knew he was there. You owe me ten bucks, by the way."

"How would I know he was there?" I asked, my voice still strident.

Oscar didn't make a peep but crawled back into the footwell so passersby wouldn't see him.

"Hey, thanks again for your help last night, Oscar," Sailor said.

I glanced in the back and saw my gobgoyle shrug in reply.

"Didn't I tell you not to come?" I demanded, still annoyed.

Grunt.

"You're not a pig at the moment, Oscar. Why are you grunting?"

I glanced back again to see him shrug. This was

unusual for my talkative familiar. Something occurred to me: "Are you okay, Oscar? Were you hurt?"

"No, course not. A bozo like that isn't gonna hurt a guy like Oscar." There was a slight pause. "No offense, Sailor."

"None taken."

"What's bothering you, then?" I asked.

He mumbled something I couldn't understand.

"What?" I asked.

"I *said* they thought I was *ugly*."

"Who . . . ?"

"Everybody," he muttered.

"You mean the coven sisters?"

"Yeah."

"Oh . . . They didn't mean it, Oscar. They were just so startled to see you in your natural form, is all. They didn't expect it, and they were already amped up just being at Rodchester House. They were excited to be scared, in a way."

More silence from the backseat.

I met Sailor's eyes.

"They're cowans, Oscar," said Sailor. "As a general rule, we humans are way too caught up in the outer shell; we're swayed by external beauty, and beauty's defined by the wrong things. For instance, you were certainly a beautiful sight when you came to help me."

"I woulda caught up with him, no problem, if I still had my *wings*," he said in a sullen reference to the wings I had destroyed in an attempt to save him a while ago.

I sighed.

"Hey, it was *awesome* the way he screamed when he saw me—you remember, Sailor?" Oscar said, his voice regaining his familiar upbeat tone. "Heh!"

"It was truly awesome," Sailor said with a nod. "And *you* are truly awesome."

"Ya know somethin', mistress? I mean, I know he lost the fight and all, but this Sailor guy just might be a keeper."

Unfortunately, Oscar couldn't tell us what the assailant looked like, or even recall the color and make of the motorcycle. It had been too dark, and it had all happened too fast. When we got back to Aunt Cora's Closet he made a beeline for his pillow, and I brewed a pot of very strong coffee to help motivate me to open the shop. Brownyn had the day off, but Maya arrived with Loretta, and Conrad was at his post outside on the curb.

I gave Maya a rundown of the sleepover as we straightened the racks and shelves, preparing for the day's customers.

"This is why I opted for empanadas," she said. "Is Sailor going to be okay?"

"He has a black eye but otherwise seems fine." I had dropped a decidedly grumpy Sailor at his apartment in Chinatown. "I think I was annoying him by suggesting medical care, or even willow bark tea for his headache. I guess it's not manly to feel pain."

She smiled. "My brother's like that. Oh, hey, Mom's coming by today to take measurements next door at Sandra's. She talked to the landlord and I guess they're ready to go. She's so excited about the new shop."

"As am I. It'll make a great addition to Aunt Cora's Closet, and to the Haight."

"It was an inspired idea. Thank you. Also, it looks like Loretta has won over everybody's hearts and minds at the Bayview house. Since she's up for grabs . . . I think she has a new home."

"Oh, that's wonderful news!" I said, getting down on the ground to pet Loretta's silky coat. She thumped her tail at me.

"I put Selena's new charm on her collar," Maya said. "She's got quite the collection now. I wondered if the jingling would bother her; but *nothing* seems to bother her."

I scratched Loretta's neck and checked out her charms. There was a little soccer ball, a retro dress—appropriate for a vintage clothing store—a top hat, a Maltese cross, the state of California, a witch's hat, a book, the shiny silver bee, and a tiny little almond-shaped bottle.

"It occurred to me to wonder if the charms might have significance," said Maya. "Like, beyond just being cute. I noticed a witch's hat, and that little cross . . . you once said the Maltese cross was used as protection."

"That's true. Where I'm from, people put it on their barns so witches wouldn't curdle the milk."

"Why would you curdle anyone's milk?"

"I never quite figured that part out. Like a lot of traditions that get handed down over generations, the original intent might be outdated, though the behavior remains. The Maltese cross never put *me* off—I'll tell you that much. But then, I didn't bother with my neighbors' milk. Except that one time, but that was totally called for."

Maya smiled. A pair of young women came into the store and started trying on hats, so we suspended our discussion of witchcraft and got back to work, sorting through inventory and helping our customers find the perfect vintage outfit.

A few hours later, the phone rang. It was Inspector Carlos Romero.

"Someone named Scarlet just tried to sell Riesling a ball gown. Riesling said she didn't look very good."

"Where is she?"

"On her way to the hospital. UCSF. I'll meet you there."

Chapter 24

I paused and stroked my medicine bag to ground myself before passing through the sliding glass doors. Hospitals are difficult places for most people to enter; repositories of pain and anxiety and grief, the halls are also crowded with confused spirits and errant vibrations. So for sensitive folks, they're even more challenging. Though I can't communicate with the dead, their energy is attracted to mine. Just as in museums, but more so, I could feel the whispery sensations along my skin, like cold little puffs of breath on my arms and the back of my neck, seeking recognition, yearning for connection.

I entered the ICU waiting room. A middle-aged woman sprawled on a bank of chairs, sleeping. A man stared blankly into space; two young children were coloring together on the floor at his feet. A television tuned to a news channel was muted, the closed captioning informing whoever was interested that the president had signed a new bill into law.

Beside the door leading to the actual ICU, a sign over a telephone told family members they must speak with the nurse before entering.

Carlos stood in the middle of the room, gazing up at the television. He looked exhausted.

"Hi," I said.

"You made good time," he said in a low voice, checking his watch. "The nurse is supposed to notify us when she's able to talk."

"What happened?"

"Like I told you, she showed up at Parmelee Riesling's place. I assume she knew about her from Jennings. She tried to sell the gown, said she needed cash. She was experiencing visible symptoms, so Riesling tried to explain to her that she needed to see a doctor, and she collapsed right there. Riesling called an ambulance, and then me."

"Do they think she'll be all right?"

He shrugged. "Sounds complicated. There's a chelating process they can do, but there could be lasting kidney damage, neuropathy, all sorts of nasty stuff. Poor kid. Anyway, apparently it's not difficult to test for arsenic. Riesling has already determined the ball gown was loaded with the poison."

"Does she still have it? Could I look at it?"

He reared back and fixed me with a look. "What are you planning to do, feel for vibrations? This thing's so loaded with arsenic it'd be like hugging a toxic powdered donut. Matter of fact, she already called in hazmat to deal with it. They'll take it to the lab, redo the tests, but I don't doubt Riesling's findings."

"Hard to believe the old dyes would still be so toxic. After all, this wasn't slow; it was acute poisoning, right?"

"Here's the thing," Carlos said, dropping his voice to a whisper. "Riesling said this amount of arsenic was way off the charts, much more than what she would have expected to find."

"Which means?"

"It looks like someone *added* arsenic to the gowns. Sprinkled it on like so much Parmesan cheese on pasta."

"Are you hungry, by any chance? All your metaphors are food based."

"Skipped breakfast."

"Oh! I have leftovers from the birthday sleepover." I brought out a pack of brownies Starr had wrapped up for me.

"That looks delicious. Thanks." He took the goods from me and started to munch, letting out a soft appreciative moan.

"Did you have anything for lunch?"

"I might have missed that, too."

"Tough day? Or . . . night?"

"Not as tough as some. But busy, definitely. Homicide in the Tenderloin."

"And now you're pulling overtime with me."

He shrugged. "It's a living."

"So, what happens now?"

"As we both know, this isn't my case, so it's not up to me. But I think Stinson is going to have to reopen the homicide investigation. I imagine now he'll be going through Jennings's place with a fine-tooth comb." Carlos cast me a glance. "You didn't happen to remove any pertinent evidence from the scene, did you?"

"I looked through a few things, but that's about it."

"Good. We'll see if they come up with any clues

from her place. They really should have processed the scene long ago, for crissakes, if they had the time to go through Aunt Cora's Closet. . . ." He trailed off, shaking his head.

A nurse came out. "Inspector? She's awake and able to answer a few questions. But please remember: She's a very sick girl."

"Let's go," Carlos said to me. He was clearly going out on a limb here; surely it would get back to Inspectors Stinson and Ng that Carlos Romero had been here with a woman in tow. But I was going to leave that to Carlos. He was smart, and more than able to take care of himself. And this was my chance to get some answers.

The air in the ICU was loaded with spirits. I could feel them. Everything was white and sterile looking, and everywhere I turned there was the incessant *beep*ing and *bloop*ing and *whoosh*ing of machines, nurses with running shoes and scrubs in pastel colors and cartwheeling teddy bears.

Scarlet was almost unrecognizable as the young woman I had seen a few days ago. Her skin was ashen; her eyes had dark circles around them; they darted around the room, as though agitated. She had tubes sticking out of her arms and oxygen in her nose.

Carlos introduced himself and told her we wanted to help but that she would need to be honest with us. His voice was incredibly gentle, yet firm, in a tone that would have gotten me to confess any number of things.

Scarlet seemed to sense the same thing. She started talking.

"I'm so sorry. I know we shouldn't have done it. . . ."

"Done what?"

"We stole the trousseau from the House of Spirits. They said it was cursed but we didn't believe them, so we took it."

"How did you manage it?" I asked. "That was a lot of stuff."

"We were at the house for volunteer day, so we just packed everything up in cardboard boxes labeled plates and napkins and stuff and carried them out with the caterer. It was easy. And she paid us well."

"Who paid you?" asked Carlos.

She hesitated.

"You need to tell us so we can help you," he said.

"Autumn Jennings."

"Autumn paid you to steal the trousseau? Why? How did she even know about it?"

"I guess it was once in her family, or something?" She started to cry softly, tiny tears glistening at the corners of her eyes and rolling down her temples. She turned to stare at me. "Please, I know you killed Autumn. Please take the curse off me!"

"I didn't . . ."

She was getting agitated. The indicators on the machine beeped as her blood pressure and pulse ratcheted up.

"Is that why you ran from me that day with the dogs? You think *I* cursed Autumn?"

"And you're killing me now because I stole the trousseau! I'm sorry; I needed the money!"

"It wasn't me, Scarlet, I promise you," I began. "Was Brad the one who helped you to steal the trousseau?"

She shook her head and started to cry in earnest. The nurse came scurrying in, checking her vitals.

"You're going to have to leave," she said sternly.

"But—," I began.

"Come on, Lily. In here, the medical professionals reign," Carlos said. He turned to the nurse. "Thank you for letting us speak to her."

"Feel better, Scarlet," I said over my shoulder as Carlos led me out. I doubted the young woman heard me—or would accept my good wishes—caught up as she was in her own emotions and illness.

I insisted on taking Carlos to the cafeteria and buying him a sandwich, a small bag of chips, and a mango smoothie. I got myself a cup of coffee. We took our orange plastic tray to a table by the window, which looked out over a meditation garden.

He wolfed down half the sandwich before he said a word.

"I worry about you sometimes," I said. "I know you're a one-man army against the ne'er-do-wells in San Francisco, but you won't do anyone any good if you're six feet under."

"At least I know you'll still talk to me when I'm in the grave, right?"

"I really don't have that kind of talent. You'll be stuck with Sailor."

"*That's* a thought that'll fester. Now, just for the record," he said, washing down another bite of sandwich with a swig of the smoothie and sitting back in his chair, "you did not in fact place a curse upon either Autumn Jennings or Scarlet Funk, right?"

"Can you believe she's called Scarlet Funk? On the other hand, it'd be a great band name."

"Answer the question, please."

"*No*, Carlos, of course I had nothing to do with placing a curse upon anyone. I never hex."

He stared at me for a long moment.

"*Almost* never. And certainly not in this case."

"Why would Scarlet think that you had?"

"I've been wondering that myself. Maybe she heard the trousseau was cursed, which seems to be the rumor around the neighborhood. And then maybe she heard I was a witch, and put it all together . . . ?" I trailed off and sipped my coffee. "I really don't know."

Carlos finished the rest of his sandwich and chips.

"What really bothers me, though, is that it doesn't make any sense. Why would Autumn Jennings have hired someone to steal a cursed trousseau, especially if she had family ties to it somehow? Unless . . . it's possible Jamie told her to get hold of it, and he would use it to remove the curse."

"Let's back up so you can explain that one to me. Who's Jamie?"

I told him about my meeting with Jamie and what we had found out at Rodchester House about the trousseau being stolen.

"And why would it have wound up in the attics of Rodchester House of Spirits?"

"The Widow Rodchester was a spiritualist, and interested in all sorts of occult things. It was rumored to be cursed long ago, so I suppose she just collected it. It's hard to tell since it wasn't intact in its trunk anymore, but it didn't look as though she'd done anything with it. Maybe she was keeping it in the attic hoping to prevent it from harming anyone. Who knows?"

"Okay, so far the story is this: Autumn Jennings

thinks she's cursed because everyone she loves dies. So she contacts a little weasel named Jamie and maybe he tells her to steal this trousseau because it's the cause of the curse. She hires Scarlet and her boyfriend to steal it, so Scarlet's made sick, too. How's the boyfriend?"

"Brad seemed fine the other day, but it might be worth checking on him again."

Carlos nodded, pushing the tray away from him. He'd eaten every bite. "The only problem with this little story is that they aren't in fact dying of a curse; they're dying of arsenic poisoning. *Intentional* arsenic poisoning."

"Good point. Carlos, how are you going to convey all of this information to Stinson and Ng?"

He cocked his head. "Not sure yet. But they need to know everything, so I'll find a way. I'll for sure insist they test the entire trousseau, see what we're dealing with."

"There were some stockings in a box there, too—I think they should be sure to check everything in that place. Just in case."

Carlos nodded. "And I'm going to need the contact information for this Jamie fellow."

"All I have is a phone number, and I was told it was a burner."

Carlos lifted his eyebrows slightly. "This guy a drug runner?"

"No, just a run-of-the-mill curse lifter. He's unlicensed, but he promised to get the paperwork started."

"I'm staying out of that," said Carlos. "Anything else?"

"I wonder . . . it's probably nothing, but . . ."

"Tell me."

"Jennings's next door neighbor, Renee Baker—"

"This the cupcake lady?"

"Yes, that's her. She's interested in moving into Autumn's shop space."

"And?"

"The body's not even cold, as they say. Isn't it a little soon?"

He shrugged. "The real estate market these days—you snooze, you lose."

"I suppose."

"You think she's suspicious in some way?"

"I was just thinking, wouldn't it be awfully easy to put arsenic into a cupcake and then blame it on old dresses?"

"I suppose, if you *knew* about the old dresses."

"She had heard about the alleged curse on the trousseau. Not sure if she knew about the arsenic per se, but . . ."

"But you're suspicious."

"Just thought I should mention it. Just in case. Maybe Stinson and Ng should poke around a little."

I wanted to talk with Jamie before the cops contacted him and scared him off. This was the sort of thing that drove Carlos insane. But this wasn't even his case, and I wasn't entirely sure Stinson and Ng would follow up, at least in a timely fashion. And a burner implied it would be tossed soon, didn't it? So then if I wanted to talk with him I'd have to harass Russians out in the Avenues for a while trying to track him down.

Or worse, try to get Renee to cough up his information. But that look she had given me when I mentioned him to her in Aunt Cora's Closet . . . it still made me shiver.

There was something about her. Could she, indeed, be casting, somehow? Those cupcakes would be an effective way to influence folks, if she was skilled with brewing or botanical charms. Sailor and Oscar and I had eaten them without any ill effects, but if she set out to influence someone, it would be an easy way to do so. But . . . why?

Could she be the reason the police had largely avoided looking at Jennings's place?

Or was my admittedly overactive imagination going wild? I used to think I could distinguish magical from nonmagical types, but over the past several months I'd learned just how easily I could be fooled. And it was true that my skittishness was a learned behavior. I was going to have to thank my mother, my father, and my hometown for teaching me that it was dangerous to trust people.

Luckily I had Graciela to teach me otherwise; else I'd truly be in trouble.

I called Jamie and left a message that I had some news about the necessary licensing. I figured I'd keep the satchel as the ultimate threat, though I still didn't know exactly how that worked.

He called me back at Aunt Cora's Closet in twenty minutes.

"Meet you at Ghirardelli Square in an hour," he said. "At the Mermaid Fountain."

"Right outside the chocolate factory?" I asked.

"That's the place."

When I hung up, Oscar was sitting right in front of

me, eyes huge and butt wriggling in excitement. No doubt he'd heard those magic words: chocolate factory.

Maya laughed. "Methinks *somebody* wants to go for a ride."

"I suppose you're right. You're okay here by yourself?"

"Sure; Conrad's outside, and Mom has been in and out all day. And I've got Loretta for company, of course."

"All right, see you in a bit. Chocolate in hand."

Chapter 25

"You have a thing for tourist spots, I see," I said as we approached. I had called to tell Sailor where I was headed, and he insisted on accompanying me.

"Force of habit," Jamie said with a shrug. "Lots of people around, no locals to recognize a person."

I supposed, given the way my life was heading, I should spend more time with the criminal element and learn some basic skills such as this.

Jamie was sitting on a low brick wall by a big fountain with a white paper bag in one hand. He held it out: "Chocolate?"

"No, thanks. I'll buy some before we leave."

He took an irregular chunk of chocolate out and broke off a piece. "Ghirardelli. Not really the best chocolate in the world, but it brings back my childhood."

"You grew up around here? Really?"

"Yeah, Potrero Hill. Why?"

"You speak like you're from Jersey or New York maybe."

"*You* talk like you just walked out of the Alamo and you're making fun of my accent? You got some nerve, lady."

Sailor chuckled.

"I wasn't making fun. And for your information, *no one* walked out of the Alamo alive. Anyway, let's go over it again," I said. "What *exactly* did Autumn Jennings say? Try to remember as closely as possible. And remember, Sailor's a human lie detector. He'll know if you're holding back."

"Look, lady, not for nothing, but I think you got a screw loose, maybe."

"Remember, I have control of the satchel."

Jamie muttered something under his breath.

"What was that?" I asked.

"Nothin'. Like I said, she comes to me thinking she's cursed on account of everyone in her life dies. Says it's some sort of family deal; I guess her great-grandfather got cursed by some shoeshine boy."

"And was this connected to the cursed trousseau? Did you tell her she had to get it back so you could lift the curse somehow?"

"What? No, of course not. That's not how these things work; you should know that. Being near a cursed object would make things worse."

"Then why did she have someone steal it?"

"She didn't have no one *steal* it. She got it from one of her neighbors. It was only afterward she realized the family connection. And then she was afraid it had come to her on purpose."

"*Wait*. She got it from one of her neighbors? Which one?"

He shrugged. "I dunno."

"Was it Renee?"

"I. Don't. Know. You got a hearing problem?"

"And how do you know Renee, exactly?"

He gave me a funny look. "We go way back. What's it to you? Look, lady, as a fellow practitioner and someone who might be just a tad too invested in 'by the book,' you should know that the practitioner-client relationship is sacred. I don't tell stories out of school."

"I thought Scarlet told you Autumn hired her to steal the trousseau," Sailor said as we headed back to the car, bag of chocolate in hand. We each had a piece, savoring the sweet cocoa taste.

"She did," I said. "But it never made sense to me. If you already think you're under a curse, why would you invite more bad juju into your life? And even if Autumn did it because she thought Jamie might help her, would she go around trying on cursed dresses? It makes no sense. I'm sure Scarlet was lying to me."

"Why would she lie at this point?"

"Because she's afraid of whoever hired her to steal the trousseau. Easy enough to blame it on a dead woman."

"She said she stole the trousseau with her boyfriend, right? Let's go chat with Brad—I've been meaning to check in with him since we left San Jose. I called to check; his shift started half an hour ago."

We got back to the car and handed the bag to Oscar; he was in chocolate bliss.

"How are you feeling?" I asked Sailor as I drove us back to Union Square.

"Fine."

It didn't take a mind reader to know he was lying.

"Still," I said, "you look pretty macho with that black eye. It's a good look for a bodyguard."

He gave me a reluctant smile. "Yeah, well, wait till you see the other guy."

We stowed the car in the garage, Oscar snuggled down in his nest in the backseat for a nap. Then Sailor and I walked to David Gallery.

Brad did not seem pleased to see us.

"It wasn't *me*, man! I was on a date last night. *All* night, if you catch my drift. The girl was pretty chill; she can vouch for me."

"I thought you were in love with Scarlet," I said.

"She took my bike! And then someone said they saw her with another guy." He shrugged. "Not saving myself for her. I got a good job; I got options."

"Who was this other guy she was with?"

He shrugged. "I dunno. Some guy she met while she walked those dogs. Life's too short, man. Time to move on. I even reported the motorcycle as stolen."

"Could you lift your shirt for me, please?" asked Sailor.

"What? Why?"

"I want to see if you have any bruises or marks from a fight."

"Yeah, looks like somebody sucker-punched *you*, huh?" He yanked his shirt up to display a white, hairless, well-padded torso. It looked completely untouched. "There, that good enough for you?"

"Yes, thank you," said Sailor.

"That about it? 'Cause I got work to do, and I gotta tell you I'm getting tired of being harassed. I could, like, report you."

"Thank you for your time," I said. "And if you have a change of heart, Scarlet's at UCSF in the ICU. She's very sick."

That stopped him. "Really? What's wrong with her?"

"It looks like arsenic poisoning. It could be serious. So if you still care for her at all, you might want to visit."

"Aw, maaaan," he said, shaking his head as he walked back to his station.

"You believe him?" I asked Sailor as we left.

Sailor nodded. "And I know for a fact I landed a few good hits on the guy's ribs. Unless Brad's a remarkably good healer, it wasn't him at the Rodchester House last night."

"He seems to have rebounded from his heartache pretty quickly."

"Well, she did take his bike. You can't mess with a man's bike."

"I'll keep that in mind," I said with a smile. "You know . . . there's someone connected to the Rodchester House who also frequents the dog park."

"Has anyone seen Cody around? Or Eleanor, with Mr. Bojangles?" I asked.

Lots of shaking heads. I recognized a few familiar faces from the other day, but there were new ones as well. Not everyone went to the park every day, of course, nor did most people keep to a strict schedule for dog walking.

"I saw Cody yesterday, and he totally shaved his beard!" said a man I had seen here before, named Rolando.

"Dude, I *saw* that," said another. This prompted a long discussion among the group about the relative merits of facial hair. "I'm keeping my mustache, though."

"A lot of us are new to the neighborhood," said one woman, getting back to my point. "You should ask one of the old-timers, like Mrs. Morgan."

"Mrs. Morgan is newer than I am," said Rolando. "She just moved in last year."

"Really?" asked the woman. "I guess I just assumed she had been here a while."

Me, too, I thought. Why would she have moved into a house with so many stairs? But, then, perhaps she didn't have mobility problems a year ago.

Sailor and I thanked them for their time and headed back to the parking lot.

"It really might have been Cody, then," I said. "I wondered how you wouldn't have noticed such a bushy beard, even in the dark. But if he shaved it . . ." I blew out a frustrated breath. "Still, I don't even know his last name. I guess this was a bust. I suppose I could stake out his apartment house, maybe, or just start ringing doorbells. . . ."

"Not necessarily. You know his first name, and he runs the Web site for Rodchester House of Spirits. Maya should be able to track down his full name in about five seconds. And if he's not listed, get Sam Spade to find his exact address. And then I'll go with you to talk to him." He tugged my ponytail very gently. "You've got some good old-fashioned detective skills now, you know, not just of the witchy variety."

I smiled up at him. "You're right. Thanks for reminding me. For now, I guess I'll head back to Aunt Cora's Closet and see if Maya can do some Internet sleuthing for me. See you later?"

On our way to the dog park I had dropped Sailor at his place in Chinatown so he could get his motorcycle;

he had an appointment not far away, on this side of town.

"You can bet on it."

We kissed, and I watched as he pulled on his helmet, swung his leg over his bike, and zoomed off.

It occurred to me to stop by and talk with Renee, but I didn't want to be stupid. If she was involved in this somehow, I shouldn't confront her alone. Better to try to figure out what role she might have played and hand all the evidence over to the police. Like a good, smart witch.

I was about to get in my car when I noticed Mrs. Morgan hobbling down the street, leaning heavily on her walker with one hand while trying to keep Colonel Mustard in line with the other.

I hurried over to her.

"May I help you?" I asked, reaching out to take Colonel Mustard's leash.

"Oh, thank you, my dear. Why, here you are again! You really should get yourself a dog if you're going to come to the dog park every day anyway!"

"I think you might be right." I smiled. "I have a pet pig, but I don't know that he's allowed in the park."

"A what?"

I gestured toward my car, where Oscar was sprawled on the backseat in his porcine guise, snoring.

Mrs. Morgan tottered over and peered in and chuckled. "If I didn't see it with my own eyes I wouldn't believe it. A pig!"

Oscar awoke with a snort and rolled over to look at us. This made Mrs. Morgan laugh more.

"You should let him come out and play with the others."

"You think so?"

"Oh, yes, of course. This is a friendly crowd—as long as he's a friendly pig."

"Very," I said, partly lying given his encounter with Autumn Jennings.

"You want to come out and play, Oscar?"

He gave me a look. His snout was still smeared with chocolate, but nonetheless I realized I was going to pay for this one. He gave a quick shake of his head, then snorted and curled up with his butt to us, wiggling his little tail.

"I guess he's not up for it," I said. I should have known. Oscar found it humiliating to be lumped in with dogs and other pets. "Would you like me to stay with you, and then I could give you a ride home?"

"Oh, would you? That would be wonderful. Thank you."

Mrs. Morgan and I sat on a bench and watched the dogs play with one another and their humans. Rolando threw the ball for Colonel Mustard over and over; his dog and the Colonel seemed like good canine buddies.

It was a beautiful Bay Area summer day, warm and sunny but with a pleasant breeze. Nothing like the summers I had grown up with: hot and sticky. On the other hand, there were no fireflies here, and rents were exorbitant. Everything had its pluses and minuses.

"You know," said Mrs. Morgan. "I don't mean to be presumptuous, but if you love dogs and coming to the park, I could pay you to walk Colonel Mustard for me."

"Oh, I wish I could, but I actually have a job, across town. I have my own vintage clothing shop."

"Oh, of course you do, so silly of me. You already told me that. I'm sorry; I forget things."

"Actually I was here today looking for a young man named Cody who comes here often with his dog Bojangles. Do you happen to know him?" I had asked her before but hoped her memory might have been jogged.

"Oh, I wouldn't know. I've met a few people here, but truth to tell, they all run together! I'm terrible with names. I'd like to blame it on age, but the truth is I was never much good at remembering names. Faces, now, that I remember."

"Cody's a young man, probably midtwenties, with a full black beard, at least until recently."

"I'm sorry, but I really don't know."

"You know, Rolando mentioned that you were new to the neighborhood, just moved in a year ago." She nodded, her eyes still on the dogs. "I guess I assumed you had been here a while."

"No, not long. It's a lovely neighborhood, though, isn't it?"

"It is." I wanted to ask why she would buy a house with so many steps but decided it was none of my business. She wasn't my grandmother, after all. But I hated to think of her struggling with them every day.

We watched the dogs for a few more minutes, and then I gave Mrs. Morgan a ride back to her house. Oscar was disgruntled at having to share the backseat with Colonel Mustard, but in response to a stern look he moved out of the way.

I pulled into Mrs. Morgan's very small driveway, parked, and came around to help her out.

"I'm just fine at the moment, but thank you," she said as she started climbing the stairs. "It's the Parkinson's. It comes; it goes. Sometimes I swear I feel a mere sixty years old, like I could walk miles! People find it odd, sometimes, think I'm faking. But it's the way of this disease."

"I'm sorry. That must be very difficult."

"I'm much luckier than many. Look at what happened to poor Autumn! One never knows what's in store. That's why it's so important to appreciate every day."

"So true," I said as I followed her up the stairs, holding Colonel Mustard's leash. When we got to the door Mrs. Morgan searched her handbag for her key.

I noticed a package had been left on the landing, so I picked it up to bring it inside, barely glancing at the name.

Mrs. Morgan opened the door and let us in.

"I would be happy to help you take those catalogs down for the recycling, if you like," I said, setting the package on the foyer table and reaching for an armful of catalogs.

"No, thank you. There's really no need— Put those down," said Mrs. Morgan.

I had glanced at the name on the package, but it hadn't registered. Now I looked back at it and read: *Mrs. Mildred Parr Morgan.*

Parr. Unlike Mrs. Morgan, I was usually pretty good with names. And that one rang a bell.

"The nob's name was Clark. The shoeshine boy was Thomas Parr."

Not that it was a particularly rare name. But she had that catalog from Rodchester house. . . .

"I wondered if you'd figured it out," said Mrs. Morgan. She was holding a gun trained on me, and unlike when something similar happened just a few days ago with Autumn Jennings, her hands were steady. So steady, in fact, it made me wonder if the whole Parkinson's thing had been an act. Like everything else about Mrs. Morgan, apparently.

I stood very still, trying to think through my options. Oscar was out in the car and often had a kind of psychic awareness of when I needed help. But he wasn't faster than a speeding bullet, so if Mrs. Morgan was actually intent on killing me here and now, I'd better think fast.

"I do know Cody; of course I do," she said. *Good*. At least she wasn't in any hurry to end this. That was good. "In fact, when he mentioned you were going to be at the Rodchester House of Spirits I sent him down there to take care of things. Made him shave first—that ridiculous beard made him so conspicuous. I expected he'd push you down a flight of stairs or something— My word, there must be a thousand easily explainable accidents that could happen to a person at an overnight in a place like that! But no, he gets into a scuffle with some sort of *bodyguard*? I know it's trite to say, but it really is hard to find good help these days."

"Why would you want to kill *me*?"

"I didn't. Not at first. You didn't have anything to do with this. But then you got involved and made the connection between the stolen trousseau and Scarlet, and I knew that stupid girl would talk. She's not very bright."

"Just FYI, she didn't rat you out. And she seemed bright enough to me. Granted, last time I saw her she was suffering under the effects of arsenic poisoning. But prior to that, she served me with legal papers, and apparently she was smart enough to steal that trousseau for you."

She scoffed. "She and Cody are so easy to manipulate. He was afraid I would tell his precious Eleanor that he and Scarlet were having an affair, and Scarlet fancied herself in love, would do anything for Cody—also, that girl will do just about anything for cash. Rents are terrible in the city, aren't they? It's such a scandal."

"How did you find the trousseau?"

"Scarlet told me all about falling in love with a wonderful man—the only hiccup being that he was *married*, of course. But she was enamored and showed me the catalog he had put together for the Rodchester House. Poor thing was so in love, she treated that catalog like a diamond ring. I convinced her to leave it here for safekeeping and looked through it, as I do the catalog for every antique auction I come across, and lo and behold, after all these years! The very trousseau I had been looking for, right there in the Rodchester attics. It really was fate that brought Cody to me, I feel sure."

"But why would you want to harm Autumn with a cursed trousseau?"

"Autumn's maiden name is Clark; didn't you know that? Somehow she escaped the curse my great-grandfather laid upon hers."

"I don't know if that's true. Everyone she loved died, after all. That's a curse."

She shrugged. "It wasn't enough. Not nearly enough. It came to me a couple of years ago, after my husband committed suicide. No children, no friends. And I was afflicted with old age and ill health: *This* was why I'm still alive. This was my purpose. I tracked Autumn down and spent my life savings to move into this house right across the street. But then what? I can barely get around. How could I enact this final curse, avenge the death of my great-grandfather?"

"And then you discovered the trousseau."

"Exactly. I almost gave up, more than once. But then Autumn came over here, whining about losing her husband, everyone she loved, as though *I* haven't lived a life full of pain. That's what life is. My great-grandfather was *poisoned* by the shoe polish he used every day. Do you have any idea how painful that was for him to be slowly killed by nitrobenzene while he polished the shoes of wealthy men?"

I shook my head. I certainly didn't, but I was pretty sure she didn't, either.

"So you paid Scarlet and Cody to steal the trousseau from Rodchester House of Spirits, and then what?"

"Then I gave the curse a little boost. I know a lot about poisons—something else that was passed down through the family."

"You added powdered arsenic to the dresses."

She nodded. "And I called and told Autumn I had some very old dresses to sell, from an old trousseau. She didn't make the connection that it was attached to the family curse. She was blinded by her own greed— she thought she was getting something over on me, that I didn't know how valuable the clothes were."

I remembered Jamie saying Autumn had bought the trousseau from a neighbor, only realizing afterward that this might be related to the family curse. I had thought "neighbor" referred to Renee, but I had been wrong.

"Don't feel too sorry for her," continued Mrs. Morgan, shaking her head and tsking. "Willing to take advantage of a little old lady. Who *does* that? And she was no saint; she used to sew fake designer labels into her clothes to boost the prices. Scarlet's old boyfriend, Brad, helped her sell them over the Internet."

"Did you at least warn Scarlet about the dresses?"

She made a dismissive sound. "Unlike Autumn, *Scarlet* knew that trousseau was cursed. What kind of fool tries on dresses she knows to be cursed?"

"Cody doesn't believe in curses. He probably scoffed at the idea."

Mrs. Morgan shrugged. We stood there for a moment, two adversaries assessing each other in her front entry, which smelled of lemon polish and potpourri. The place was beautiful, with a warm redwood trim and a small tiled fireplace. Colonel Mustard was curled up on the stair landing. It could have been a beautiful, welcoming home, if not for the madwoman intent on vengeance for a great-grandfather she'd never even known.

The hand holding the gun began to sag, and Morgan used her left hand to help support it. And then her head began to shake. Were these the off-again, on-again tremors she had told me about?

And then I saw an ugly gargoyle face in the window. My knight in shining armor.

"What are you smiling about?" Morgan demanded.

"You know how sometimes something—or someone— is physically attractive but truly a terrible person, and once you realize that, all you can see is the ugliness? And sometimes it's the other way around: Someone is a truly wonderful soul but just as ugly as a mud fence. And you'd rather have their ugly than the beauty, any day?"

"What on earth are you going on about, child?"

"Mrs. Morgan, your world is about to be taken apart. And I'm not your child."

"What—"

Before she could get the sentence out, Oscar crashed through the window and bowled her over. Morgan cried out in pain as she went down. The gun skittered across the tile of the foyer; I lunged for it, then pointed it at the old woman, who lay, frail and pathetic, on the floor.

"My arm!" she cried out. "That . . . that thing *head-butted* me!"

"Heh," said Oscar. Then he looked at me. "It was okay this time, right, mistress?"

I nodded. "It was just fine, Oscar, just this once."

Chapter 26

When the police arrived I told them I had disarmed the old woman myself and that I had no knowledge of how the window had been shattered, shaking my head about the things that happened in urban neighborhoods these days. Mrs. Morgan tried to tell the paramedics about the horrifying creature that had crashed through her window and head-butted her, but they assumed she was hallucinating.

Oscar waited patiently in the car, in pig form, while I told Inspectors Ng and Stinson what I knew about Morgan's belief in a family curse and how she'd admitted to adding arsenic to the dresses to be sure the curse came true. I suggested they speak to Scarlet and track down Cody for the rest of the story.

"What do we do with the dog?" asked a young uniformed officer.

"Call animal control," said Inspector Stinson.

"Maybe someone at the dog park wants him," I suggested.

"You want to take care of it?"

"Not really, but I feel bad for the poor thing; he just lost his person and now he gets shunted off to the pound?"

Stinson shrugged. "I got much bigger things to worry about."

"All right," I said, giving in to the inevitable. Maybe I could find yet another hapless friend to take Colonel Mustard. He was a sweet dog.

It was a long time before they'd finished asking their questions. When Colonel Mustard and I finally descended the stairs, drained from the grilling and exhausted by the emotions of the day—not to mention the lack of sleep last night—my gaze alit on a welcome sight across the street: Sailor, straddling his motorcycle. His helmet was off and he appeared to be simply waiting, arms crossed over his chest, eyes fixed on Mrs. Morgan's house.

I stashed Colonel Mustard in the car with Oscar and made a beeline for him.

He enveloped me in a hug. I could feel myself letting go, relaxing, savoring the strength of his arms around me, the scent of his leather jacket and the indescribable aroma of citrus and spice that always seemed to linger on his skin.

Neither of us said a word for a very long time.

"You drive me absolutely insane—you know that?" he said finally, his voice gruff with emotion. "I thought you were going straight back to Aunt Cora's Closet."

"I was, but then I saw Mrs. Morgan. She's an old lady, I thought. It never occurred to me that she would be any kind of danger."

"Doesn't take much to pull a trigger."

"I know. I have to stop underestimating people."

"That you do," Sailor said. "Listen . . . I know this

isn't the best time for this. In fact, I've been trying to figure out the right moment for a while . . ." He cleared his throat. "Something's been on my mind, and when I realized what happened here, it dawned on me that I can't put this off any longer."

I pulled away from him.

"I know what you're going to say," I said, my voice breaking. "It's fine. Really, Sailor, it is. You have your own life; you can't continue to put your training on hold for me, to keep sticking your neck out for me. I mean, we make jokes about you being my bodyguard, but you're right: It's because of me that you're wounded all the time. I got you attacked at the Rodchester House just last night, and today I had an encounter with a killer. I'm like a bad penny, but, you know, a coin bad enough that it will get you killed."

"What are you talking about?"

"It's fine, really. We've had a good run, certainly better than I've ever had with any other man, and—"

"*Dammit*, woman, I meant nothing of the sort. I've never met someone so intent on breaking up with the man who loves her."

That stopped me.

"I'm . . ." He cleared his throat. "Look, I know this is a hell of a time, right out here on the street. And I'm not talking right away, not until we're both ready . . . but . . ." He ran a hand through his hair and gazed into my eyes.

"Dammit, Lily, I'm asking you to marry me."

Chapter 27

After a long moment I realized my mouth was agape. I tried to speak, but the words refused to coalesce in my brain.

"I'm going to give that a minute to sink in," said Sailor. After another long pause he added, "Or maybe two."

"I . . . but . . . you . . . ," was all I could manage to say.

"I'm guessing this comes as a surprise to you."

"It's just . . . I . . ." Again, speech failed me.

And then I saw the shift, the moment his eyes shuttered, and the sardonic look I knew too well came back on his face. "Or perhaps I misjudged your feelings for me. It's a ridiculous idea, anyway. Who's ever heard of a pain-in-the-ass witch meeting up with a psychic and—"

I flung myself into his arms.

"Is that a yes?" he demanded. Then he held me away from him: "Lily, tell me. Tell me *something*."

"I love you."

His face softened; he gave me a crooked grin. "Call

me a stickler, but I'm afraid I need actual verbal confirmation here: Is that a yes? Will you marry me?"

I swallowed, hard. "It's just . . . marriage is supposed to be a lifetime thing."

"That's what I hear."

"That means . . . you're willing to be saddled with the likes of me, forever?"

He nodded.

"Really? I'm not easy."

He started to chuckle. "Did you think I haven't thought this through, Lily? It's not like we're on a bender in Vegas. I've known you, through thick and thin, for quite some time now."

"Almost a year."

"Almost a year." He nodded. "I've tried talking myself out of being in love with you, over and over again. And I fail. I can't see my future without you at my side. I can't see *your* future without me at *your* side. And . . . I've been married before, remember? I realize now that I wasn't ready. Not nearly. And she wasn't the right woman for me."

"And now you're ready?"

"Yes."

"And . . . *I'm* the right woman for you?"

"Heaven help me. *Yes.*"

"Aidan says we won't be good for each other."

"I think you know my feelings about Aidan—and especially with regard to his thoughts about our relationship."

Ever since Aidan proclaimed that I would never be able to experience true romantic love, I had been insisting I was strong enough to break the trend, to love someone, to have a partner. Was I ready to put my magic where my mouth was and take the plunge? Sailor stood in front of me now, motorcycle gear and black eye, sardonic expression . . . and he was the most welcome sight in the world.

I nodded.

"I need you to say it."

"Yes," I breathed finally. "I do. I want to marry you."

We stared at each other for a long moment. I thought I spied the glint of tears in his eyes.

"Oh! Almost forgot." When he spoke his voice was gruff.

He pulled a velvet box from his pocket.

"Bronwyn helped me with the size, and she thought you'd like it. So did Maya. And Selena shined it for you. It's a druzy, which I was told is like the inside of an agate, with a glittering effect due to the growth of tiny crystals atop a colorful mineral. But if you don't like it we can get a different one. I know a diamond's traditional, obviously. Also, I know you don't wear rings, so if you'd prefer a necklace—"

I opened the box. Nestled in a velvet bed was a ring with the stone in a convex teardrop shape. It glittered pink, purple, blue, and green within its antique silver filigree setting.

I caught my breath. "How did you know?"

"Know what?"

"This marriage isn't going to work out if you can read my mind. I can already tell you that."

"I *can't* read your mind, Lily, and I wouldn't even if I could. Not unless you wanted me to. What kind of person do you think I am?"

"Then how did you know about the ring?"

He cocked his head, a questioning look on his face.

"When I was a girl, Graciela gave me one just like this. But it was lost—or taken from me—when I went to visit my father. I've always mourned it."

"So, is it a good thing or a bad thing that this ring is just like it?"

"A very good thing." My voice was thick with emotion.

He took the box from me. "Then let's do this properly, shall we?"

He got down on one knee and held the box out in front of him. "Lily Ivory, sorceress extraordinaire, pain in my butt, and mistress of my heart, will you do me the honor of taking my hand in marriage?"

"Yes. I *will.*"

The next day I was still floating on air. Autumn's murderer was in police custody, and Sailor and I were engaged. *Engaged.*

Me. Lily Ivory, engaged to be married to a wonderful man.

I looked down at the ring for the thousandth time since Sailor had slipped it on my finger. The tiny crystals glittered in the afternoon light, warming my heart.

"I told him you'd love it," said Bronwyn. No customers were in the shop, so Maya, Bronwyn, and I were enjoying a peaceful day at Aunt Cora's Closet. Oscar snored on his pillow, Loretta lay on her rug behind the counter, and Colonel Mustard was curled up by the dressing rooms.

"I can't believe you all kept the secret from me!" I said. "Selena, too. Very impressive."

"It was so hard!" Bronwyn exclaimed. "We were all so excited for you. Even Maya."

"True," said Maya with a smile. "Though you made

me wonder, when you reacted so strongly to the idea of living together, much less marrying."

"I'm not going to lie: It's still pretty scary. But we can't go around avoiding scary things, now, can we?"

"No, we certainly can't," Bronwyn said, beaming.

The only flies in the ointment were what to do with Colonel Mustard—Oscar was not pleased, to say the least, and kept coming up with suggestions of whose doorstep to leave him on—as well as a few lingering questions: How—and why—had Mrs. Morgan kept the police from thoroughly investigating Autumn's store and apartment? And why had Renee reacted so oddly to me when I asked her about Jamie, and lied to me about going to San Jose with Scarlet?

Although upon reflection I realized that Mrs. Morgan was the one who'd told me Renee had gone down to Rodchester House of Spirits. Probably Morgan had lied to deflect suspicion.

In fact . . . it occurred to me to pass by Vintage Visions, one more time, to see if the police were processing the scene. I wasn't sure why it bothered me so much, but it kept niggling at the back of my mind.

"I think I'll take these two pups to the dog park," I announced. "I need a little fresh air. I'll be back in an hour."

In the back of my mind I thought Rolando might be at the park; I remembered him—and his dog—playing with Colonel Mustard, and I held out a small flicker of hope that he might be interested in adopting the dog.

Of course, I supposed there might be paperwork involved. I wasn't sure how it worked when someone was arrested: Could their pets be adopted out? But even if it was only temporary, Colonel Mustard needed fostering; Oscar's attitude aside, he was really too big and rambunctious to be happy in my little apartment.

A man with a little white moppet of a dog was there when I arrived, but otherwise the park was empty. He left soon after we arrived, looking askance at my two big canine companions.

So I threw the ball for Colonel Mustard for a while, simply enjoying the way my ring glinted in the sunshine, and thinking about how fortunate I was.

Loretta lingered by the oak tree, a bee buzzing around her head. I went to shoo the bee away. When I scratched Loretta's neck, her collar tinkled.

I could feel the faint vibrations of Selena's power in the silver bee charm hanging from her collar. But there was something else. Something more. I crouched down to inspect the charms. The Maltese cross didn't draw my attention this time, but the little almond-shaped bottle did.

It reminded me of the receptacle that I had seen in my vision, when I was in Aidan's hexagonal chamber: The sky had rained tears of blood into it.

I studied the bottle. It was tiny. But when I cradled it in my palm, I could feel it: It hummed. It was filled with the energy of grief. Great sorrow and anguish.

This was a lacrimatory.

A bee buzzed by and returned, then flew around and around my head. *Are you trying to tell me something, Beatrice Beech?*

Could this be Jedediah Clark's lacrimatory? Had he shed tears over his fiancée into this bottle, and tucked it away in her trunk? Had Autumn found it along with the trousseau, thought it pretty, and attached it to Loretta's collar? Or had she somehow known it was powerful and tried to hide it in plain sight, on her dog's collar?

A man arrived at the park. But he didn't have a dog with him.

"Jamie? What are you doing here?"

"Just happened by, thought I recognized you."

"Nice to see you," I said, straightening. What were the chances that Jamie was just happening by? I looked around, hoping some other dog lovers might be arriving. We were in a public place, but still.

"Those your dogs? Hey there, pup," he made kissy sounds. Colonel Mustard came trotting up to him; Jamie scratched his neck, then threw the ball. Then he crossed over to Loretta, who lingered by the oak tree. He crouched down in front of her and started stroking her under her chin.

"You look like you're a dog lover," I said. "I don't suppose you'd be interested in adopting Colonel Mustard, the poodle?"

But Jamie wasn't listening. His hands froze, still on Loretta's neck.

"Well, I'll be a monkey's uncle. She was right," he said.

"Who was right?"

"Here's the thing," he said, taking off Loretta's collar. "I need to borrow this."

"No," I said.

But for the third time that week, a gun was pointed at me.

"Hey, I'm really sorry. I gotta tell you, this is a desperate situation, so I wouldn't push it if I were you. I gotta do what I gotta do, if you know what I mean."

"Who do you work for?"

He shook his head. "Not for me to say. You'll find out

soon enough. We'll meet again, and then, I dunno, I guess you can try to get your revenge, or whatever. Listen, I'm sorry. I got no choice."

He backed away, gun in one hand, collar in the other. Then he turned and ran.

The bee buzzed by, and Loretta let out a howl.

I got the dogs in the car and pulled around the corner to drive by Vintage Visions. Sure enough, the store was now covered with crime scene tape and appeared, from what I could see through the windows, to be a mess inside.

So the police were finally investigating. Unfortunately, there didn't seem to be any cops currently on the premises.

Next door, Renee's cupcake shop was open. I parked in a shady spot and cracked the windows.

"I won't be long," I said. "Be good pups."

I took a moment to stroke my medicine bag and center myself before entering the cupcake shop. The scents of cinnamon and orange enveloped me. But I thought I sensed something acrid underneath the heavenly aroma.

"Well, hello there!" said Renee, smiling and radiating welcome. "*Lily*, how lovely to see you."

"Does Jamie work for you?" I blurted out.

Her smile froze. "I can't believe he told you that."

"He didn't tell me. I guessed."

"Well, you work for Aidan, right? We all work for someone. Unless, of course, we're in charge."

"Okay . . ." I wasn't sure why that was pertinent. But if she knew about my association with Aidan, it was clear I was on the right track. "Jamie stole a dog collar from me."

"He *did*? Good for him! Well, now, that's wonderful

news!" A big metal sifter made a metallic clanking noise as Renee applied a dusting of powdered sugar to a plate of frosted cupcakes.

"Stop playing around, Renee. Tell me what's going on. How are you involved in what happened to Autumn?"

She stopped what she was doing, set down the sifter, and focused on me. The pleasant smile never left her face, but her eyes seemed to glitter with malice. And I caught another faint whiff of something putrid under the sweet smells emanating from the cupcakes.

"I had absolutely *nothing* to do with poor Autumn's demise. Haven't you figured that one out yet? From what I gathered, the lovely Mrs. Morgan—the one with the poodle, right down the street?—had a bee in her bonnet over some ridiculous curse from her ancestors. I'd wager she was involved somehow. I could tell there was something a little *off* about her, first time we met. You didn't notice?"

"I don't have the best track record when it comes to little old ladies," I admitted. "I never think they're capable of something so . . . violent."

She wagged a finger in my direction. "Well, now, you'll need to rectify that way of thinking, wouldn't you agree? No way for someone in your position to be acting."

She chuckled and continued to speak while decorating the already sugar-topped cupcakes with little marzipan apples. "I tell you what, running a cupcake shop—everyone comes in here at some point or another. I hear *all* the neighborhood gossip. So one day Cody comes in here, all upset, poor thing. I fed him a cupcake—one of Renee's *special* fairy cakes—and he told me the whole story: that he'd been having an affair, and now he had to steal a trousseau from the Rodchester House. Mrs. Morgan had found out about it and was blackmailing him—but she also promised to pay his girlfriend a pretty penny, and Scarlet really needed the money."

"There's a lot of that going around. Autumn needed money, too—was that just so she could stay where she was, with rent increases?"

Renee nodded. "That, and the fact that she had spent a fortune on inventory she was having a heck of a time unloading—I mean, really, who wants an Edwardian dress with a bustle? They're fun to look at, but to spend thousands on? I don't think so. Also, she was paying out a lot of cash trying to rid herself of a family curse. Imagine that—then she goes and buys the contents of that trousseau without even realizing its connection to her own family! She thought it was just a bunch of old clothes."

"Why did you send Autumn to speak with Jamie about lifting the curse?"

"I brought her some cupcakes one day, hoping to encourage her to move her store out so I could expand into that space. I didn't even realize she had the trousseau until she insisted on showing me upstairs. I could tell right away this was no average trousseau. She sat right there on the floor, clad in that beautiful gown, and started crying and telling me she was suffering under a curse. I still hadn't put it all together, but I figured there was something very special about this trousseau, some reason dear Mrs. Morgan would orchestrate its theft and then turn around and sell it to Autumn. So I told Autumn I knew a man who could help with her curse. I hoped she'd spill the beans."

"But then she died."

"Exactly. Can you *imagine*?" She sighed and rearranged some minicupcakes on a tiered display plate. "At first I thought perhaps she had been right after all, that there *was* some sort of terrible curse on her family. But I wanted the opportunity to look through the trousseau at leisure—"

"So you kept the police from thoroughly investigating her store."

She winked and gave me a huge smile. "I offered them cupcakes—no one refuses cupcakes, am I right? Simple enough banishing spell. They looked around a little, but they could sense they weren't welcome. *Anyway*"—she sounded slightly annoyed that I had interrupted her story—"I wanted to look through the trousseau at my leisure, and guess what I found?"

I waited.

"Guess," she urged.

"Oh! Sorry—thought that was rhetorical. Um . . . I don't know . . . old stockings full of arsenic dye?"

She looked peeved. "It's no fun if you're not even going to *try*. No, I found this."

Renee opened a cookie jar and pulled out a very old, yellowed piece of paper encased in a plastic sleeve. She handed it over.

The letterhead was from an auction house in San Francisco. A list, written in faded ink, enumerated the contents of *An Intact Trousseau, Beatrice Beech, circa 1890s*. At the bottom of the long list of gowns, lingerie, and linens was *One lacrimatory, thought to have been added subsequent to the demise of the young lady*.

"A lacrimatory," I said, looking up at Renee.

"Can you *imagine*? I don't give a damn—pardon my

French!—about old clothes. But a lacrimatory? That's a whole different batch of cupcake batter, if you catch my drift. They're adorable! I collect them. Have quite the assortment, right next to my little souvenir teaspoons."

"How did you figure out it was on the dog collar?"

"Got one of Jamie's crazy Russian psychics to read for me. She kept seeing a dog bone; I couldn't figure it out, until I remembered you had taken Autumn's dog." She shrugged. "I sat right down and had a lemon chiffon fairy cake and pondered, and then I remembered about those charms Autumn was forever attaching to the poor dog's collar." I blew out a breath, wondering where this left us. Yes, she had interfered with a police investigation, broken into Autumn's apartment—but then, so had I—and ordered a lackey to steal a dog collar with a lacrimatory. But she hadn't killed anyone—that had been Mrs. Morgan's doing. So what was going on?

"Lily, think about this. You don't have to work for Aidan. You have other choices."

"Such as?"

"Working for me."

I laughed.

"I'm serious. Aidan is weak. He's off now looking for a fountain of youth, if you can believe that. But as we both know . . ."

I leaned forward, wondering what we both knew.

She cocked her head. "There's no such thing."

"Oh. Oh, right."

She narrowed her eyes and focused on me, as though trying to read my mind. "You're saying there *is* a fountain of youth?"

"Heck if I know," I said with a shrug. "Frankly, I'm not even all that sure about vampires."

Renee gave me a strange look. She pushed a pink cup-cake across the top of the case. It was sprinkled with red-and-white striped crumbles.

"A new flavor. Peppermint Patty. Try it."

"I'm good at the moment, but thank you. No more eating between meals or I won't fit into my own vintage clothes anymore."

"Is that a crack about my weight?"

I had to laugh. It was all so absurd. We were talking about Autumn's untimely death, a toxic trousseau, and facing some sort of supernatural showdown for the soul of San Francisco, but Renee was talking about cupcakes and her weight.

"I promise you," I said, "that was *not* a crack about your weight. I would think you were a beautiful woman, except for the fact that you're trying to take over this city."

"Why do you assume I'd be any worse for San Fran-cisco than is Aidan Rhodes, of all people? Who died and made *him* dictator?"

That was a good question. Why would I assume Renee was less equipped than Aidan to deal with this city? When I first met Aidan, I thought a woman should be in charge. So here was a woman ready, willing, and apparently able to mount a challenge. And she made a hell of a cupcake. So what was I so afraid of?

Rain turning to blood. A cup of snakes. The coming storm.

I couldn't get the visions out of my mind. I was going to have to trust my admittedly weak third eye on this one: Renee was no good, cupcakes or no.

"I guess I'll take the devil I know," I said.

"I mean that quite literally, though. Do you know

who died and made him boss? You should ask him that. This is the way of it, Lily: The weak are taken out for the good of the herd. There can only be one leader."

"We're talking metaphorically, here, right?"

She paused for a long time before smiling sweetly and saying, "Whatever else could I possibly mean?"

"It has begun," said Aidan.

He had flabbergasted me by walking into Aunt Cora's Closet immediately after I had returned with the dogs. And Sailor arrived right behind him.

I had never before invited Aidan into my apartment. But we needed to talk in private. So I left Maya in charge of the shop, and now our trio sat in my small living room: Sailor and I on the couch, Aidan in a chair facing us.

Oscar, still nervous around Aidan, had gone to hide in his cubby over the fridge.

I told Aidan and Sailor about my encounter with Renee, and what happened with Loretta's collar.

"'It has begun'? Isn't that a little . . . melodramatic?" I glanced over at Sailor's unsmiling face, then back at Aidan. "I mean, know I was the one who first suggested it, but I guess I'm having a hard time wrapping my mind around the idea that the big showdown we're all so afraid of is with the cupcake lady."

"Don't underestimate her," said Aidan. "She's excellent at cloaking. We really don't have any way of knowing how powerful she is until she launches the challenge. And now she has the lacrimatory."

"If it's that powerful, why didn't I feel it earlier?"

"It's not that powerful by itself, but it seems Renee's been tracking and collecting lacrimatories for some time. And as a group . . . yes, they're powerful. There's a lot of energy in grief. And she has the residual salts from the tears, of course. You should know, better than I, how those could be used as a basis for powerful spells. Renee's abilities to brew might rival your own."

I chafed at that idea—I'd gotten used to being the acknowledged local expert on brewing. I couldn't scry worth a darn, and my soothsaying left a lot to be desired. But I could brew. But it looked like there was some new competition in town.

"Still," I said. "I guess it's the cupcakes that are throwing me."

"I'm going to assume you never saw *Ghostbusters*," said Sailor. "Ultimately, it doesn't matter if you're killed by a puffy marshmallow man or a bad guy with a gun: You're just as dead."

We all let that sink in for a moment.

"All right," said Sailor, standing. "Now that we know a little more about who, and what, we're dealing with, I'm going to go talk with my relatives. The Rom will be able to rally some troops."

"Good idea," said Aidan. And then, as though it pained him to say it: "Thank you."

Sailor nodded, gave me a kiss on the cheek, squeezed my hand, and left.

"While he's doing that," Aidan said, sitting forward in his chair, "you and I should divide up the folks in the satchel and start making the rounds, make sure people fall in line."

"Sure, good idea. But first, I had a couple of questions. What was Autumn Jennings's name doing in your satchel?"

"She asked me for a favor. A long time ago."

"What was it?"

"That's confidential, as I'm sure you're aware. It was nothing outrageous—most people want help with their finances, or love life, or both. But she was keeping an eye on a few things for me, until . . ." He trailed off, shaking his head.

"Until what?"

"She started asking others for help. It's not done."

"Jamie mentioned Autumn originally found him through Renee."

Aidan inclined his head. "I didn't know it was Renee at the time, obviously. But I knew she had gone elsewhere. She was impatient."

"So you cut her off?"

"Not exactly, but she knew I wasn't happy. I believe she was looking for you, perhaps to try to win you over to her side. Probably assumed since you had vintage clothes in common, you had a basis for an alliance."

"She filed a lawsuit against me!"

"Leverage. She thought she could use it as leverage, I believe. As I said, she was impatient." He paused. "The truth is, I haven't been tending well to everyone lately. As I told you before, my powers have been compromised, and I've had to concentrate on the most important threats. These petty concerns are the least of my problems—until folks start getting out of line. That's why I asked for your help while I was out of town."

"That satchel is a lot of work."

"That it is."

"Listen, I wanted to tell you something, Aidan. Sailor proposed."

Aidan looked at me for a long moment. Maybe Renee

was right; he looked younger and healthier than he had last time I saw him. Had he gone somewhere looking for youth and vitality? Now didn't seem the best time to ask. I read anger but also sadness in those mysterious, too-blue eyes. They were as cool and beckoning as a turquoise Caribbean Sea. The kind with an invisible riptide that could pull you into the depths before you even realized what was going on.

"Proposed what, exactly?"

"Marriage, of course," I said, barely refraining from rolling my eyes.

"You can't be serious."

"I am."

"I sincerely hope you told him no."

I just looked at him.

Aidan gave a disgusted toss of his head and threw his hands in the air. "What *is* it with you two? You're like a couple of hormonal teenagers. I rue the day I introduced you; I tell you that much."

I shrugged.

"What did I tell you about your chances in a romantic relationship?"

"I don't believe you."

"You think you aren't subject to the same rules as the rest of us?"

"Not in this case. Besides, who made up those rules?'

"No one made them up, any more than someone 'made up' gravity. It's just the way it is."

I shrugged again. "Your concern is that the relationship will make me vulnerable, right? But I'm powerful enough that a little chink in my armor isn't going to do me in."

A ghost of a smile played on Aidan's lips. After a moment he reached up and very slowly started clapping.

"Well, I have to hand it to you, Lily. When you first arrived in San Francisco you were unsure of yourself, afraid of your own power. And now here you are, considering yourself so powerful that it doesn't matter who challenges you."

"I've learned a lot since I arrived. And I've been introduced to the Ashen Witch, my guiding spirit."

He shook his head. "It's not that. It's her nemesis that's giving you this confidence—or dare I say it: this *arrogance*."

"What are you talking about?"

"I told you, you defeated the demon known as Deliverance Corydon too easily. She left a bit of herself with you."

I shook my head. I didn't want to accept that possibility. Deliverance was evil incarnate.

"I was worried about it," Aidan continued. "The first time I felt it was when we combined our powers that time on the Golden Gate Bridge, do you remember?"

"Of course I remember."

"I felt it then. A definite vibration . . ." He studied me, as if he could read the future in my face. Then he nodded and let out a long breath. "Maybe you're right, at that, Lily. Magic is all about powers in balance. The male, the female, the androgyne. Good and evil, the ancient and the contemporary. *Coincidentia oppositorum.*"

"That Latin phrase—I heard it when I was in your vision chamber."

He nodded. "Male and female, united together. We have this advantage over Renee, unless she finds a male practitioner to work with her."

"I thought our society was moving past this whole male-female dichotomy."

"Not in this case. Anyway, who's to say? Maybe you really are made of tough enough stuff. But do me a favor: Don't ever think yourself strong enough to do without me. We're going to have to work together to make sure Selena is safe, not to mention San Francisco as a whole."

"You're saying you and I are the essential primordial female and male forces?"

"We're the best we've got."

Chapter 28

"Lily, it's for you," said Bronwyn the next day, holding up the telephone. "She says she's your grandmother!"

I froze. I had been arranging some newly carved and charged talismans in a display cabinet.

"My grandmother?" Graciela didn't call me. Ever.

I raced to the phone. "Graciela? Are you all right?"

"No," she said, her gruff voice coming through loud and clear. "What's this about *una boda*? A wedding? *¿Estás prometida?* You're engaged and you didn't tell me?"

"How did you—"

"My whole coven insists on coming. And your mother, if you can believe that. *No lo puedo creer.* Did you know she has been sewing a trousseau for you?"

"A what, now?"

"You don't know what a trousseau is?"

"Of course I do, but my mother—"

"*Ya sé, m'ija.* I know. Who could have imagined? But all these years she has been pouring her thoughts to you into her sewing. It will be a powerful trousseau, just right for your wedding. Or will it be a handfasting?" A handfasting was a sort of witchy wedding, usually performed in a natural setting, often under a full moon. "Either way, it will be perfect. It doesn't take a witch to imbue something with power, as you know too well."

"But how did you—"

"Rosa's son has an old school bus he will let us use. We're going to stop at In-N-Out."

"You never leave your land," I said, still amazed. How did she know I was to be married? "And I can't believe my mother—"

"This is good, *m'ija*. Trust me. Be strong, *m'ija*. I want to meet this man who has won your heart and puts you at risk. What's his name?"

"Sailor."

"Marinero?"

"Yes, sort of. It's just a name, not a profession. He's a psychic, as a matter of fact. He's very special."

"He will need to be. And you will need all your womenfolk behind you. You are facing a challenge, but never forget, *m'ija*: We witches take care of our own."

As I hung up the phone, I pictured the faces I hadn't seen since I fled my hometown at the age of seventeen: my grandmother's stubborn chin and near-black eyes gone foggy with age; my mother's soft round face with its sweet but stunned expression, as though life had left her betrayed and bewildered. My grandmother's whole coven, thirteen impossibly old women who cackled and gossiped and worshipped and practiced their magic together, with the insight and knowledge borne of age and experience. It made me smile to imagine what that road trip would look like, an old school bus full of ancient witches stopping for burgers and fries. Excitement and warmth filled my core. I couldn't wait to see them, to hug them and share stories and ask magical questions late into the night. And to have them stand with me as I entwined my life with Sailor's.

On the other hand, if these witches were all coming to San Francisco, they must be very worried indeed. On that unlikely road trip would be thirteen witches, and my *mother*.

All these years she had been sewing me a trousseau. My mother, who never answered my letters or acknowledged the checks I sent to her. Who had cast me out of her home when I was a child for fear of my magical abilities. Who had once loved my father. My *mother*.

Oh, yes, we had some catching up to do.

Keep reading for a preview of the next book in
Juliet Blackwell's bestselling
Haunted Home Renovation Mystery Series,

A GHOSTLY LIGHT

Available in December 2016!

The tower reached toward the gray sky. A faint—dare I say ghostly?—glow emanated from the lighthouse's narrow windows. No doubt a trick of the afternoon sun, reflecting off the Bay Light's old stone walls.

"I'm thinking of calling it 'Spirit of the Lighthouse' or maybe simply 'A Bay Light,'" Alicia Withers said as she checked an item off the list on her clipboard. Alicia was big on lists. And clipboards. "What do you think, Mel? Does that sound like a good name for an inn? Is 'A Bay Light' too boring? I think it may be too boring."

"I think you need to figure out your plumbing issues before worrying about names," I replied. I'm Mel Turner, a general contractor and the head of Turner Construction. Otherwise known as a killjoy.

Alicia and I were in the main hallway of the former lighthouse keeper's house, a charming but dilapidated four-bedroom Victorian home adjacent to the lighthouse tower. The Bay Light lighthouse had been built on the small, rather unimaginatively named Lighthouse

Island, in the strait that connected San Francisco Bay to San Pablo Bay. Barely visible to the southwest loomed the San Francisco–Oakland Bay Bridge, linking Oakland to Treasure Island and San Francisco. The nearest shoreline was Richmond, while San Rafael—and San Quentin State State Prison—was across the sparkling waters of the placid bay.

It was a view to die for.

For years the Bay Light was operated and maintained by full-time lighthouse keepers and their families, the blaring foghorn and sweeping light assisting ship captains in navigating the surprisingly tricky shallows and rocky shoals of the bay. But the humans have long since been replaced by less costly electronics, and the structures on the island had fallen into disrepair.

The keeper's house had been a beauty and still boasted some of the original gingerbread trim as well as an adorable cupola, painted an appealing (but now peeling) creamy white. Also in the compound was a supply shed, the old foghorn building, and a huge cistern that collected rainwater for the keeper's family to use. The only other structures on the island were the docks in a small natural harbor, which were still used occasionally by boaters seeking refuge from sudden inclement weather—and by those going to and from the lighthouse.

"I'm just saying," I continued. "There's also a lot of dry rot that has to be repaired before you start inviting guests to your Lighthouse Inn."

"Oh, *you*," Alicia said with a smile, and I grinned.

The first time I met Alicia I had thought she was smart, professional—and singularly humorless. She wore her professionalism like a suit of armor, and it had taken a while before I detected the warmth and good humor that lurked beneath. She was still serious and hardworking, but had relaxed a lot since we'd met on a historic-castle restoration in Marin County. Late one night we had bonded over potato chips and home-renovation television shows, and she had saved both our lives when she had quite literally kicked the butt of a murderer. The butt-kicking had definitely improved her outlook on life.

"I haven't lost sight of the all-important infrastructure, as I'm sure you know," continued Alicia. "But according to my business plan, I need to register my domain and business names ASAP, so no, it's *not* too early to think about such things."

She whipped out a thick sheaf of lists and flowcharts and handed them to me. I flipped through the papers, which included preliminary schedules for demolition and foundation work; for electrical and plumbing and Internet repairs and installation; for the Sheetrock and mudding; for the renovation of the bathroom and kitchen; for the restoration of moldings and flooring and painting and light fixtures.

I raised my eyebrows. "Wow. Thanks, Alicia, but just so we're on the same page: I usually work up schedules with my office manager, Stan."

"I know you do, but while I was thinking through what needed to be done, I figured I might as well work up a template modeled on the schedules you developed for the Wakefield project in Marin. I can e-mail everything to Stan and you can plug in the dates and whatnot. I hope it wasn't too presumptuous—I couldn't help myself. Ever since Ellis agreed to back me on this project, I can hardly *sleep* I'm so excited!"

Several months ago Alicia's boss, the fabulously

wealthy motivational speaker Ellis Elrich, had asked if
I would mind doing him a favor and looking at a property he was considering renovating. I had spent many
months as the general contractor for Ellis's project in
Marin, renovating an ancient Scottish castle into a
state-of-the-art conference center and retreat, so I
knew he was not only a good boss and a decent human
being, but that he paid his staggering bills promptly and
without quibbling. Such clients were rare and much to
be treasured, so I'd been happy to oblige him when he
called. It wasn't until Ellis had said to meet him at the
Richmond docks that I realized this was no ordinary
property: It was the Bay Light on Lighthouse Island.

I—along with many in the Bay Area—had watched
over the years as the abandoned Victorian-era lighthouse descended into decrepitude. Every time my family
had passed over the Richmond–San Rafael Bridge my
father would shake his head and grumble, "It's a damned
shame." My mother would shush Dad for swearing in
front of my sisters and me—"Little pitchers have big
ears, Bill"—and then, craning her neck to watch the sad
little island recede from view, she would add, "You're
right, though. Someone really ought to save that place."

Never did I imagine that, decades later, *I* would be
that someone.

But historic renovation was my business, and Ellis
Elrich was filthy rich, so if he was willing to bankroll
Alicia's plans to renovate the Bay Light, I was game. I
already had the architect's detailed blueprints and had
pulled the necessary permits and variances from the
city. The Bay Light was public property, not Alicia's
private property, but some sort of public/private part-
nership had been hammered out in the interests of

salvaging a historic structure. I didn't ask too many questions. Ellis Elrich made things happen.

"So this is what I'm thinking," Alicia said, making a sweeping gesture around what had been the home's former living room. "We take down this wall here, combine this room with the small parlor next door, and make this area the inn's bar and restaurant."

I paced off the area, trying to imagine the completed space. "I'll have to check if that's a bearing wall. If it is, we'll need to pour some footings and install a steel I beam. That'll be expensive, and the additional space it creates is not substantial. Sure it's worth it?"

Alicia nodded. "I don't need a large bar and restaurant. The plans are for a maximum of ten overnight guests, which means I need at most five small tables— or maybe just one big table. I haven't decided yet."

"What about drop-in trade?"

"I doubt that'll be much of an issue—it's not as though it's easy to get here. Even with our boat making regular runs to the mainland, I anticipate we'll be more of a 'destination' inn and restaurant. I'm thinking we'll be at capacity with about twenty guests for drinks and dinner. But for those who make it, we'll be a gorgeous little oasis in the bay."

Alicia sighed with happiness.

I was glad for her, but I was too experienced not to be slightly jaded at the emotions common at this stage of a renovation. This was the phase when clients couldn't see past the stars in their eyes and the longing in their hearts. Starting a historic renovation was like falling in love: a time of a soaring, almost romantic infatuation that was followed by the grueling realities of sawdust and noise and confusion and delays and unwelcome discoveries in the walls that brought a person back to earth with a thud.

Or maybe that said more about *my* love life.

"And we'll keep and expand the kitchen, of course. It's entirely unsuitable as is or, as I like to think of it, it's a blank slate. But we'll make the study and a part of the pantry into a first-floor suite for the inn's live-in manager—"

"That would be you?"

"Oh, I dearly hope so, if I can find a replacement so Ellis isn't left high and dry."

"I can't imagine you'll be easily replaced. But Ellis is on board, right? Why else would he be bankrolling the project?"

Alicia blushed. "Yes, he is. He is very . . ."

"Sweet," I said when she trailed off.

She nodded but avoided my eyes. Now that I knew her better, and now that she had loosened up a little, Alicia was charming. A scar on her upper lip and another by one eye, relics of difficult times at the hands of her abusive (now ex) husband, only made her pretty face more interesting. The wounds on her psyche were another matter, but after years of therapy and a whole lot of emotional hard work, Alicia had made great strides in lessening their grip on her heart and mind.

And unless I was mistaken—and I was pretty sure I wasn't—Alicia had developed a serious crush on Ellis Elrich, her boss and knight in shining armor, who had helped her start her life over. Ellis was a surprisingly great down-to-earth guy, for a billionaire. Still, the situation seemed . . . complicated.

"Anyway, that leaves three guest suites on the second floor, each with an attached bath, plus one in the former attic. Oh! Did I tell you? The attic is full of old furniture and knickknacks, including the keeper's logs."

"After all this time? I'm surprised no one took them."

"I suppose that's the advantage of being on an isolated island. Can you imagine? We can put items on display to add to the historic ambiance!"

I smiled. "Of course we can. It's going to be great."

"Now, I was wondering. . . . It might be possible to create an additional bedroom in the foghorn building, unless we decide we need a separate office. The problem, though, is the noise."

"What noise?"

"The foghorn is still in use on foggy days. It's not the original horn; it's an electronic version. But still, it's loud. I mean really loud."

"Hmm, that could be an issue. Unless you throw in a free set of earplugs. Lay them out on the pillow with the mints."

"That's what I was thinking!"

"What about the lighthouse tower? What are your plans for it?"

"That's the best part! I was thinking—"

She stopped midsentence, and her face lost all color.

"Alicia? What is it? What's wrong?"

"I thought I saw . . ."

"What?"

"Nothing," she said with a shake of her auburn hair.

I looked around, paying careful attention to my peripheral vision and crossing my fingers that I would not see a ghost or a body—or both.

Because I see things. Not all the time, but often enough. Given my professional focus on historic renovations, this probably wasn't surprising. I'd inherited my sensitivity to the spirit world from my mother, and in the past few years had encountered more than a few lost souls who had been caught on the wrong side of the veil between this world and the next. I'd struggled to accept that my ability to see what others could not was simply part of my life and had gradually become resigned to it.

My tendency to trip over dead bodies, on the other hand, remained . . . disturbing.

In this moment I saw only the debris-filled main parlor of the old keeper's house. My mind's eye began to imagine the space filled with vivacious guests sharing meals and swapping stories, visitors holding their cold hands up to the fire in the raised stone hearth, and perhaps a cat lounging on the windowsill. All of them were warm and happy, safe from the chilly winds blowing off the bay, the occasional mournful blast of the foghorn or flash of the lamp atop the tower adding to the dreamy atmosphere. There was the sense that they were in another time and place instead of mere minutes from a major metropolis. Alicia was right. With Ellis's financial backing and Turner Construction's renovation skills, this place could be magical. *Would* be magical.

Who's the romantic now?

"Let's . . . I think we should go, Mel," Alicia said.

The tightness of her voice told me something was wrong. "What is it, Alicia? Did you see something?"

"No."

"Are you sure? You know you can tell me."

"It's just . . . Let's go outside." She led the way through the front door, its charming beadboard paneling buckling here and there, and out to the covered porch that ran the length of the house. Wooden boards laid over the rotting floor allowed us safe passage to the steps. "It's nothing, really."

"Yeah, I'm really not buying that. Fess up."

"I think I'm just spooked. I received a letter, not long ago."

"And?"

"It was from Thorn. He's . . . he was my husband. Thorn's my *ex*-husband."

"That must have been a shock," I said. Alicia had told me how, with Ellis Elrich's assistance, she had changed her name and had created a new identity to escape her abusive ex-husband. "How did he find you?"

"I'm not sure," she said with a humorless laugh. "For years I was careful, so careful, to stay out of the public eye. But I've let my guard down recently. When Ellis bought this island and announced the plans to renovate and open an inn, I was photographed next to him. And one thing I can say about Thorn: He's not stupid. Never was. When he puts his mind to something, he can be quite determined."

"What did Ellis's security team say about it?"

She didn't answer, instead leading the way down the shored-up front stairs to a stone courtyard designed to funnel rainwater into the underground cistern. In 1892, when the buildings were constructed, access to fresh water would have been a priority on this barren island. Lack of water was ultimately what closed Alcatraz, the federal penitentiary that still held pride of place on another island in the bay, much closer to San Francisco. When everything, even drinking water, had to be brought in by supply boat, priorities shifted.

No pizza delivery while on *this* job.

Lighthouse Island's appeal—its isolation—was also its chief liability, at least when it came to the restoration. All construction supplies—every single piece of lumber, every sack of concrete and piece of Sheetrock, and every single nail and screw and tube of caulk—would have to be brought to the island by boat, hoisted onto dock with a winch, and carted up to the building site.

The prospect was daunting but exciting. I had been running Turner Construction for a few years now, and while I still enjoyed bringing historic San Francisco homes back from the brink, it was fun to have a new challenge. Something different.

And this was a *lighthouse*.

What was it about lighthouses that evoked such an aura of romance and mystery? Was it simply the idea of the keeper out there all alone, polishing the old lamps by day, keeping the fires burning at night, responsible for the lives of equally lonely sailors passing by on the vast dark waters?

"Alicia—"

My words were cut short when I realized she was standing frozen, looking stricken. I followed her gaze.

A man stood next to a green hedge just beyond the courtyard, smiling a smile that did not reach his eyes.

My first thought: *At least it's not a ghost.*

My second thought: *Could that be Thorn, Alicia's ex? Did he manage to track her here, to a secluded island?*

It was really too bad he wasn't a ghost.

ALSO AVAILABLE FROM
NEW YORK TIMES BESTSELLING AUTHOR

Juliet Blackwell

The Haunted Home Renovation Mysteries

If Walls Could Talk

Dead Bolt

Murder on the House

Home for the Haunting

Keeper of the Castle

Give Up the Ghost

Available wherever books are sold or at
penguin.com

facebook.com/TheCrimeSceneBooks